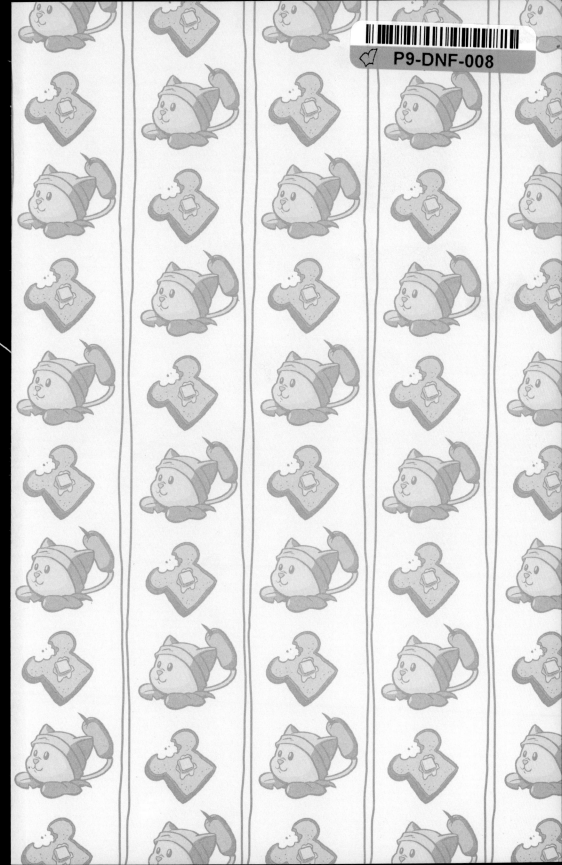

PLANTS VS. ZOMBIES™

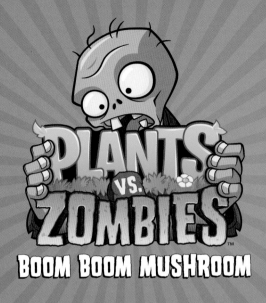

BOOM BOOM MUSHROOM

Written by **PAUL TOBIN**
Art by **JACOB CHABOT**
Colors by **MATT J. RAINWATER**
Letters by **STEVE DUTRO**
Cover by **JACOB CHABOT**

DARK HORSE BOOKS

PLANTS VS. ZOMBIES

BOOM BOOM MUSHROOM

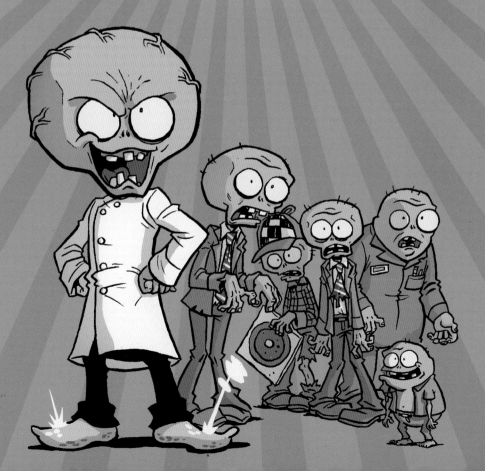

President and Publisher **MIKE RICHARDSON**
Editor **PHILIP R. SIMON**
Assistant Editor **MEGAN WALKER**
Designer **BRENNAN THOME**
Digital Art Technician **CHRISTINA McKENZIE**

Special thanks to Leigh Beach, Gary Clay, A.J. Rathbun, Kristen Star, Jeremy Vanhoozer, and everyone at PopCap Games. Editorial thanks to Sal Paradise.

First edition: January 2017
ISBN 978-1-50670-037-3

10 9 8 7 6 5 4 3
Printed in China

DarkHorse.com | PopCap.com

▷ No plants were harmed in the making of this comic. However,
numerous zombies—including Frogpants, Tugboat, and Nigel
Blimpbottom, who have immensely irritated Zomboss and can never
seem to heat up his morning Pop Smarts properly—definitely were.

NEIL HANKERSON Executive Vice President TOM WEDDLE Chief Financial Officer RANDY STRADLEY Vice President of Publishing MICHAEL MARTENS Vice President of Book Trade Sales MATT PARKINSON Vice President of Marketing DAVID SCROGGY Vice President of Product Development DALE LaFOUNTAIN Vice President of Information Technology CARA NIECE Vice President of Production and Scheduling NICK McWHORTER Vice President of Media Licensing KEN LIZZI General Counsel DAVE MARSHALL Editor in Chief DAVEY ESTRADA Editorial Director SCOTT ALLIE Executive Senior Editor CHRIS WARNER Senior Books Editor CARY GRAZZINI Director of Specialty Projects LIA RIBACCHI Art Director VANESSA TODD Director of Print Purchasing MATT DRYER Director of Digital Art and Prepress MARK BERNARDI Director of Digital Publishing SARAH ROBERTSON Director of Product Sales MICHAEL COMBOS D r of International Publishing and Lice ing

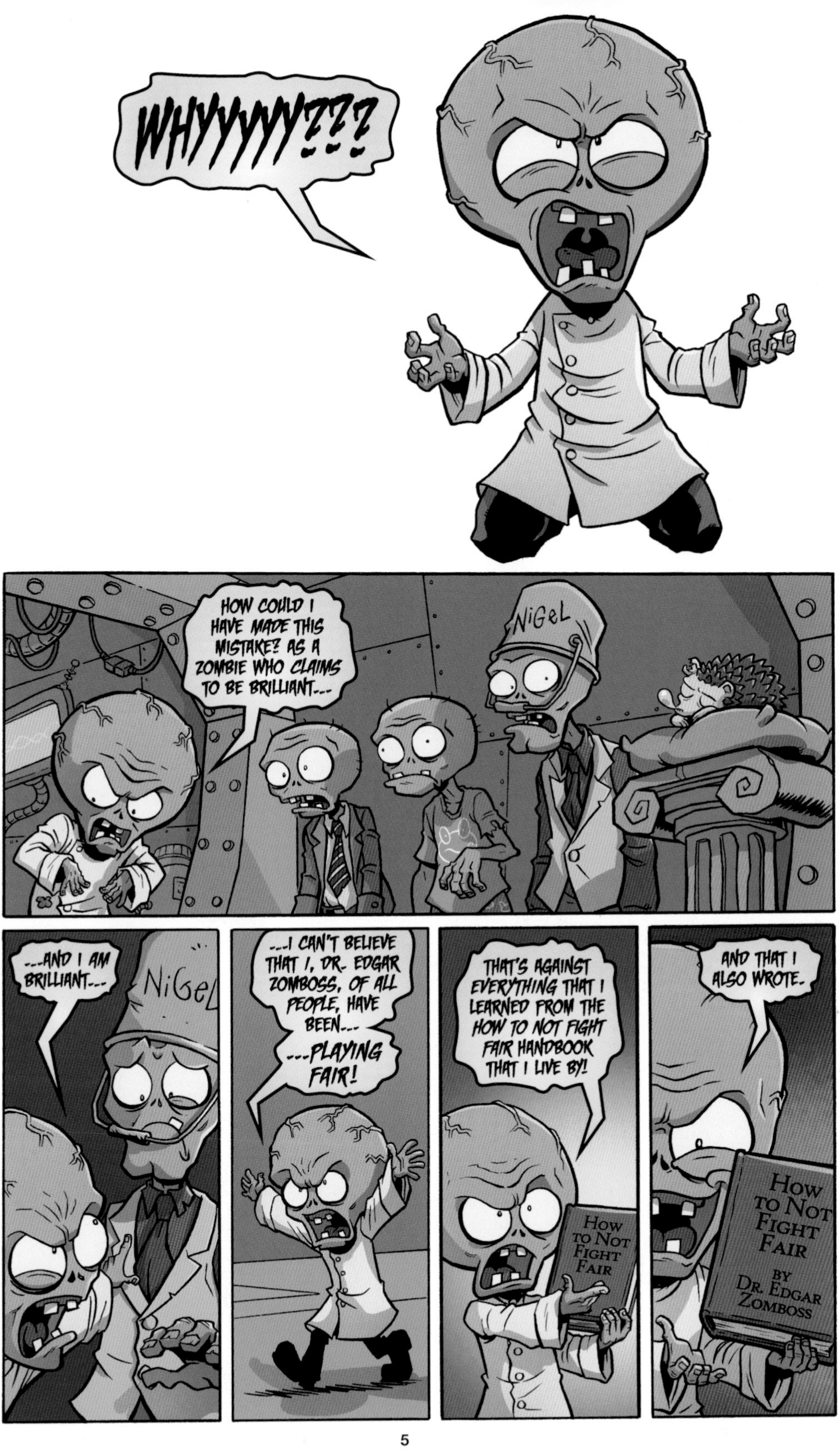
WHYYYYY???
HOW COULD I HAVE MADE THIS MISTAKE? AS A ZOMBIE WHO CLAIMS TO BE BRILLIANT...
NiGeL
...AND I AM BRILLIANT...
NiGeL
...I CAN'T BELIEVE THAT I, DR. EDGAR ZOMBOSS, OF ALL PEOPLE, HAVE BEEN...
...PLAYING FAIR!
THAT'S AGAINST EVERYTHING THAT I LEARNED FROM THE HOW TO NOT FIGHT FAIR HANDBOOK THAT I LIVE BY!
How to Not Fight Fair
AND THAT I ALSO WROTE.
How to Not Fight Fair by Dr. Edgar Zomboss

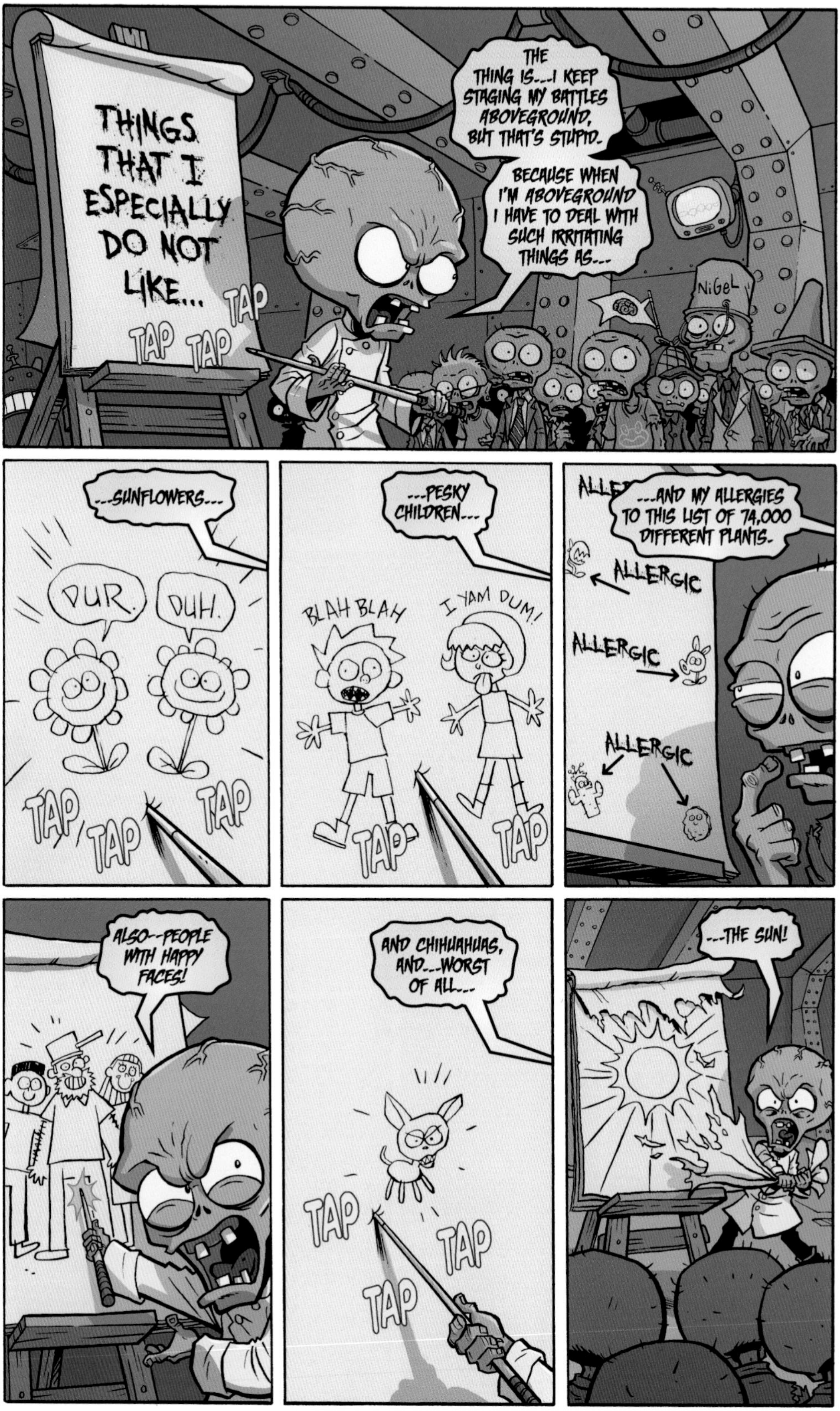
THINGS THAT I ESPECIALLY DO NOT LIKE...
TAP TAP TAP
THE THING IS...I KEEP STAGING MY BATTLES ABOVEGROUND, BUT THAT'S STUPID.
BECAUSE WHEN I'M ABOVEGROUND I HAVE TO DEAL WITH SUCH IRRITATING THINGS AS...
NiGeL
...SUNFLOWERS...
DUR.
DUH.
TAP TAP TAP
...PESKY CHILDREN...
BLAH BLAH
I YAM DUM!
TAP TAP
...AND MY ALLERGIES TO THIS LIST OF 74,000 DIFFERENT PLANTS.
ALLERGIC
ALLERGIC
ALLERGIC
ALSO--PEOPLE WITH HAPPY FACES!
AND CHIHUAHUAS, AND...WORST OF ALL...
TAP TAP TAP
...THE SUN!

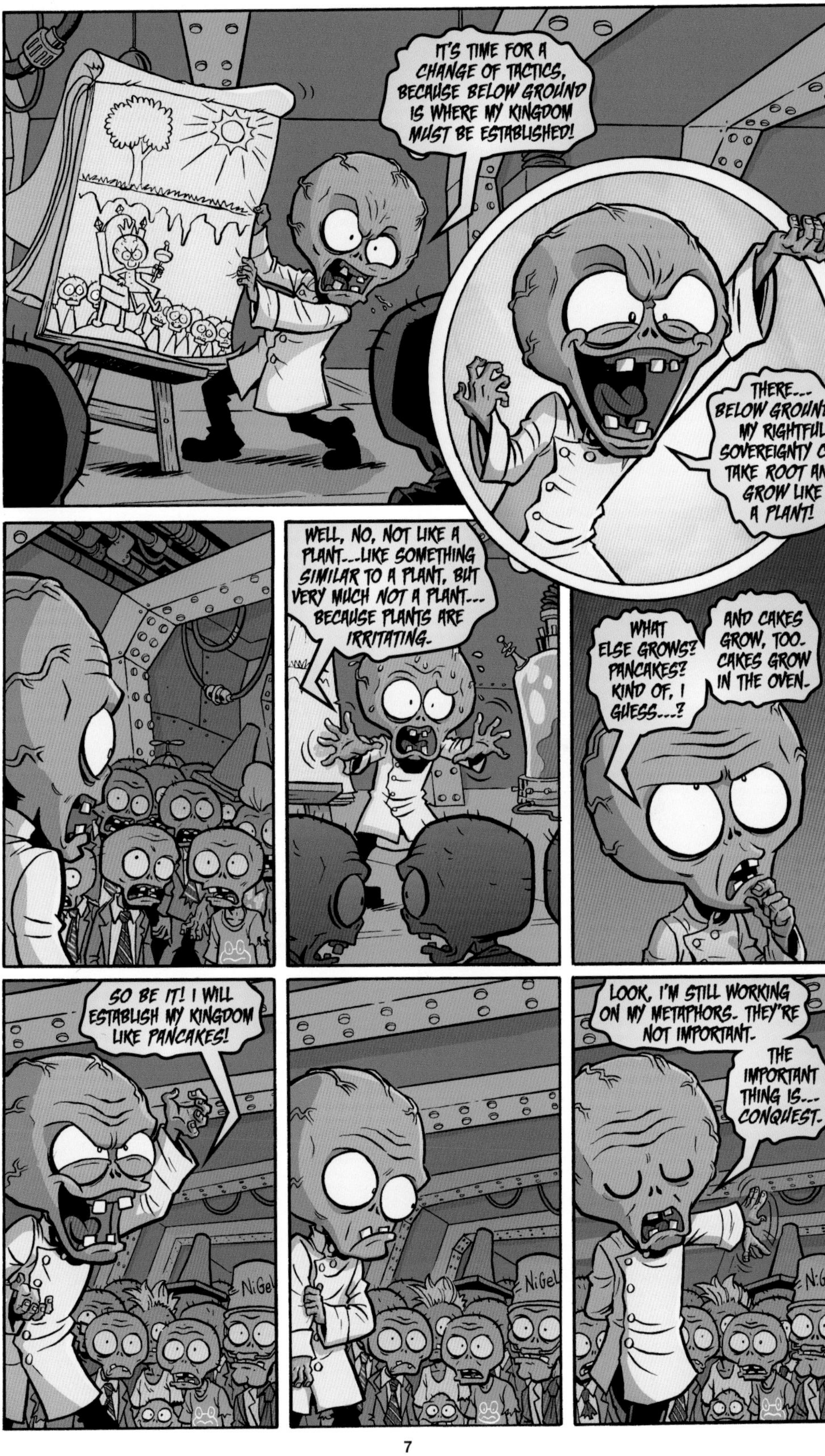
IT'S TIME FOR A CHANGE OF TACTICS, BECAUSE BELOW GROUND IS WHERE MY KINGDOM MUST BE ESTABLISHED!
THERE... BELOW GROUND... MY RIGHTFUL SOVEREIGNTY CAN TAKE ROOT AND GROW LIKE A PLANT!
WELL, NO, NOT LIKE A PLANT...LIKE SOMETHING SIMILAR TO A PLANT, BUT VERY MUCH NOT A PLANT... BECAUSE PLANTS ARE IRRITATING.
WHAT ELSE GROWS? PANCAKES? KIND OF, I GUESS...?
AND CAKES GROW, TOO. CAKES GROW IN THE OVEN.
SO BE IT! I WILL ESTABLISH MY KINGDOM LIKE PANCAKES!
LOOK, I'M STILL WORKING ON MY METAPHORS. THEY'RE NOT IMPORTANT.
THE IMPORTANT THING IS... CONQUEST.
NiGeL

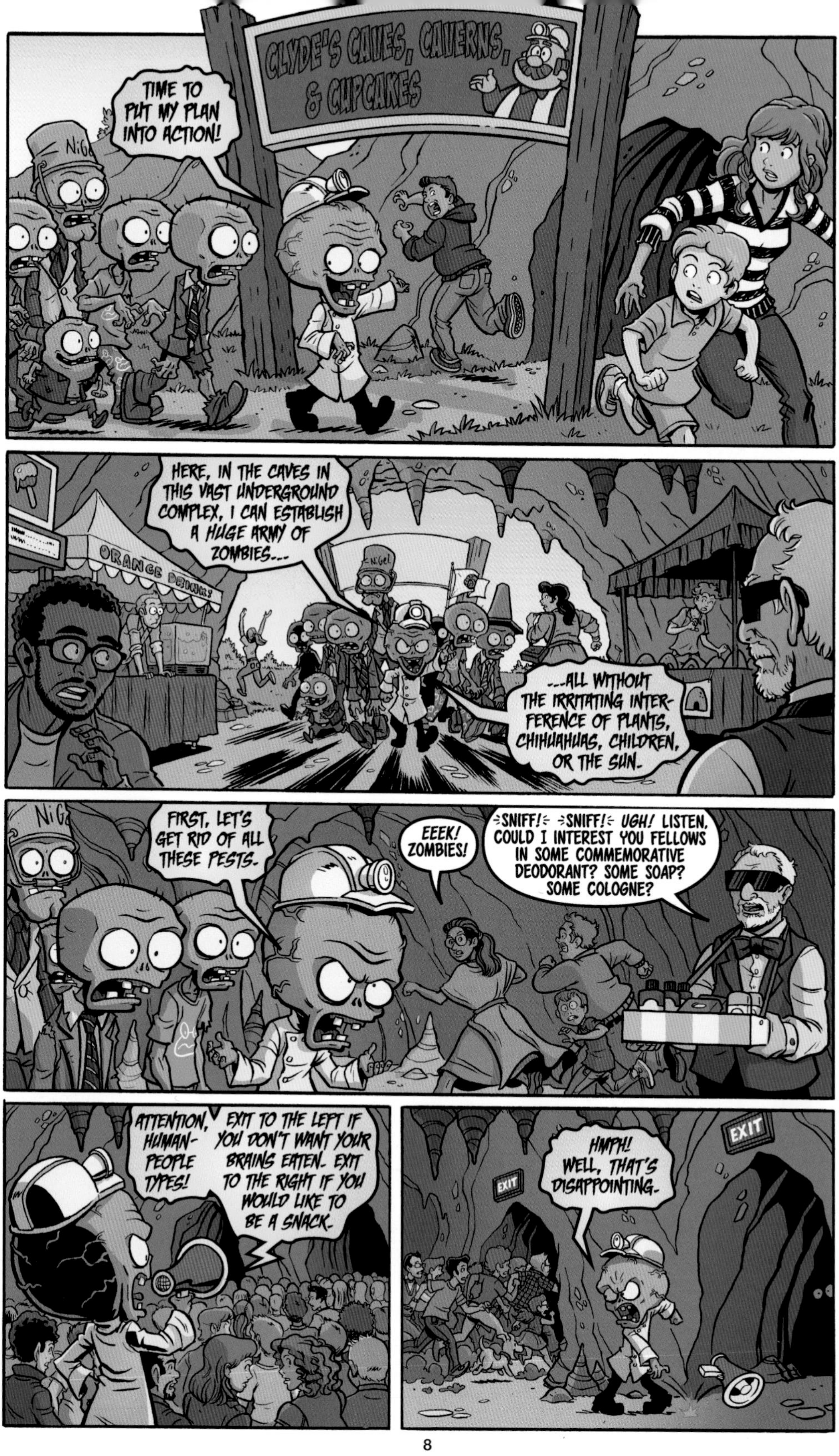
CLYDE'S CAVES, CAVERNS, & CUPCAKES
TIME TO PUT MY PLAN INTO ACTION!
HERE, IN THE CAVES IN THIS VAST UNDERGROUND COMPLEX, I CAN ESTABLISH A HUGE ARMY OF ZOMBIES...
ORANGE DRINK!
...ALL WITHOUT THE IRRITATING INTERFERENCE OF PLANTS, CHIHUAHUAS, CHILDREN, OR THE SUN.
FIRST, LET'S GET RID OF ALL THESE PESTS.
EEEK! ZOMBIES!
SNIFF! SNIFF! UGH! LISTEN, COULD I INTEREST YOU FELLOWS IN SOME COMMEMORATIVE DEODORANT? SOME SOAP? SOME COLOGNE?
ATTENTION, HUMAN-PEOPLE TYPES!
EXIT TO THE LEFT IF YOU DON'T WANT YOUR BRAINS EATEN. EXIT TO THE RIGHT IF YOU WOULD LIKE TO BE A SNACK.
EXIT
HMPH! WELL, THAT'S DISAPPOINTING.
EXIT

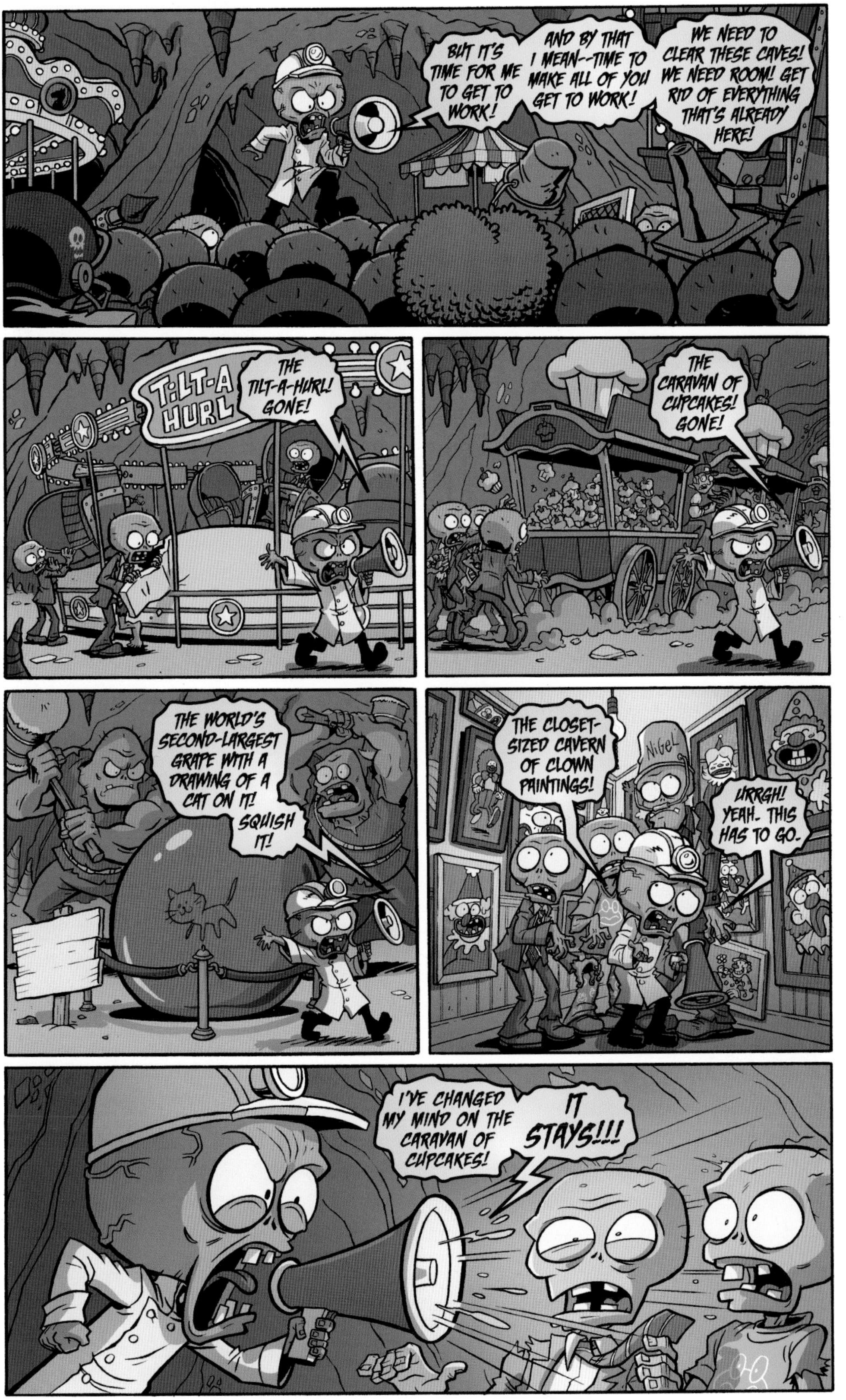
BUT IT'S TIME FOR ME TO GET TO WORK!
AND BY THAT I MEAN--TIME TO MAKE ALL OF YOU GET TO WORK!
WE NEED TO CLEAR THESE CAVES! WE NEED ROOM! GET RID OF EVERYTHING THAT'S ALREADY HERE!
TILT-A HURL
THE TILT-A-HURL! GONE!
THE CARAVAN OF CUPCAKES! GONE!
THE WORLD'S SECOND-LARGEST GRAPE WITH A DRAWING OF A CAT ON IT!
SQUISH IT!
THE CLOSET-SIZED CAVERN OF CLOWN PAINTINGS!
NIGEL
URRGH! YEAH. THIS HAS TO GO.
I'VE CHANGED MY MIND ON THE CARAVAN OF CUPCAKES!
IT STAYS!!!

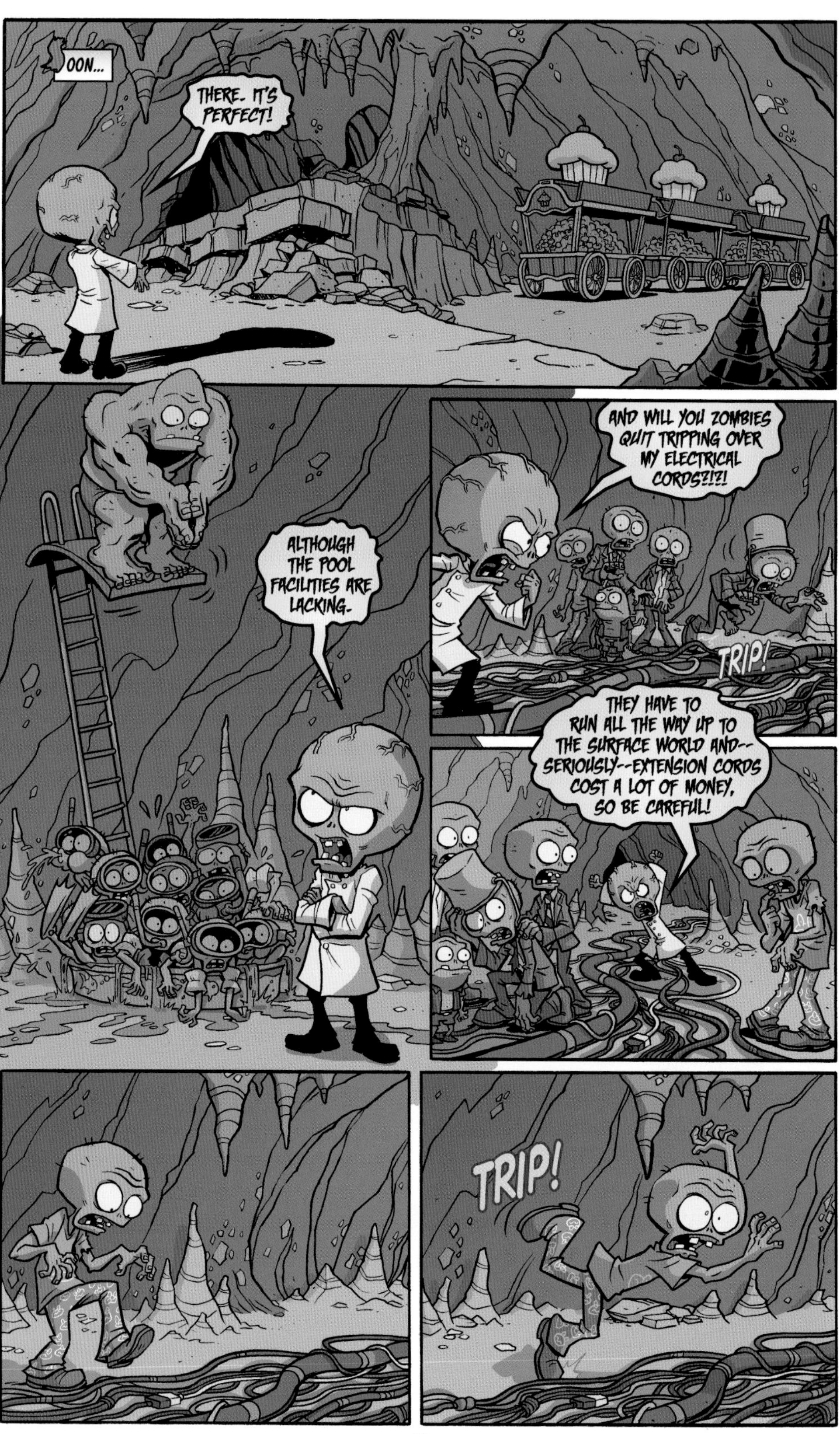

OON...
THERE. IT'S PERFECT!
ALTHOUGH THE POOL FACILITIES ARE LACKING.
AND WILL YOU ZOMBIES QUIT TRIPPING OVER MY ELECTRICAL CORDS?!?!
TRIP!
THEY HAVE TO RUN ALL THE WAY UP TO THE SURFACE WORLD AND-- SERIOUSLY--EXTENSION CORDS COST A LOT OF MONEY, SO BE CAREFUL!
TRIP!

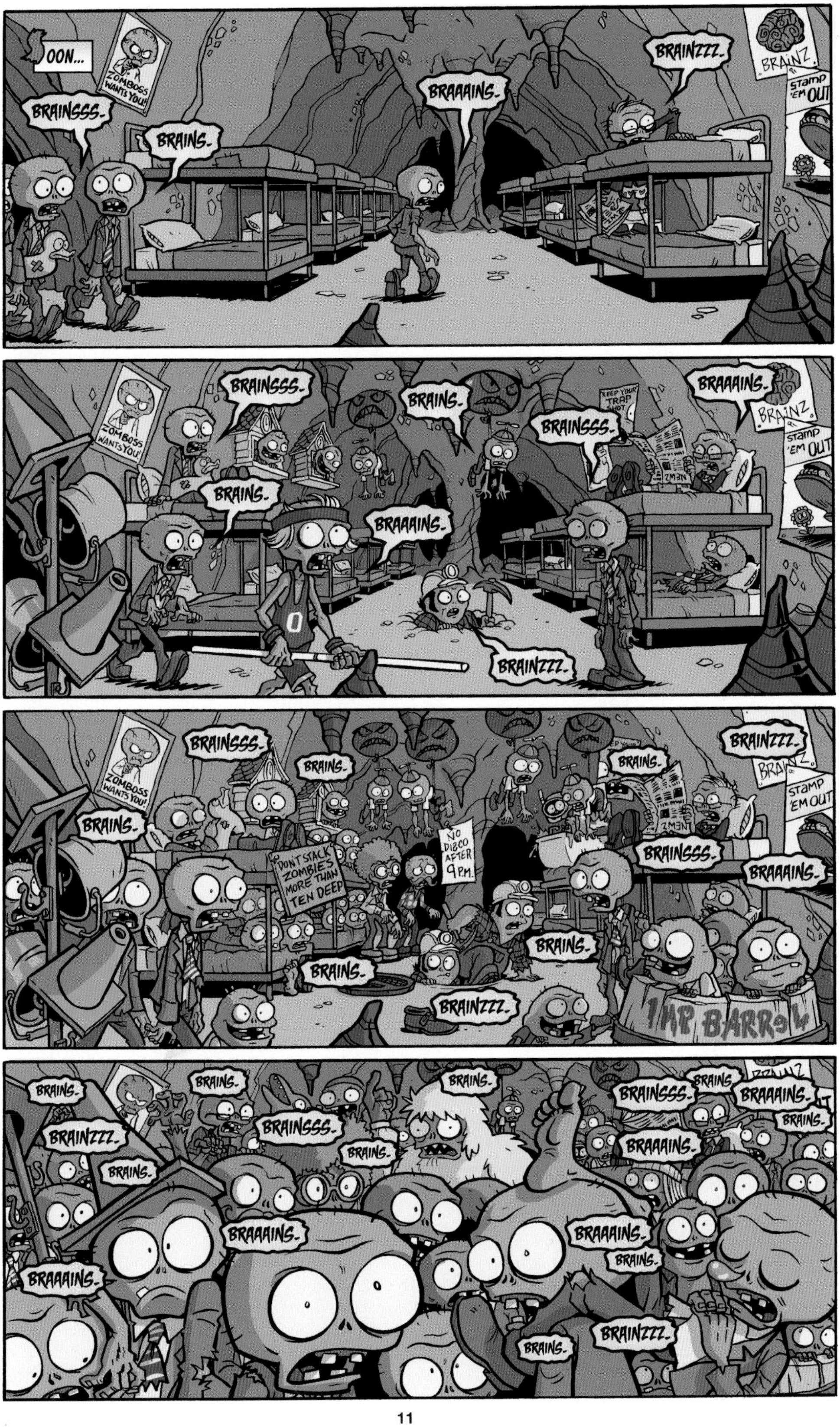
SOON...
ZOMBOSS WANTS YOU!
BRAINSSS.
BRAINS.
BRAAAINS.
BRAINZZZ.
BRAINZ
stamp 'EM OUT
ZOMBOSS WANTS YOU!
BRAINSSS.
BRAINS.
KEEP YOUR TRAP SHUT
BRAINSSS.
BRAAAINS.
BRAINZ
stamp 'EM OUT
BRAINS.
BRAAAINS.
NEWS
BRAINZZZ.
ZOMBOSS WANTS YOU!
BRAINSSS.
BRAINS.
BRAINS.
BRAINZZZ.
BRAINZ
stamp 'EM OUT
BRAINS.
DON'T STACK ZOMBIES MORE THAN TEN DEEP
NO DISCO AFTER 9 P.M.
NEWS
BRAINSSS.
BRAAAINS.
BRAINS.
BRAINS.
BRAINZZZ.
IMP BARREL
BRAINS.
BRAINS.
BRAINS.
BRAINSSS.
BRAINS
BRAAAINS.
BRAINZZZ.
BRAINSSS.
BRAINS.
BRAINS.
BRAAAINS.
BRAINS.
BRAAAINS.
BRAAAINS.
BRAINS.
BRAAAINS.
BRAINS.
BRAINZZZ.

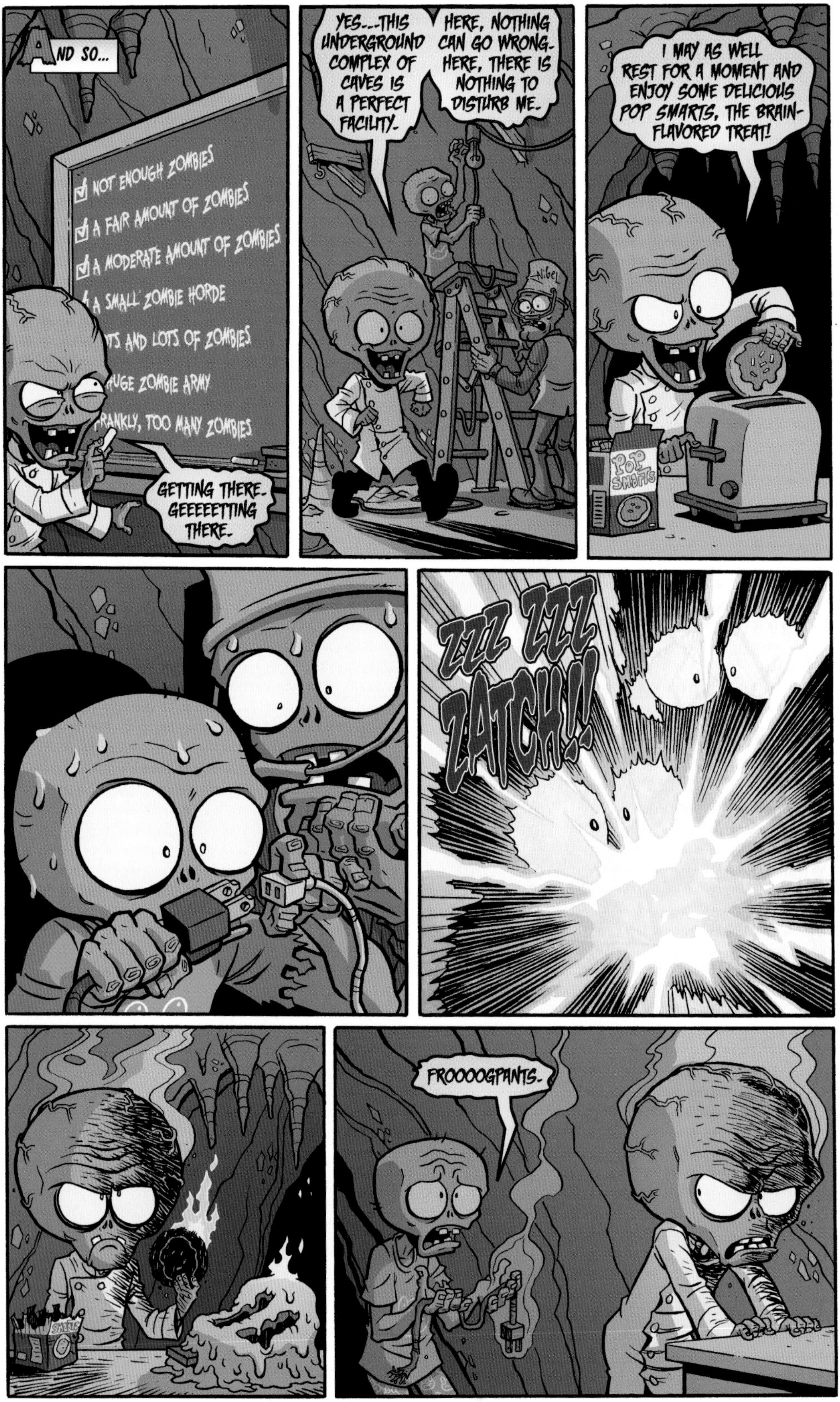
AND SO...
NOT ENOUGH ZOMBIES
A FAIR AMOUNT OF ZOMBIES
A MODERATE AMOUNT OF ZOMBIES
A SMALL ZOMBIE HORDE
OTS AND LOTS OF ZOMBIES
UGE ZOMBIE ARMY
RANKLY, TOO MANY ZOMBIES
GETTING THERE. GEEEEETTING THERE.
YES...THIS UNDERGROUND COMPLEX OF CAVES IS A PERFECT FACILITY.
HERE, NOTHING CAN GO WRONG. HERE, THERE IS NOTHING TO DISTURB ME.
NIGEL
I MAY AS WELL REST FOR A MOMENT AND ENJOY SOME DELICIOUS POP SMARTS, THE BRAIN-FLAVORED TREAT!
POP SMARTS
ZZZ ZZZ ZATCH!!
FROOOOGPANTS.

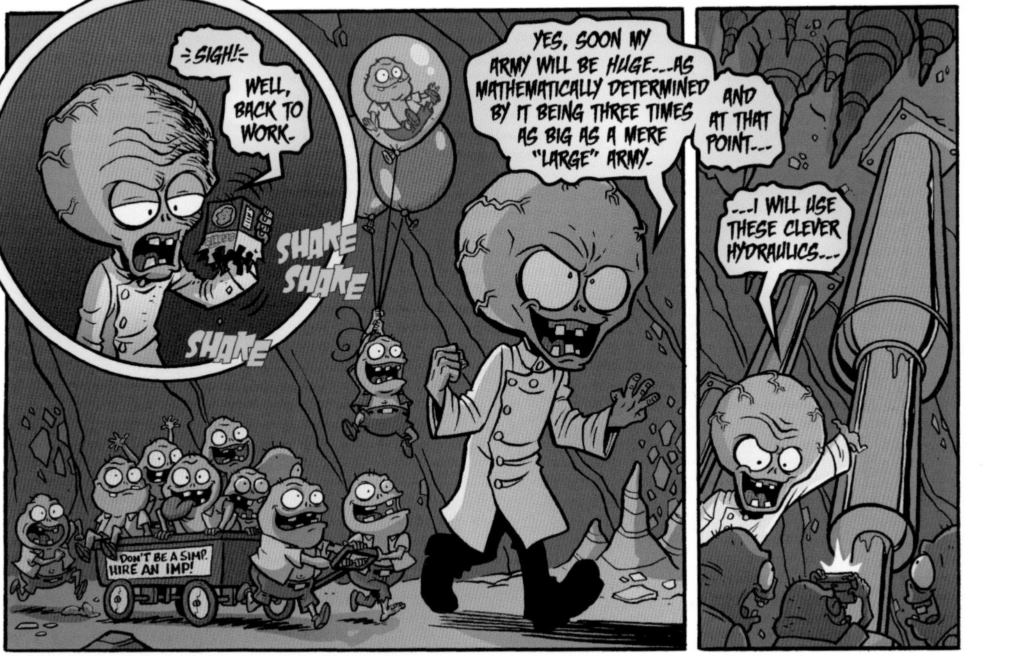
=SIGH!=
WELL, BACK TO WORK.
SHAKE
SHAKE
SHAKE
DON'T BE A SIMP. HIRE AN IMP!
YES, SOON MY ARMY WILL BE HUGE...AS MATHEMATICALLY DETERMINED BY IT BEING THREE TIMES AS BIG AS A MERE "LARGE" ARMY.
AND AT THAT POINT...
...I WILL USE THESE CLEVER HYDRAULICS...

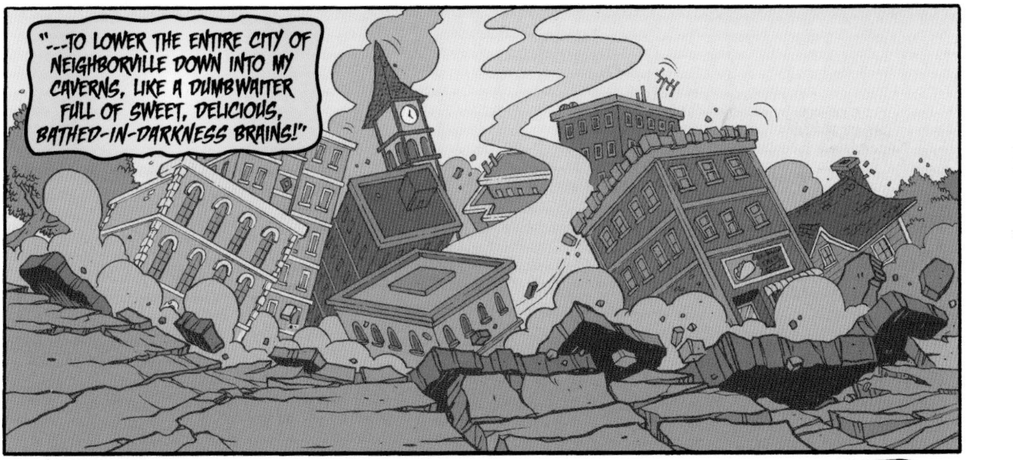
"...TO LOWER THE ENTIRE CITY OF NEIGHBORVILLE DOWN INTO MY CAVERNS, LIKE A DUMBWAITER FULL OF SWEET, DELICIOUS, BATHED-IN-DARKNESS BRAINS!"

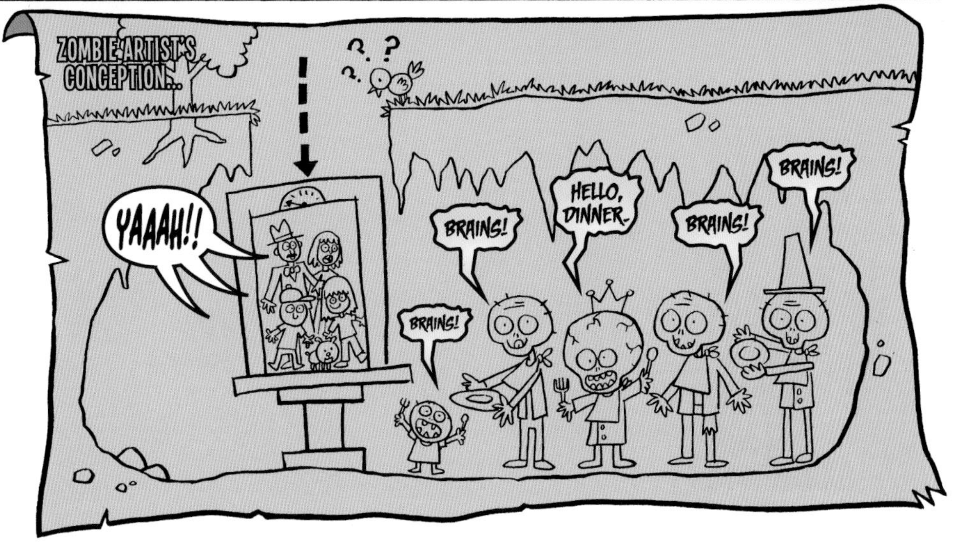
ZOMBIE ARTIST'S CONCEPTION...
? ? ?
YAAAH!!
BRAINS!
BRAINS!
HELLO, DINNER.
BRAINS!
BRAINS!

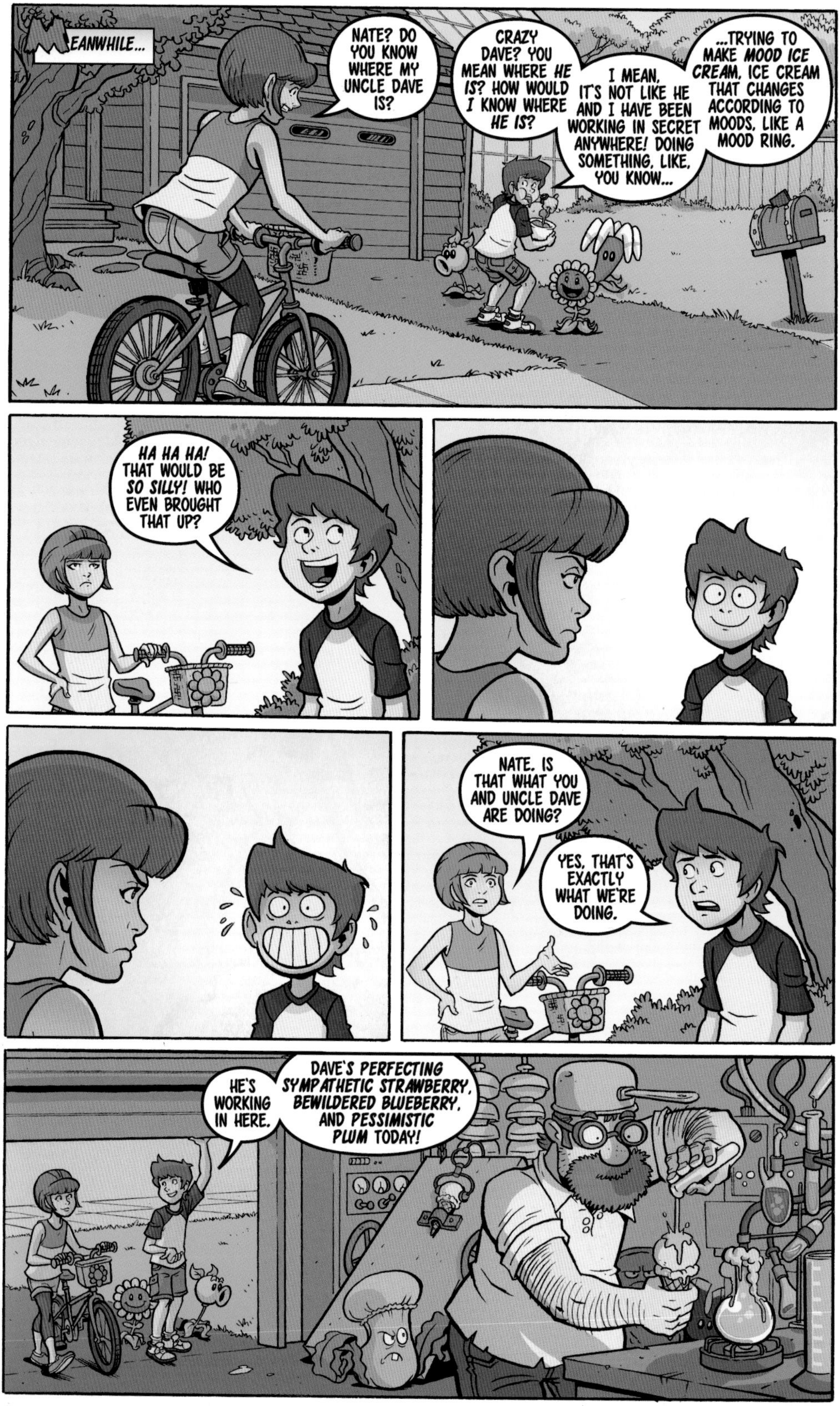
MEANWHILE...
NATE? DO YOU KNOW WHERE MY UNCLE DAVE IS?
CRAZY DAVE? YOU MEAN WHERE HE IS? HOW WOULD I KNOW WHERE HE IS?
I MEAN, IT'S NOT LIKE HE AND I HAVE BEEN WORKING IN SECRET ANYWHERE! DOING SOMETHING, LIKE, YOU KNOW...
...TRYING TO MAKE MOOD ICE CREAM, ICE CREAM THAT CHANGES ACCORDING TO MOODS, LIKE A MOOD RING.
HA HA HA! THAT WOULD BE SO SILLY! WHO EVEN BROUGHT THAT UP?
NATE. IS THAT WHAT YOU AND UNCLE DAVE ARE DOING?
YES, THAT'S EXACTLY WHAT WE'RE DOING.
HE'S WORKING IN HERE.
DAVE'S PERFECTING SYMPATHETIC STRAWBERRY, BEWILDERED BLUEBERRY, AND PESSIMISTIC PLUM TODAY!

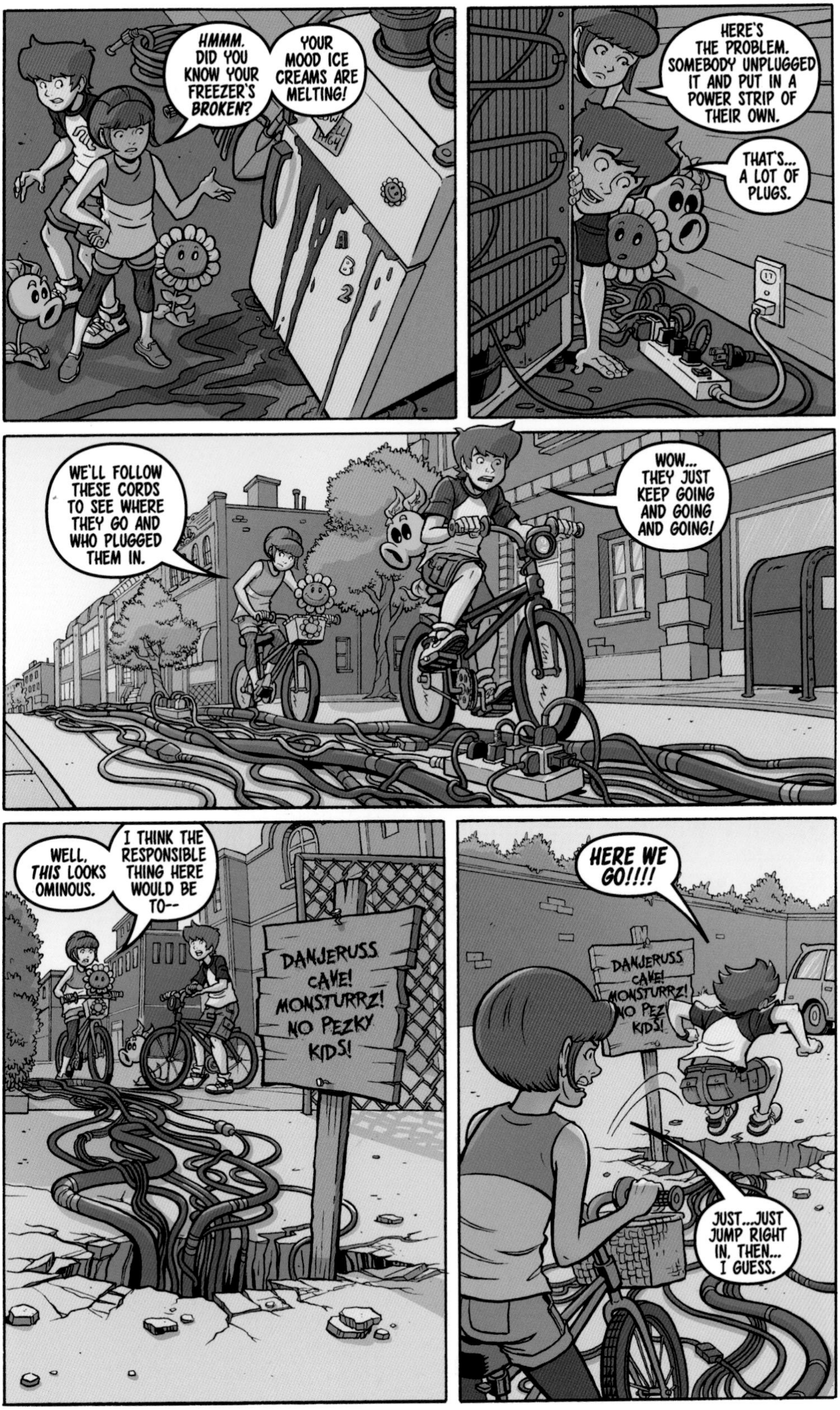
HMMM. DID YOU KNOW YOUR FREEZER'S BROKEN?
YOUR MOOD ICE CREAMS ARE MELTING!
HERE'S THE PROBLEM. SOMEBODY UNPLUGGED IT AND PUT IN A POWER STRIP OF THEIR OWN.
THAT'S... A LOT OF PLUGS.
WE'LL FOLLOW THESE CORDS TO SEE WHERE THEY GO AND WHO PLUGGED THEM IN.
WOW... THEY JUST KEEP GOING AND GOING AND GOING!
WELL, THIS LOOKS OMINOUS.
I THINK THE RESPONSIBLE THING HERE WOULD BE TO--
DANJERUSS CAVE! MONSTURRZ! NO PEZKY KIDS!
HERE WE GO!!!!
DANJERUSS CAVE! MONSTURRZ! NO PEZKY KIDS!
JUST...JUST JUMP RIGHT IN, THEN... I GUESS.

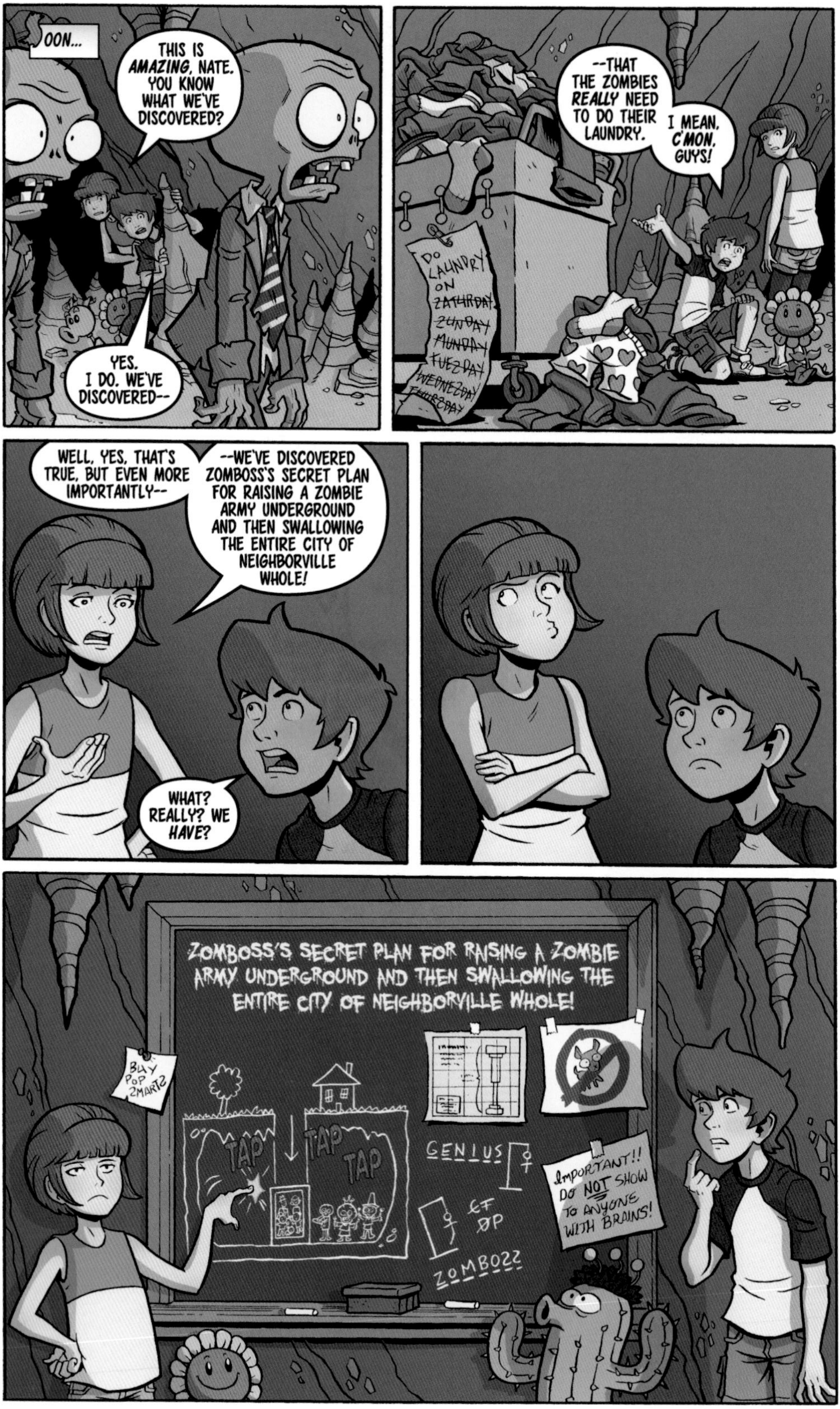
OON...
THIS IS *AMAZING*, NATE. YOU KNOW WHAT WE'VE DISCOVERED?
YES. I DO. WE'VE DISCOVERED--
--THAT THE ZOMBIES *REALLY* NEED TO DO THEIR LAUNDRY.
I MEAN, *C'MON*, GUYS!
DO LAUNDRY ON ~~ZATURDAY~~ ~~ZUNDAY~~ ~~MUNDAY~~ ~~TUEZDAY~~ ~~WEDNEZDAY~~ ~~THURZDAY~~
WELL, YES, THAT'S TRUE, BUT EVEN MORE IMPORTANTLY--
--WE'VE DISCOVERED ZOMBOSS'S SECRET PLAN FOR RAISING A ZOMBIE ARMY UNDERGROUND AND THEN SWALLOWING THE ENTIRE CITY OF NEIGHBORVILLE WHOLE!
WHAT? REALLY? WE *HAVE*?
ZOMBOSS'S SECRET PLAN FOR RAISING A ZOMBIE ARMY UNDERGROUND AND THEN SWALLOWING THE ENTIRE CITY OF NEIGHBORVILLE WHOLE!
BUY POP ZMARTZ
TAP
TAP
TAP
GENIUS
ZOMBOZZ
IMPORTANT!! DO NOT SHOW TO ANYONE WITH BRAINS!

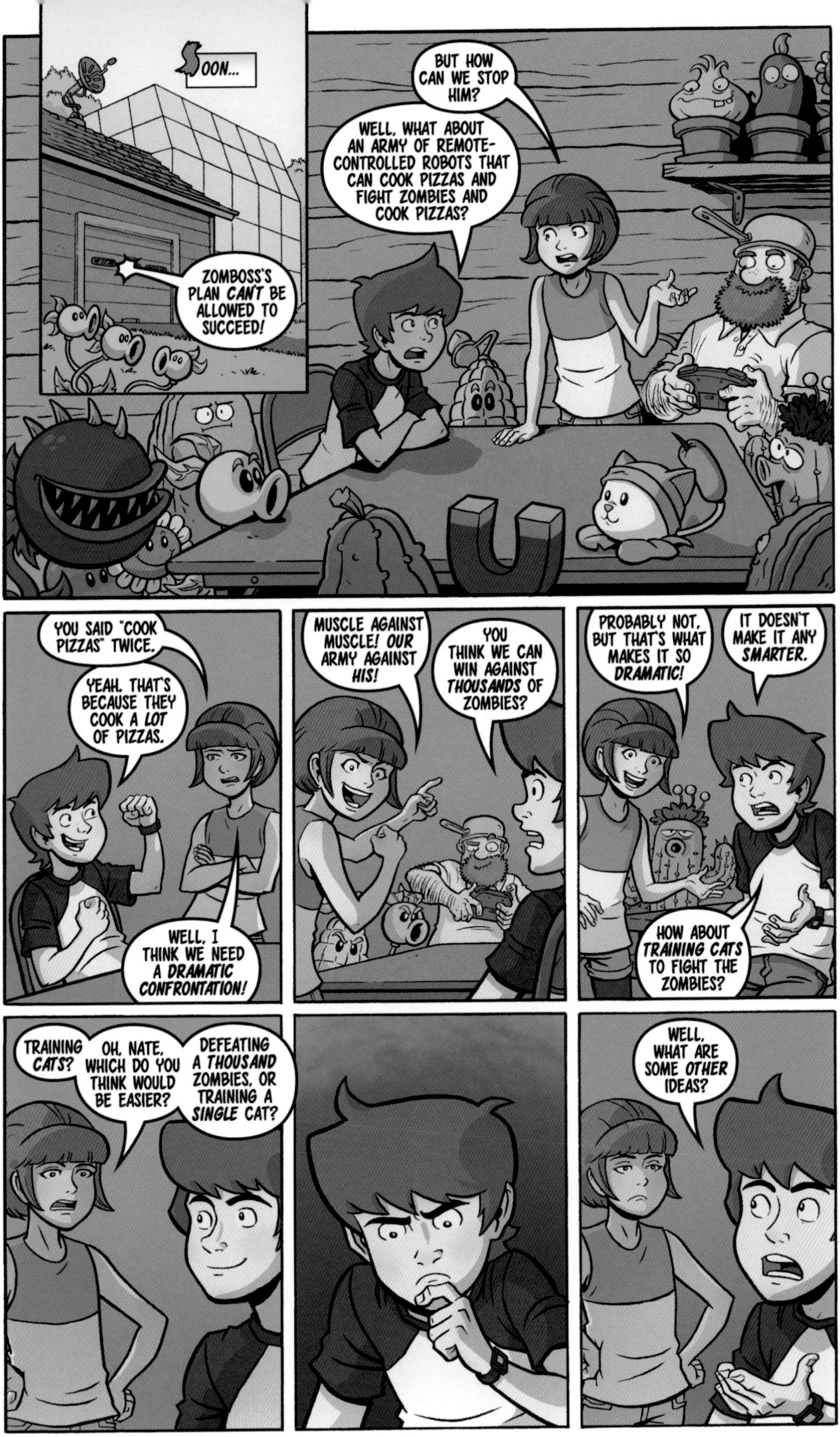
SOON...
ZOMBOSS'S PLAN CAN'T BE ALLOWED TO SUCCEED!
BUT HOW CAN WE STOP HIM?
WELL, WHAT ABOUT AN ARMY OF REMOTE-CONTROLLED ROBOTS THAT CAN COOK PIZZAS AND FIGHT ZOMBIES AND COOK PIZZAS?
YOU SAID "COOK PIZZAS" TWICE.
YEAH. THAT'S BECAUSE THEY COOK A LOT OF PIZZAS.
WELL, I THINK WE NEED A DRAMATIC CONFRONTATION!
MUSCLE AGAINST MUSCLE! OUR ARMY AGAINST HIS!
YOU THINK WE CAN WIN AGAINST THOUSANDS OF ZOMBIES?
PROBABLY NOT, BUT THAT'S WHAT MAKES IT SO DRAMATIC!
IT DOESN'T MAKE IT ANY SMARTER.
HOW ABOUT TRAINING CATS TO FIGHT THE ZOMBIES?
TRAINING CATS?
OH, NATE, WHICH DO YOU THINK WOULD BE EASIER?
DEFEATING A THOUSAND ZOMBIES, OR TRAINING A SINGLE CAT?
WELL, WHAT ARE SOME OTHER IDEAS?

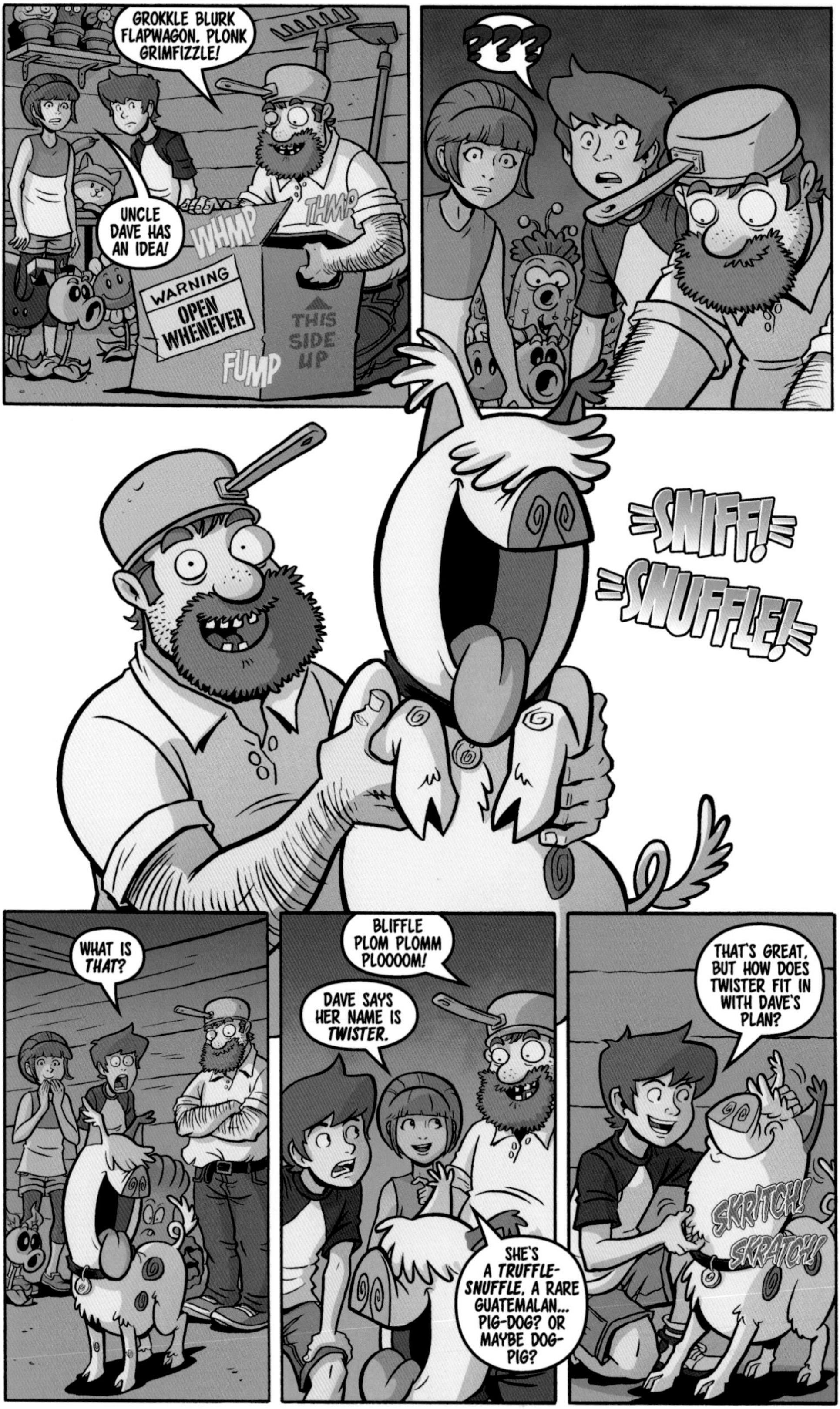
GROKKLE BLURK FLAPWAGON. PLONK GRIMFIZZLE!
UNCLE DAVE HAS AN IDEA!
WHMP
THMP
WARNING
OPEN WHENEVER
THIS SIDE UP
FUMP
???
SNIFF!
SNUFFLE!
WHAT IS THAT?
BLIFFLE PLOM PLOMM PLOOOOM!
DAVE SAYS HER NAME IS TWISTER.
SHE'S A TRUFFLE-SNUFFLE, A RARE GUATEMALAN... PIG-DOG? OR MAYBE DOG-PIG?
THAT'S GREAT, BUT HOW DOES TWISTER FIT IN WITH DAVE'S PLAN?
SKRITCH!
SKRATCH!

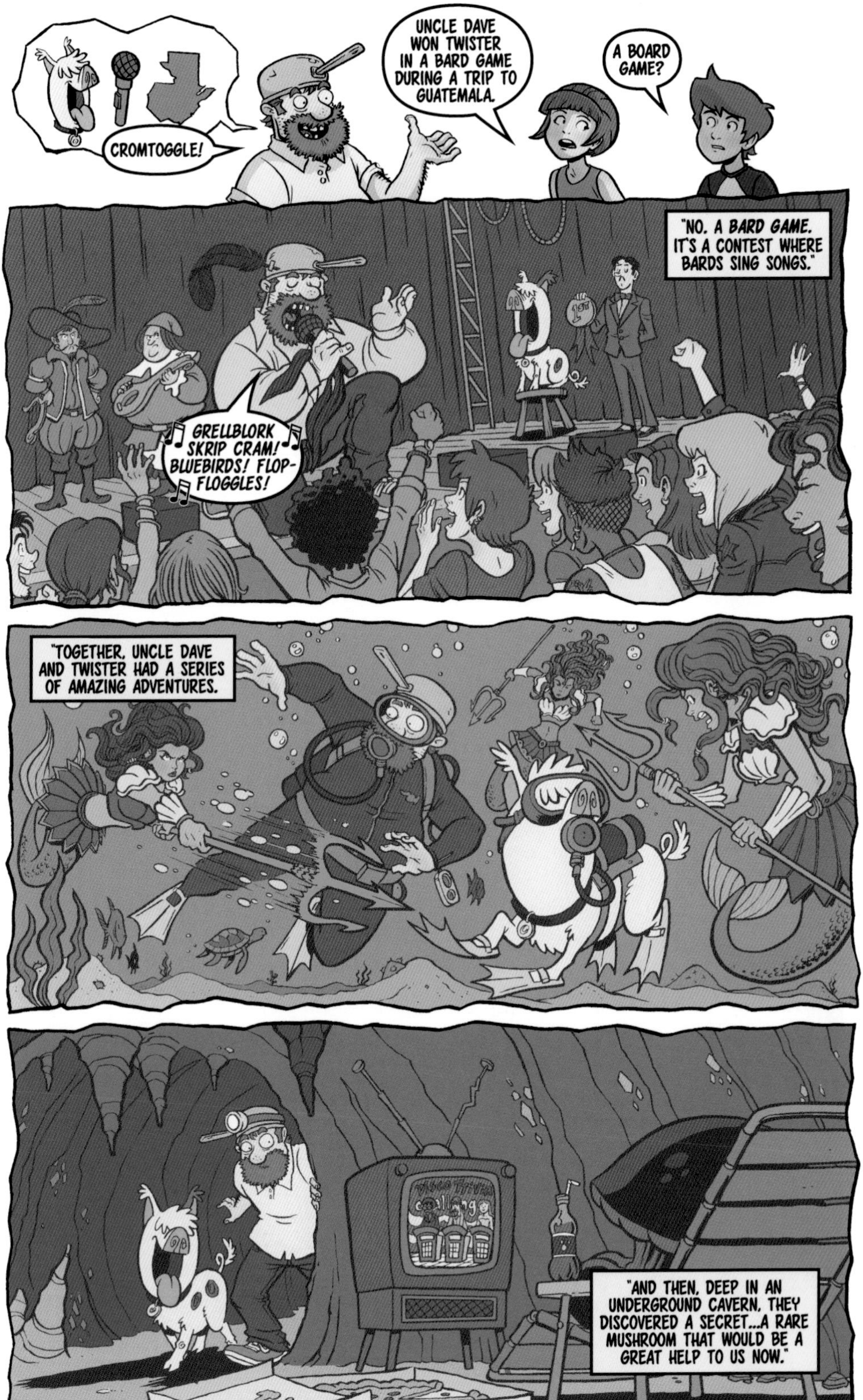
CROMTOGGLE!
UNCLE DAVE WON TWISTER IN A BARD GAME DURING A TRIP TO GUATEMALA.
A BOARD GAME?
"NO. A BARD GAME. IT'S A CONTEST WHERE BARDS SING SONGS."
GRELLBLORK SKRIP CRAM! BLUEBIRDS! FLOP-FLOGGLES!
"TOGETHER, UNCLE DAVE AND TWISTER HAD A SERIES OF AMAZING ADVENTURES.
"AND THEN, DEEP IN AN UNDERGROUND CAVERN, THEY DISCOVERED A SECRET...A RARE MUSHROOM THAT WOULD BE A GREAT HELP TO US NOW."

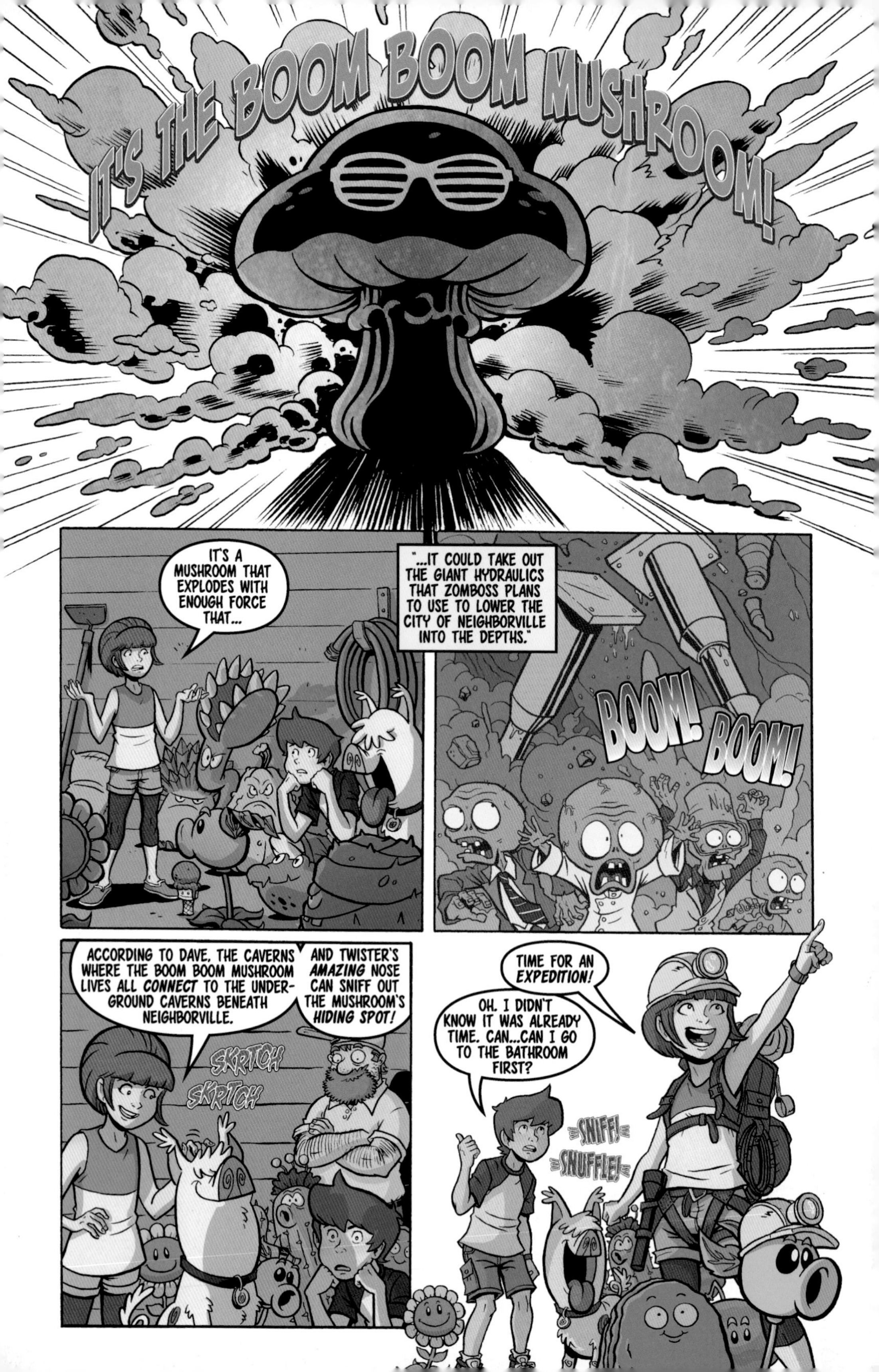
IT'S THE BOOM BOOM MUSHROOM!
IT'S A MUSHROOM THAT EXPLODES WITH ENOUGH FORCE THAT...
"...IT COULD TAKE OUT THE GIANT HYDRAULICS THAT ZOMBOSS PLANS TO USE TO LOWER THE CITY OF NEIGHBORVILLE INTO THE DEPTHS."
BOOM! BOOM!
ACCORDING TO DAVE, THE CAVERNS WHERE THE BOOM BOOM MUSHROOM LIVES ALL *CONNECT* TO THE UNDERGROUND CAVERNS BENEATH NEIGHBORVILLE.
AND TWISTER'S *AMAZING* NOSE CAN SNIFF OUT THE MUSHROOM'S *HIDING SPOT!*
SKRTCH
SKRTCH
TIME FOR AN *EXPEDITION!*
OH. I DIDN'T KNOW IT WAS ALREADY TIME. CAN...CAN I GO TO THE BATHROOM FIRST?
SNIFF!
SNUFFLE!

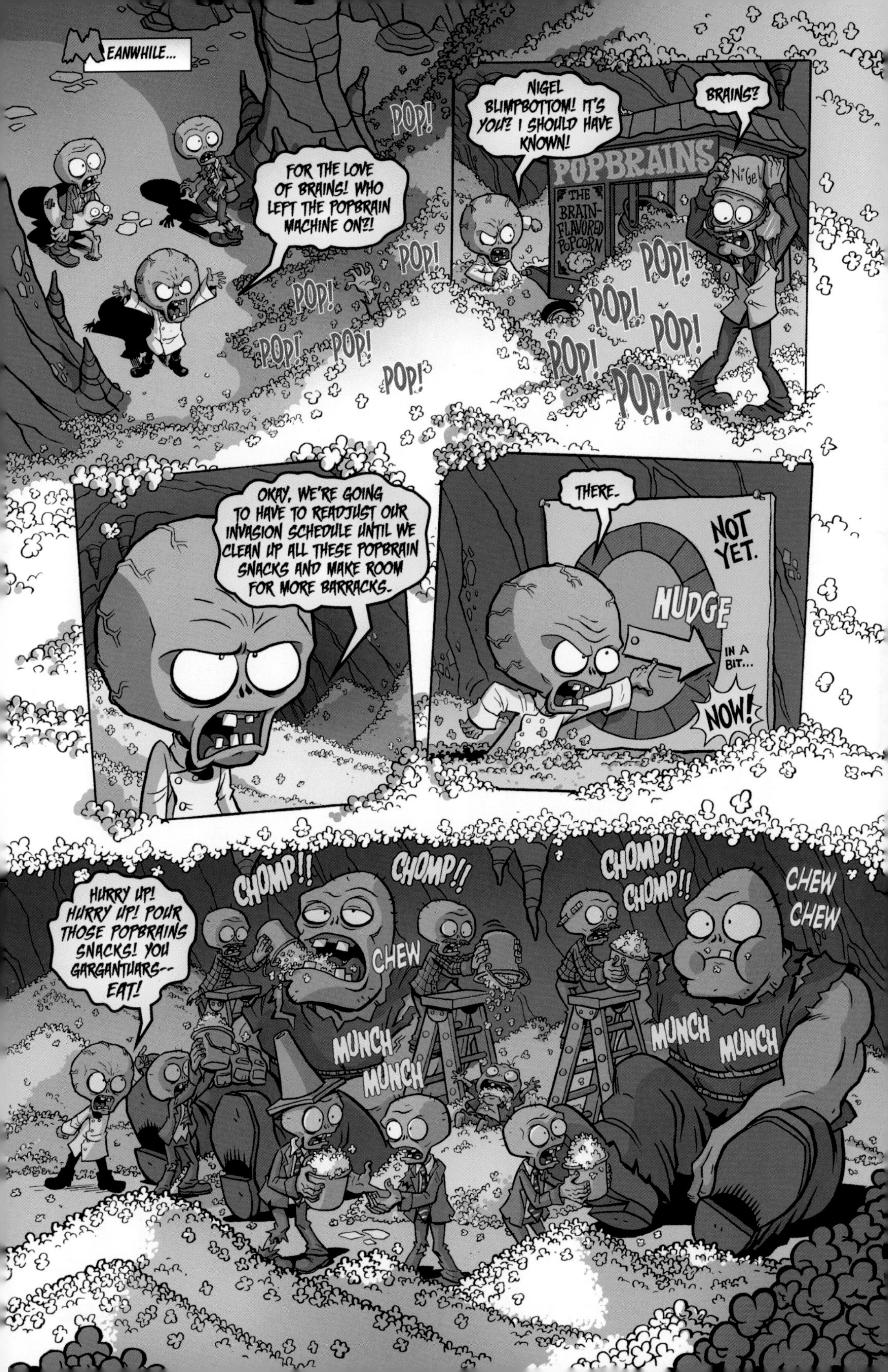
MEANWHILE...
FOR THE LOVE OF BRAINS! WHO LEFT THE POPBRAIN MACHINE ON?!
POP!
POP!
POP!
POP!
POP!
POP!
NIGEL BLIMPBOTTOM! IT'S YOU? I SHOULD HAVE KNOWN!
BRAINS?
POPBRAINS
THE BRAIN-FLAVORED POPCORN
NiGel
POP!
POP!
POP!
POP!
POP!
OKAY, WE'RE GOING TO HAVE TO READJUST OUR INVASION SCHEDULE UNTIL WE CLEAN UP ALL THESE POPBRAIN SNACKS AND MAKE ROOM FOR MORE BARRACKS.
THERE.
NOT YET.
NUDGE
IN A BIT...
NOW!
HURRY UP! HURRY UP! POUR THOSE POPBRAINS SNACKS! YOU GARGANTUARS--EAT!
CHOMP!!
CHOMP!!
CHEW
MUNCH
MUNCH
CHOMP!!
CHOMP!!
CHEW
CHEW
MUNCH
MUNCH

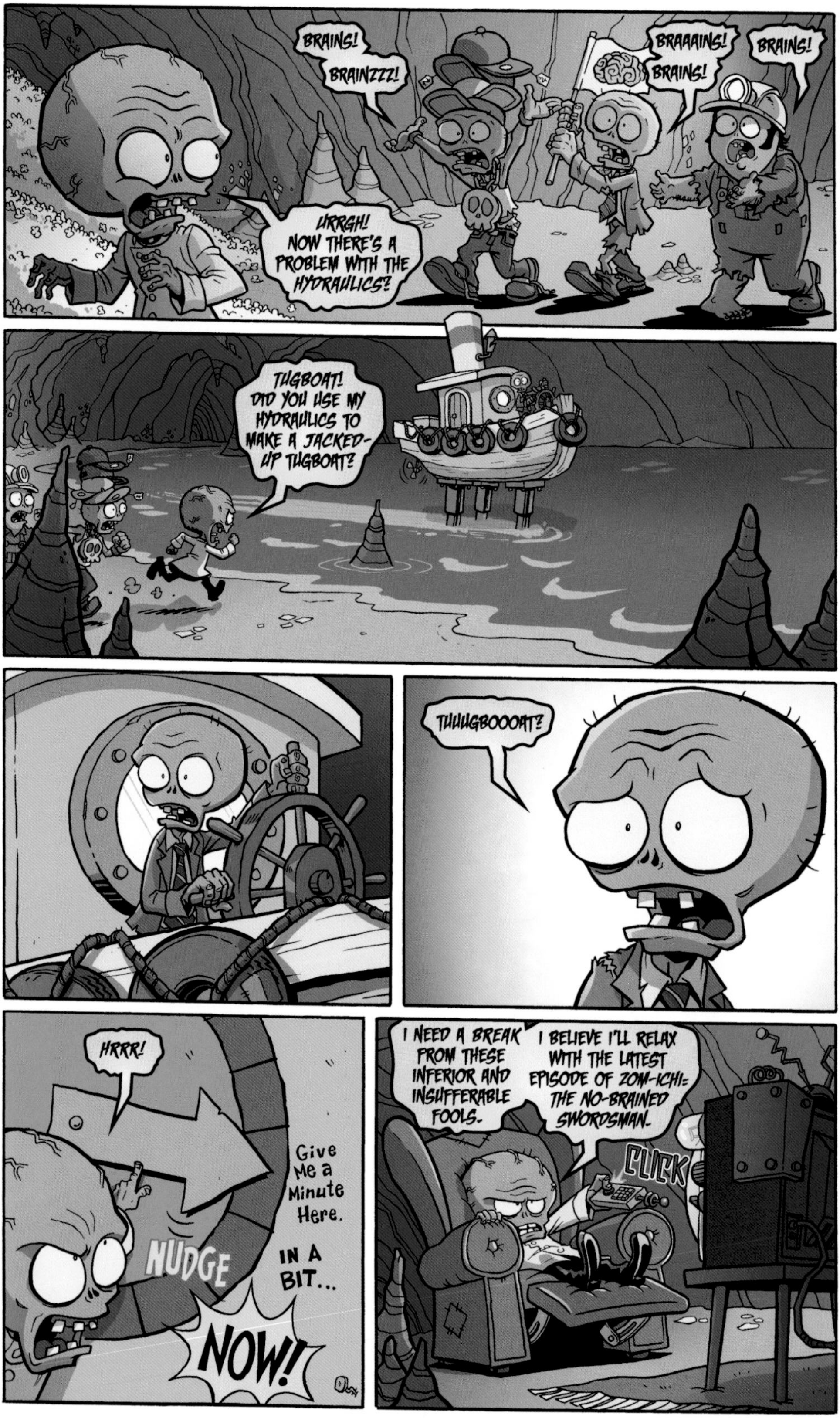

BRAINS!
BRAINZZZ!
BRAAAINS!
BRAINS!
BRAINS!
URRGH! NOW THERE'S A PROBLEM WITH THE HYDRAULICS?
TUGBOAT! DID YOU USE MY HYDRAULICS TO MAKE A JACKED-UP TUGBOAT?
TUUUGBOOOAT?
HRRR!
NUDGE
Give Me a Minute Here.
IN A BIT...
NOW!
I NEED A BREAK FROM THESE INFERIOR AND INSUFFERABLE FOOLS.
I BELIEVE I'LL RELAX WITH THE LATEST EPISODE OF ZOM-ICHI: THE NO-BRAINED SWORDSMAN.
CLICK

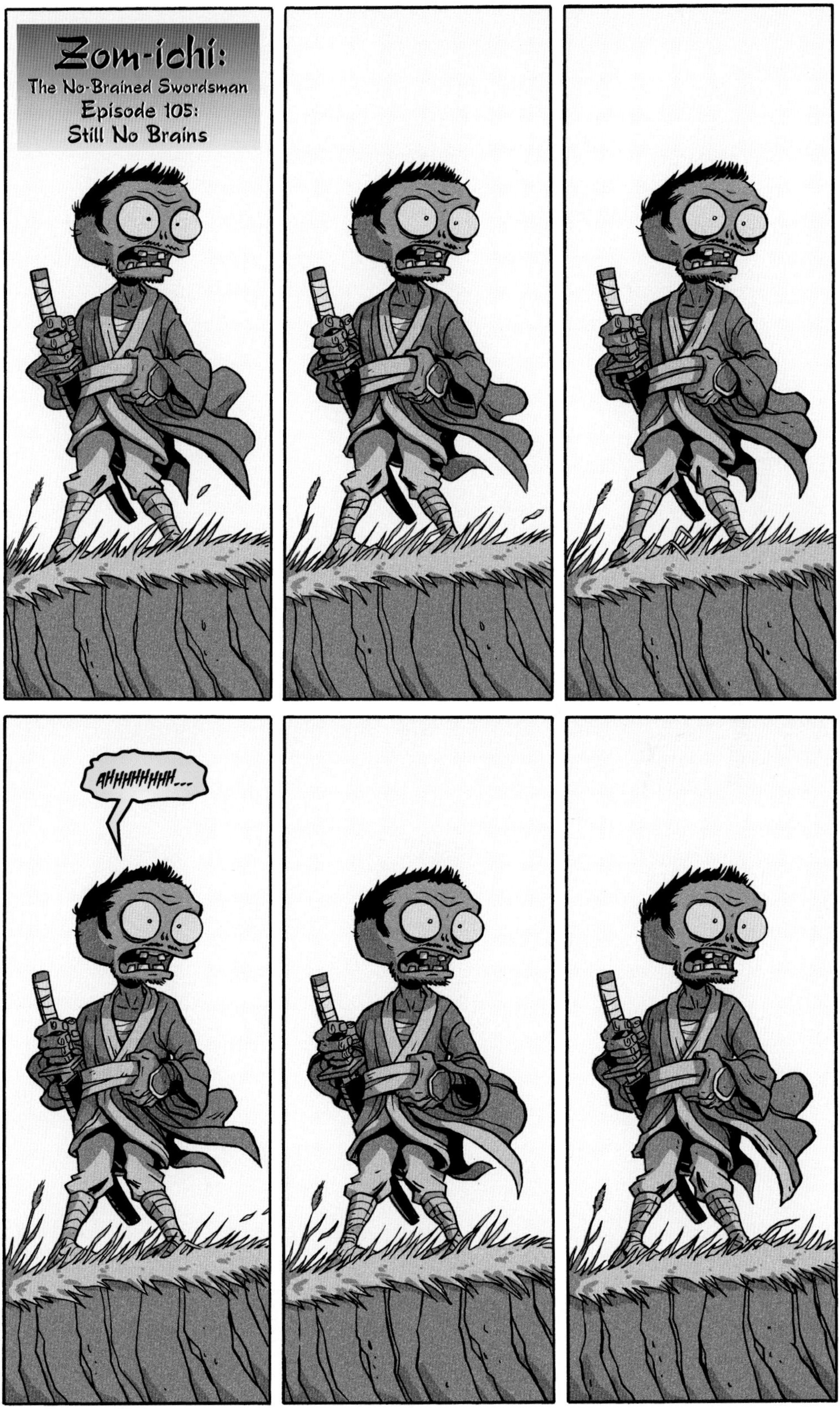
Zom-ichi:
The No-Brained Swordsman
Episode 105:
Still No Brains
AHHHHHHHH...

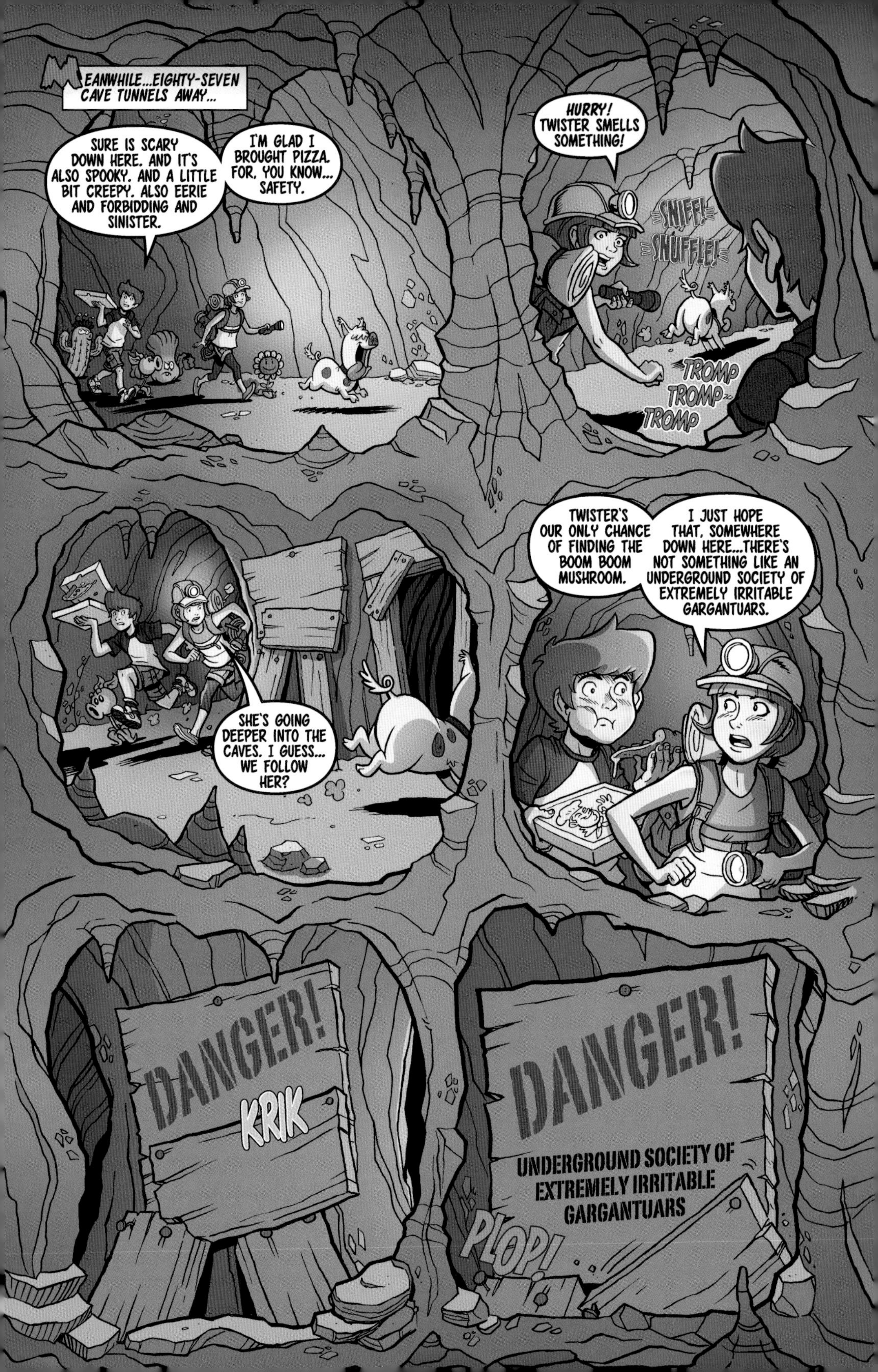
MEANWHILE...EIGHTY-SEVEN CAVE TUNNELS AWAY...
SURE IS SCARY DOWN HERE. AND IT'S ALSO SPOOKY. AND A LITTLE BIT CREEPY. ALSO EERIE AND FORBIDDING AND SINISTER.
I'M GLAD I BROUGHT PIZZA. FOR, YOU KNOW... SAFETY.
HURRY! TWISTER SMELLS SOMETHING!
SNIFF!
SNUFFLE!
TROMP
TROMP
TROMP
SHE'S GOING DEEPER INTO THE CAVES. I GUESS... WE FOLLOW HER?
TWISTER'S OUR ONLY CHANCE OF FINDING THE BOOM BOOM MUSHROOM.
I JUST HOPE THAT, SOMEWHERE DOWN HERE...THERE'S NOT SOMETHING LIKE AN UNDERGROUND SOCIETY OF EXTREMELY IRRITABLE GARGANTUARS.
DANGER!
KRIK
DANGER!
UNDERGROUND SOCIETY OF EXTREMELY IRRITABLE GARGANTUARS
PLOP!

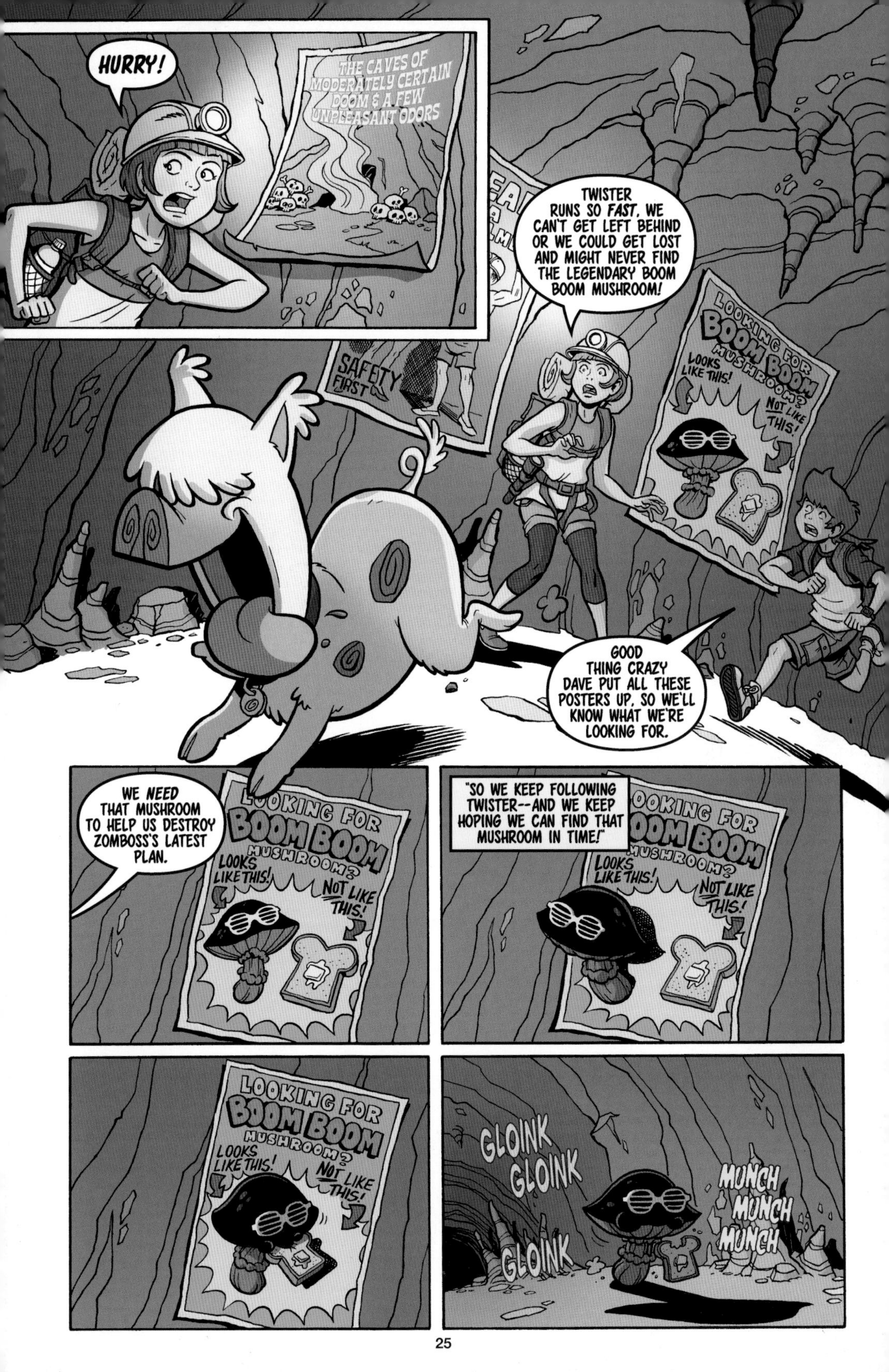
HURRY!
THE CAVES OF MODERATELY CERTAIN DOOM & A FEW UNPLEASANT ODORS
TWISTER RUNS SO FAST, WE CAN'T GET LEFT BEHIND OR WE COULD GET LOST AND MIGHT NEVER FIND THE LEGENDARY BOOM BOOM MUSHROOM!
SAFETY FIRST
LOOKING FOR BOOM BOOM MUSHROOM?
LOOKS LIKE THIS!
NOT LIKE THIS!
GOOD THING CRAZY DAVE PUT ALL THESE POSTERS UP, SO WE'LL KNOW WHAT WE'RE LOOKING FOR.
WE NEED THAT MUSHROOM TO HELP US DESTROY ZOMBOSS'S LATEST PLAN.
"SO WE KEEP FOLLOWING TWISTER--AND WE KEEP HOPING WE CAN FIND THAT MUSHROOM IN TIME!"
GLOINK
GLOINK
GLOINK
MUNCH
MUNCH
MUNCH

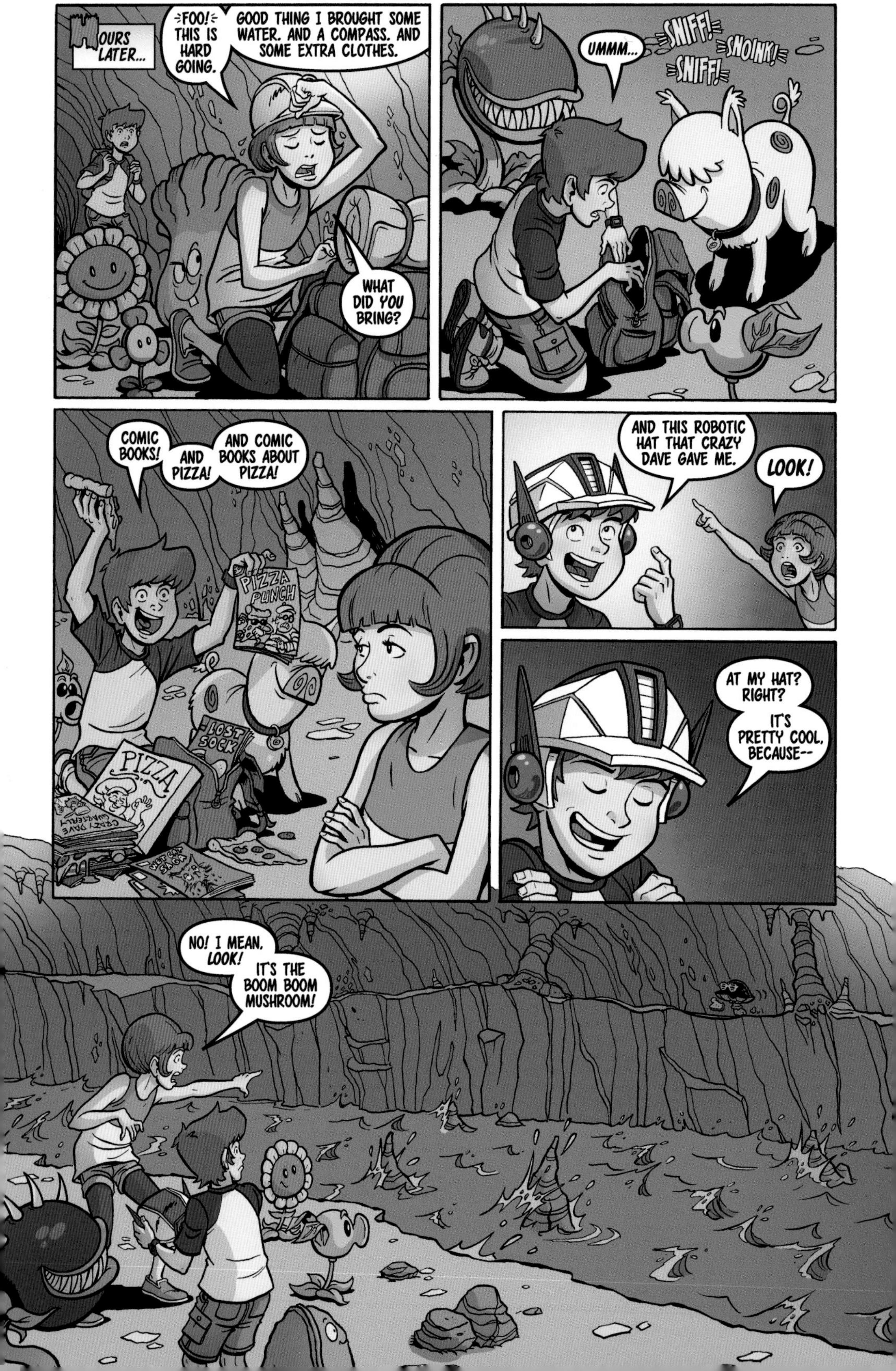
HOURS LATER...
FOO! THIS IS HARD GOING.
GOOD THING I BROUGHT SOME WATER. AND A COMPASS. AND SOME EXTRA CLOTHES.
WHAT DID YOU BRING?
UMMM...
SNIFF!
SNOINK!
SNIFF!
COMIC BOOKS!
AND PIZZA!
AND COMIC BOOKS ABOUT PIZZA!
PIZZA PUNCH
LOST SOCK
PIZZA
CRAZY DAVE
AND THIS ROBOTIC HAT THAT CRAZY DAVE GAVE ME.
LOOK!
AT MY HAT? RIGHT?
IT'S PRETTY COOL, BECAUSE--
NO! I MEAN, LOOK!
IT'S THE BOOM BOOM MUSHROOM!

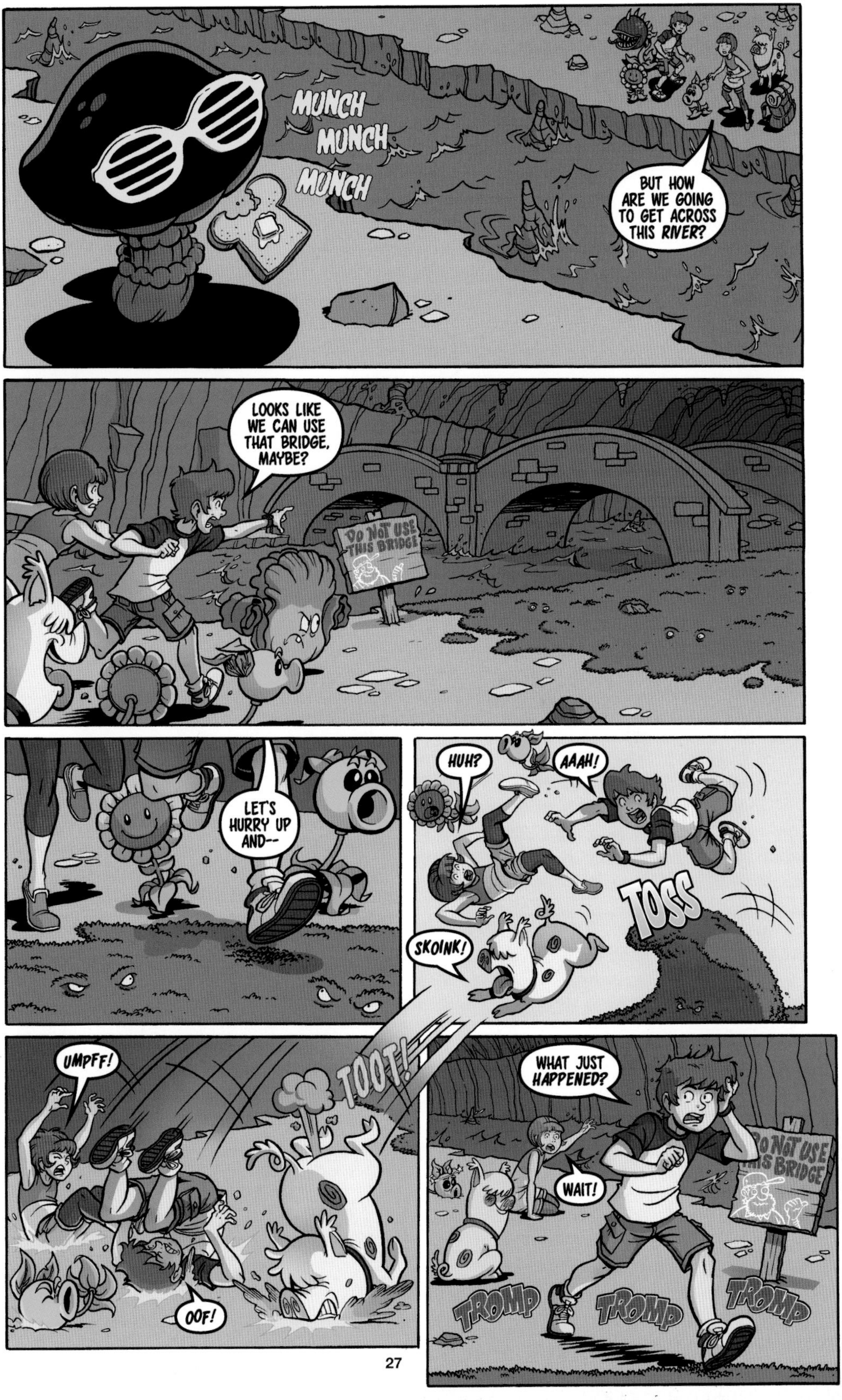
MUNCH
MUNCH
MUNCH
BUT HOW ARE WE GOING TO GET ACROSS THIS RIVER?
LOOKS LIKE WE CAN USE THAT BRIDGE, MAYBE?
DO NOT USE THIS BRIDGE
LET'S HURRY UP AND--
HUH?
AAAH!
TOSS
SKOINK!
UMPFF!
TOOT!
OOF!
WHAT JUST HAPPENED?
WAIT!
DO NOT USE THIS BRIDGE
TROMP
TROMP
TROMP

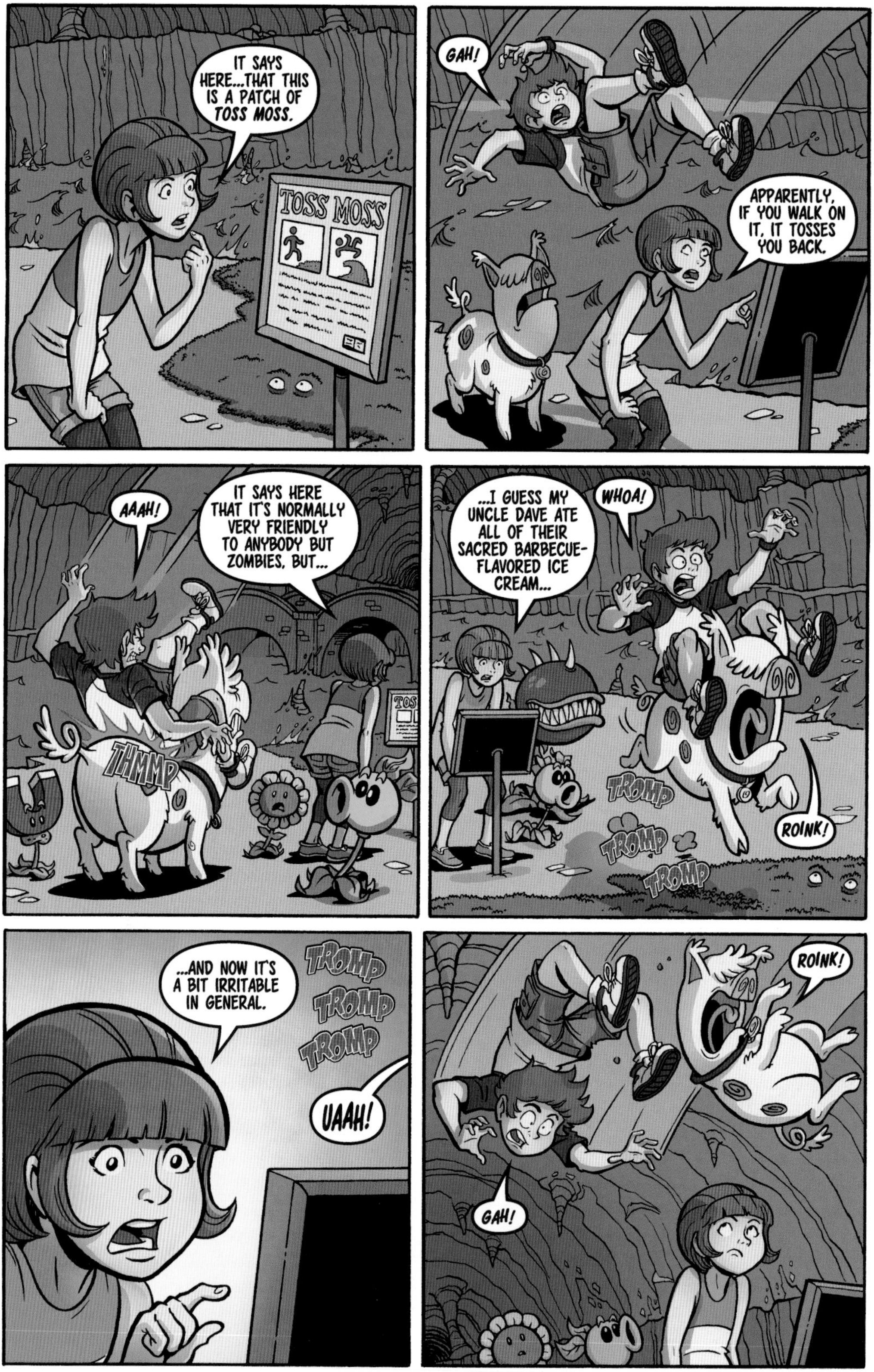
IT SAYS HERE...THAT THIS IS A PATCH OF TOSS MOSS.
TOSS MOSS
GAH!
APPARENTLY, IF YOU WALK ON IT, IT TOSSES YOU BACK.
AAAH!
IT SAYS HERE THAT IT'S NORMALLY VERY FRIENDLY TO ANYBODY BUT ZOMBIES, BUT...
THMMP
...I GUESS MY UNCLE DAVE ATE ALL OF THEIR SACRED BARBECUE-FLAVORED ICE CREAM...
WHOA!
TROMP
TROMP
TROMP
ROINK!
...AND NOW IT'S A BIT IRRITABLE IN GENERAL.
TROMP
TROMP
TROMP
UAAH!
ROINK!
GAH!

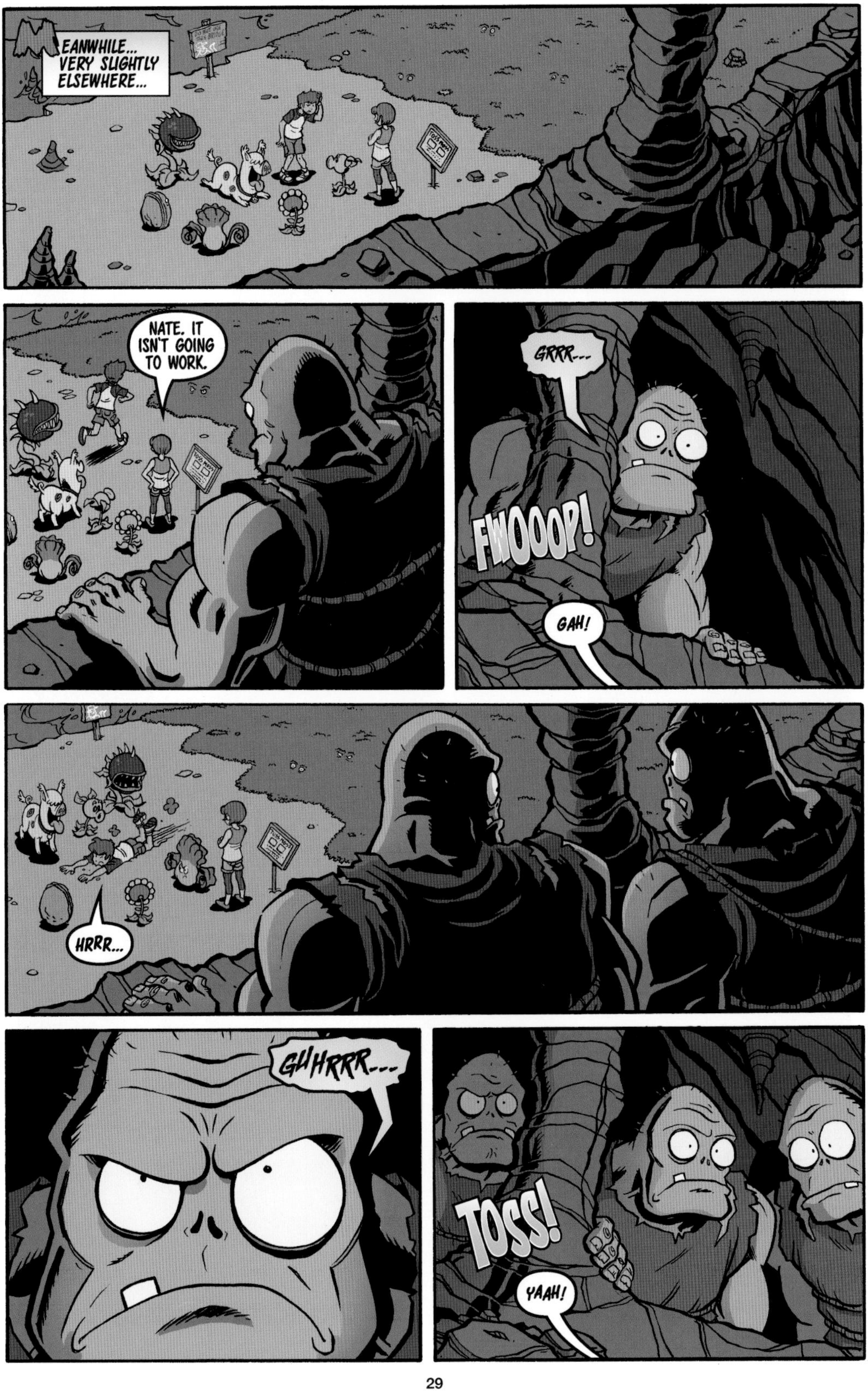
MEANWHILE... VERY SLIGHTLY ELSEWHERE...
NATE. IT ISN'T GOING TO WORK.
GRRR...
FWOOOP!
GAH!
HRRR...
GUHRRR...
TOSS!
YAAH!

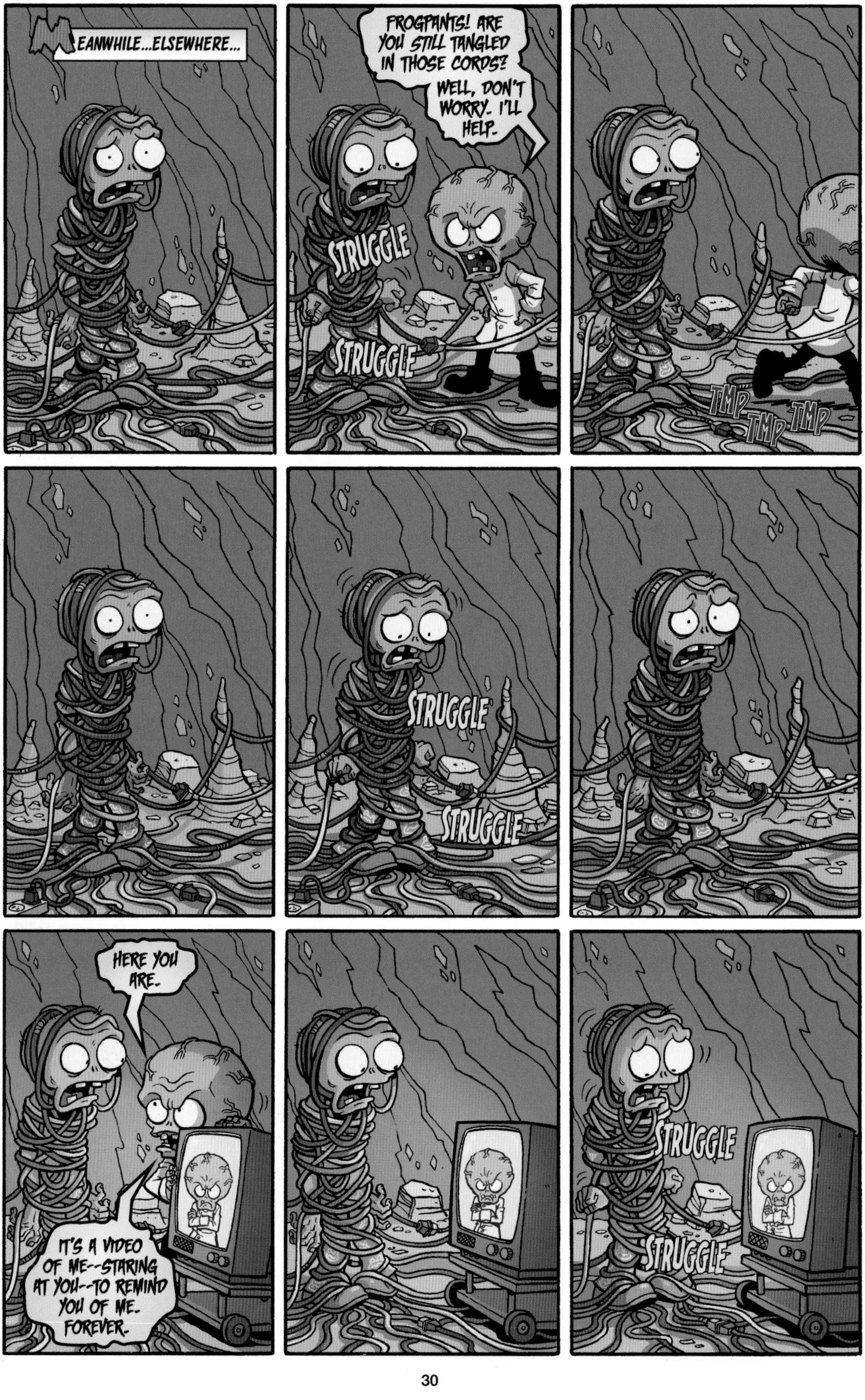
MEANWHILE...ELSEWHERE...
FROGPANTS! ARE YOU STILL TANGLED IN THOSE CORDS?
WELL, DON'T WORRY. I'LL HELP.
STRUGGLE
STRUGGLE
TMP TMP TMP
STRUGGLE
STRUGGLE
HERE YOU ARE.
IT'S A VIDEO OF ME--STARING AT YOU--TO REMIND YOU OF ME. FOREVER.
STRUGGLE
STRUGGLE

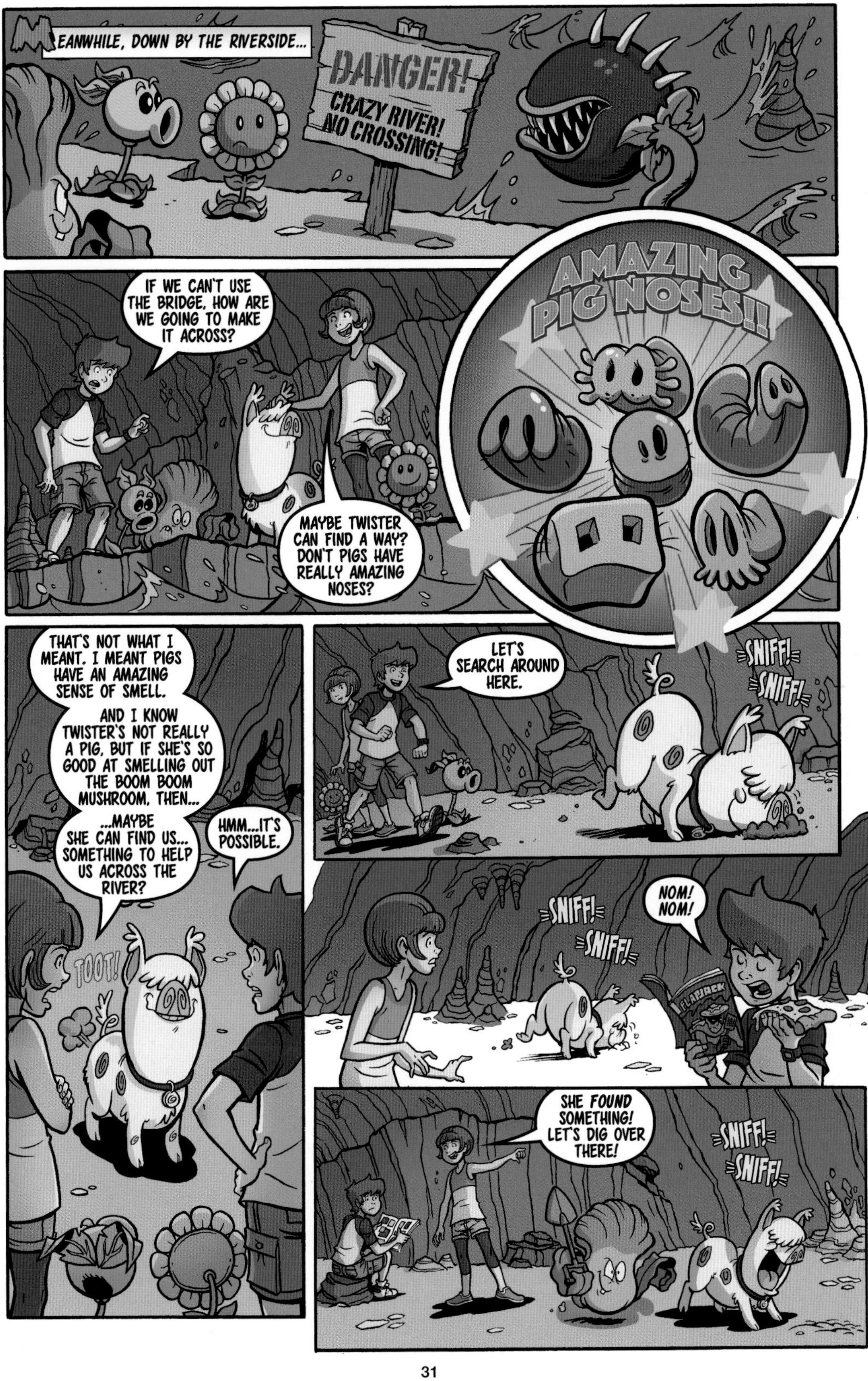
MEANWHILE, DOWN BY THE RIVERSIDE...
DANGER! CRAZY RIVER! NO CROSSING!
IF WE CAN'T USE THE BRIDGE, HOW ARE WE GOING TO MAKE IT ACROSS?
MAYBE TWISTER CAN FIND A WAY? DON'T PIGS HAVE REALLY AMAZING NOSES?
AMAZING PIG NOSES!!
THAT'S NOT WHAT I MEANT. I MEANT PIGS HAVE AN AMAZING SENSE OF SMELL.
AND I KNOW TWISTER'S NOT REALLY A PIG, BUT IF SHE'S SO GOOD AT SMELLING OUT THE BOOM BOOM MUSHROOM, THEN...
...MAYBE SHE CAN FIND US... SOMETHING TO HELP US ACROSS THE RIVER?
HMM...IT'S POSSIBLE.
TOOT!
LET'S SEARCH AROUND HERE.
SNIFF! SNIFF!
SNIFF! SNIFF!
NOM! NOM!
FLAPJACK
SHE FOUND SOMETHING! LET'S DIG OVER THERE!
SNIFF! SNIFF!

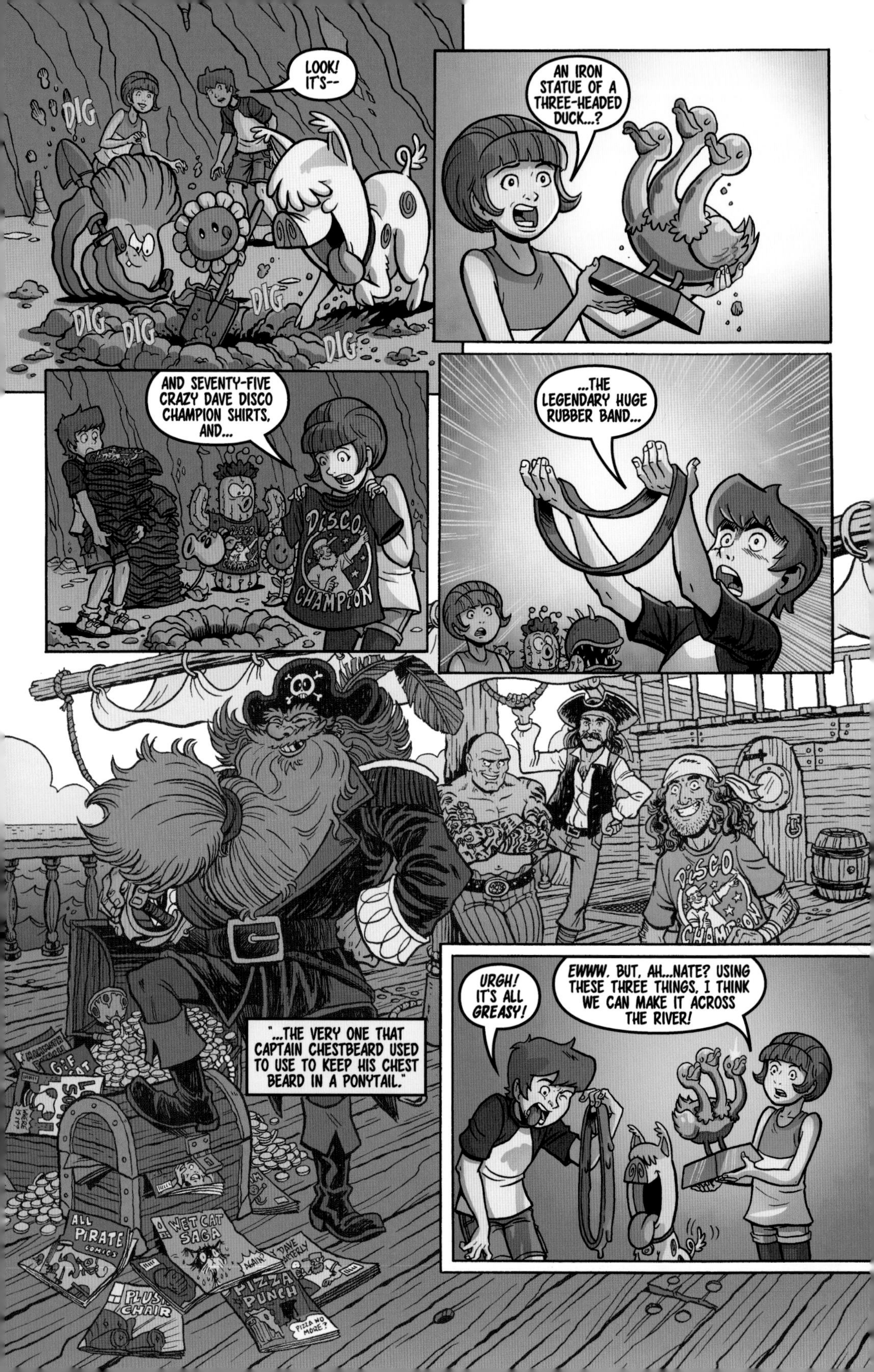
DIG
LOOK! IT'S--
DIG
DIG
DIG
DIG
AN IRON STATUE OF A THREE-HEADED DUCK...?
AND SEVENTY-FIVE CRAZY DAVE DISCO CHAMPION SHIRTS, AND...
DISCO CHAMPION
...THE LEGENDARY HUGE RUBBER BAND...
"...THE VERY ONE THAT CAPTAIN CHESTBEARD USED TO USE TO KEEP HIS CHEST BEARD IN A PONYTAIL."
DISCO CHAMPION
ALL PIRATE COMICS
WET CAT SAGA
PIZZA PUNCH
PIZZA NO MORE?
PLUSH CHAIR
URGH! IT'S ALL GREASY!
EWWW. BUT, AH...NATE? USING THESE THREE THINGS, I THINK WE CAN MAKE IT ACROSS THE RIVER!

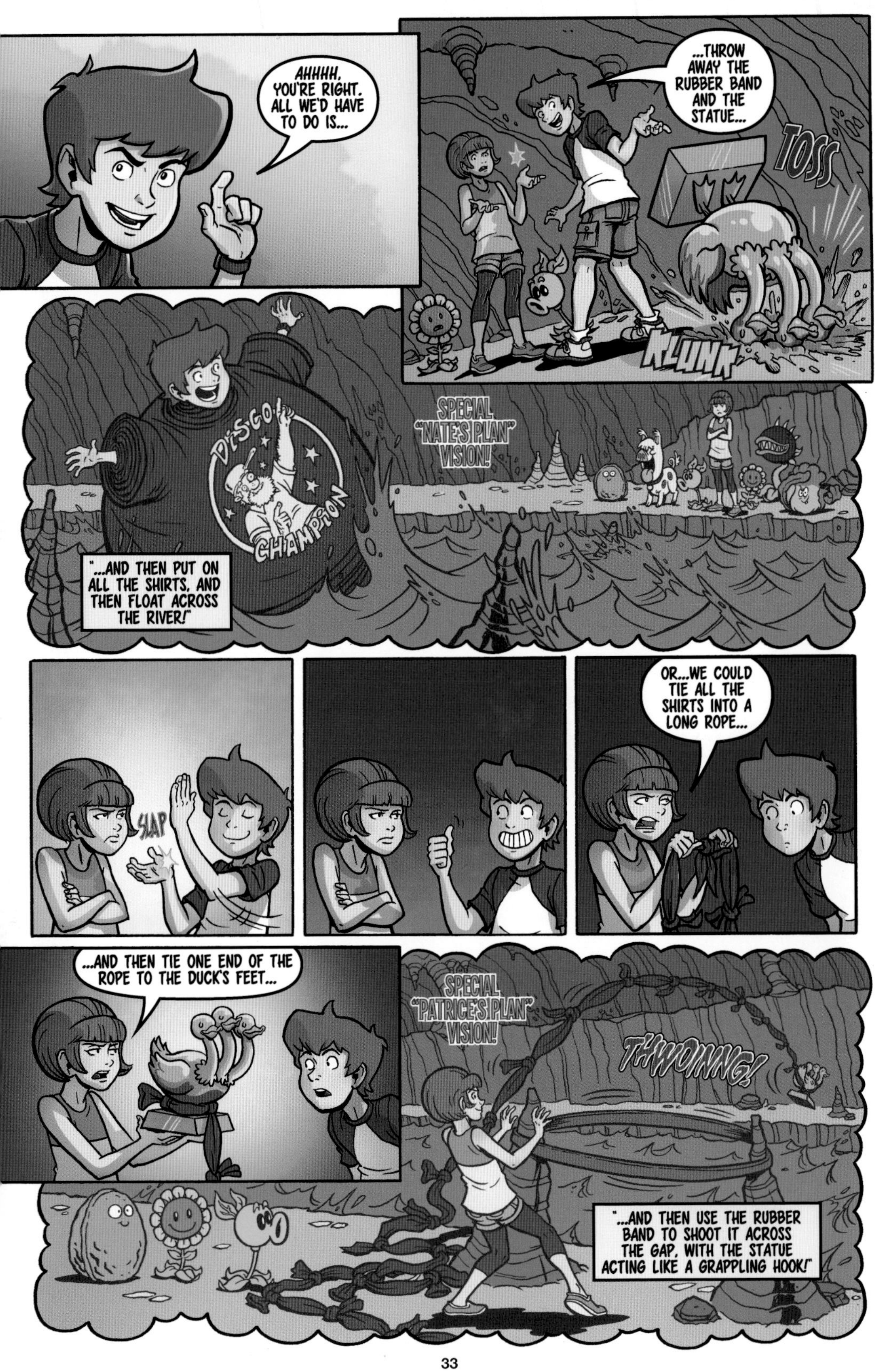
AHHHH, YOU'RE RIGHT. ALL WE'D HAVE TO DO IS...
...THROW AWAY THE RUBBER BAND AND THE STATUE...
TOSS
KLUNK
SPECIAL "NATE'S PLAN" VISION!
DISCO CHAMPION
"...AND THEN PUT ON ALL THE SHIRTS, AND THEN FLOAT ACROSS THE RIVER!"
SLAP
OR...WE COULD TIE ALL THE SHIRTS INTO A LONG ROPE...
...AND THEN TIE ONE END OF THE ROPE TO THE DUCK'S FEET...
SPECIAL "PATRICE'S PLAN" VISION!
THWOINNG!
"...AND THEN USE THE RUBBER BAND TO SHOOT IT ACROSS THE GAP, WITH THE STATUE ACTING LIKE A GRAPPLING HOOK!"

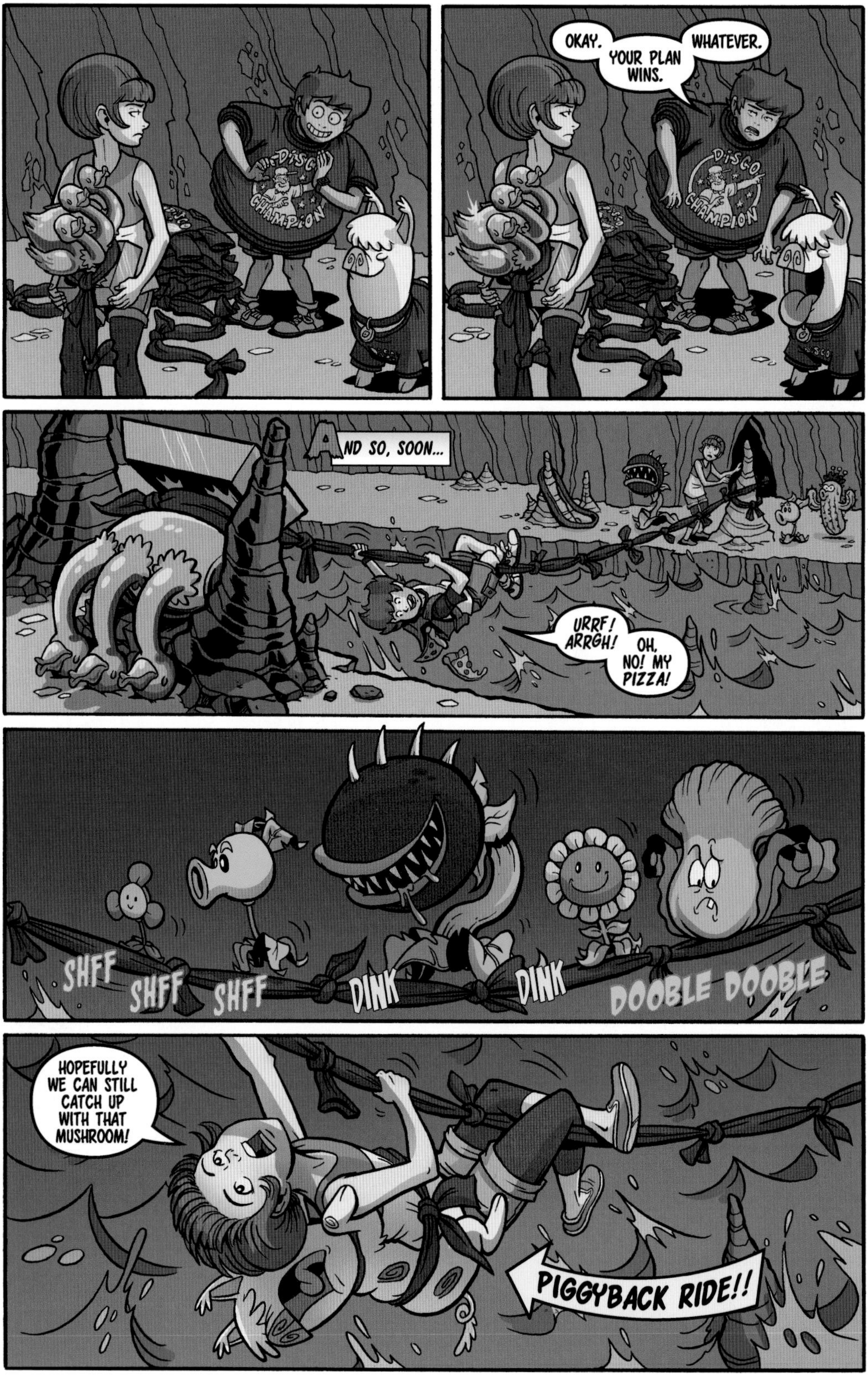

OKAY.
YOUR PLAN WINS.
WHATEVER.
AND SO, SOON...
URRF! ARRGH!
OH, NO! MY PIZZA!
SHFF
SHFF
SHFF
DINK
DINK
DOOBLE DOOBLE
HOPEFULLY WE CAN STILL CATCH UP WITH THAT MUSHROOM!
PIGGYBACK RIDE!!

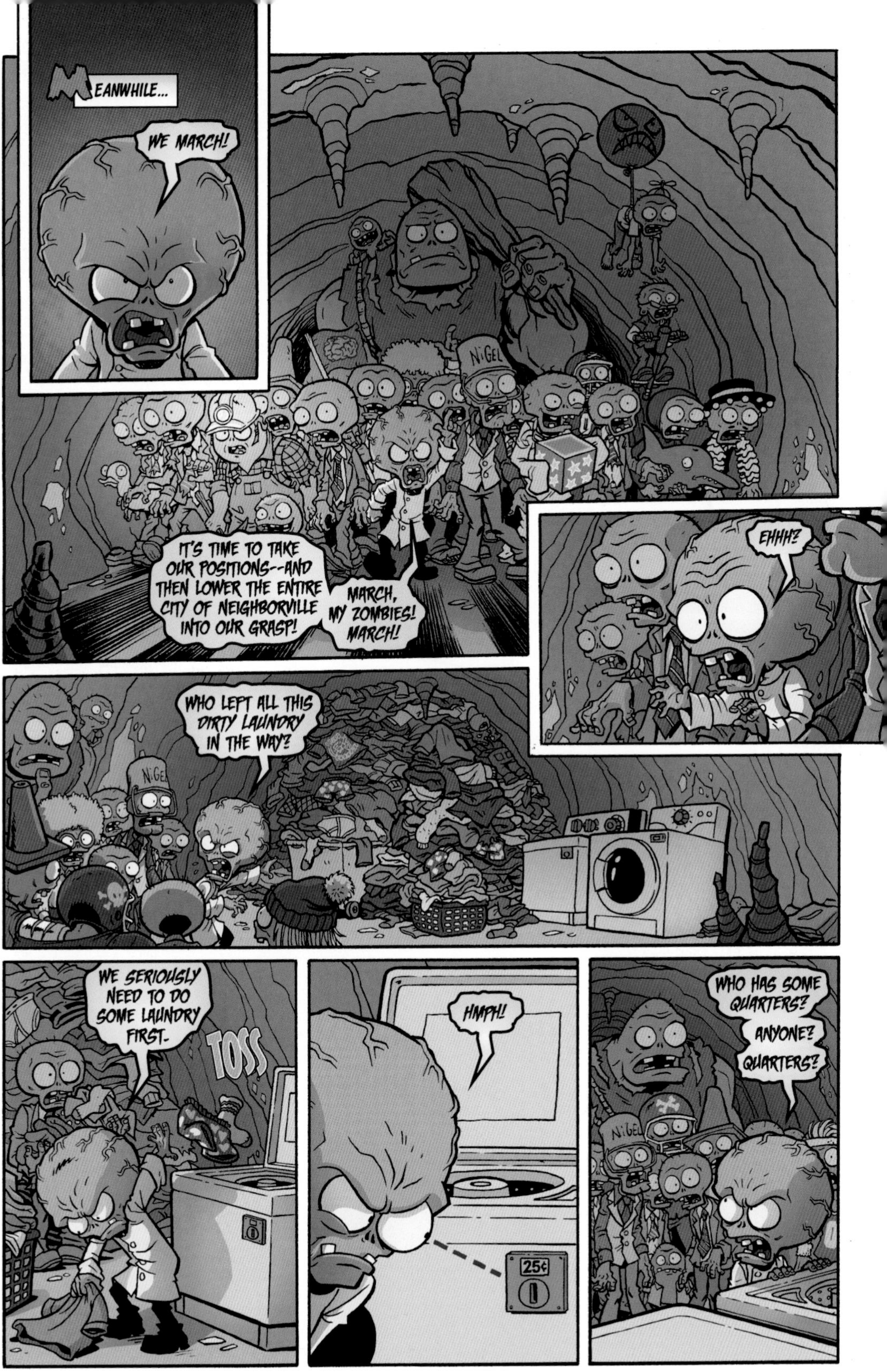

MEANWHILE...
WE MARCH!
IT'S TIME TO TAKE OUR POSITIONS--AND THEN LOWER THE ENTIRE CITY OF NEIGHBORVILLE INTO OUR GRASP!
MARCH, MY ZOMBIES! MARCH!
EHHH?
WHO LEFT ALL THIS DIRTY LAUNDRY IN THE WAY?
WE SERIOUSLY NEED TO DO SOME LAUNDRY FIRST.
TOSS
HMPH!
25¢
WHO HAS SOME QUARTERS?
ANYONE?
QUARTERS?

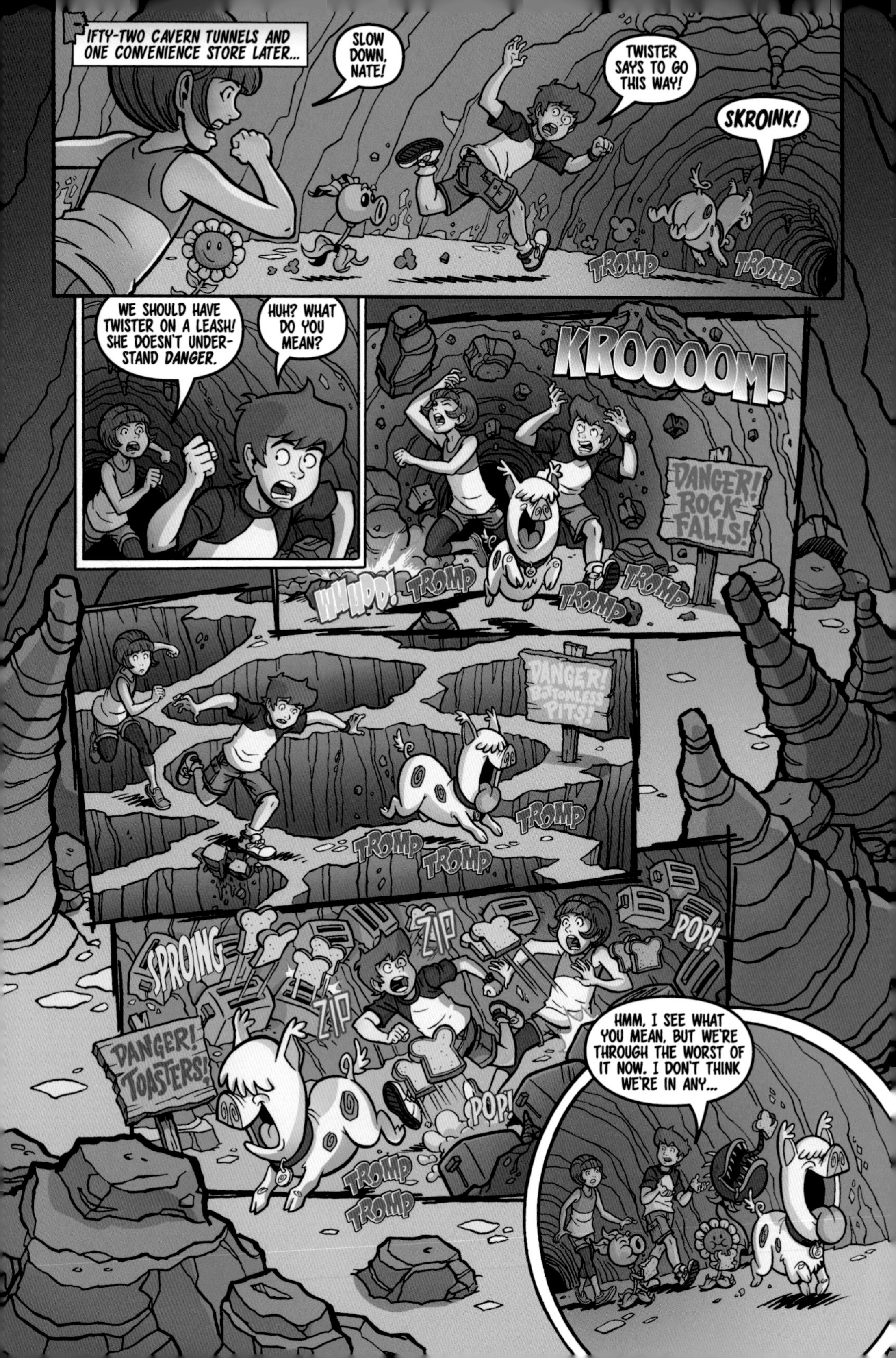
FIFTY-TWO CAVERN TUNNELS AND ONE CONVENIENCE STORE LATER...
SLOW DOWN, NATE!
TWISTER SAYS TO GO THIS WAY!
SKROINK!
TROMP
TROMP
WE SHOULD HAVE TWISTER ON A LEASH! SHE DOESN'T UNDER-STAND DANGER.
HUH? WHAT DO YOU MEAN?
KROOOOOM!
DANGER! ROCK FALLS!
WHUDD!
TROMP
TROMP
TROMP
DANGER! BOTTOMLESS PITS!
TROMP
TROMP
TROMP
SPROING
ZIP
POP!
ZIP
DANGER! TOASTERS!
POP!
TROMP
TROMP
HMM, I SEE WHAT YOU MEAN, BUT WE'RE THROUGH THE WORST OF IT NOW. I DON'T THINK WE'RE IN ANY...

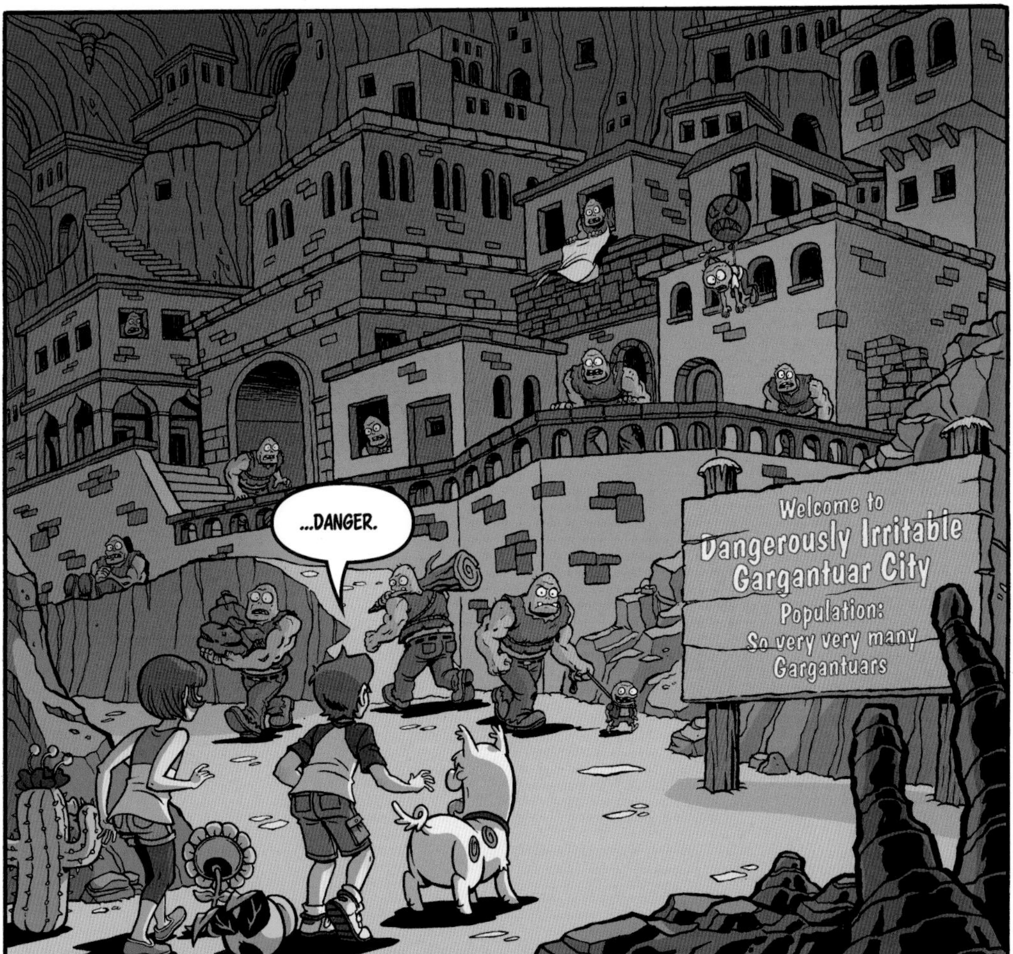
...DANGER.
Welcome to
Dangerously Irritable
Gargantuar City
Population:
So very very many
Gargantuars

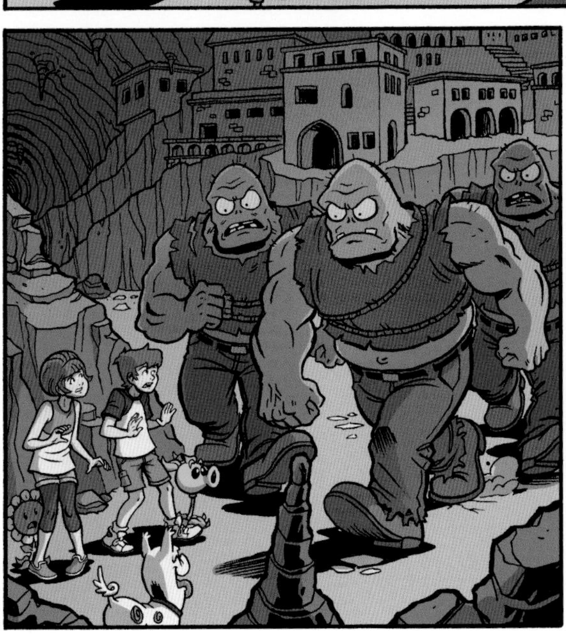

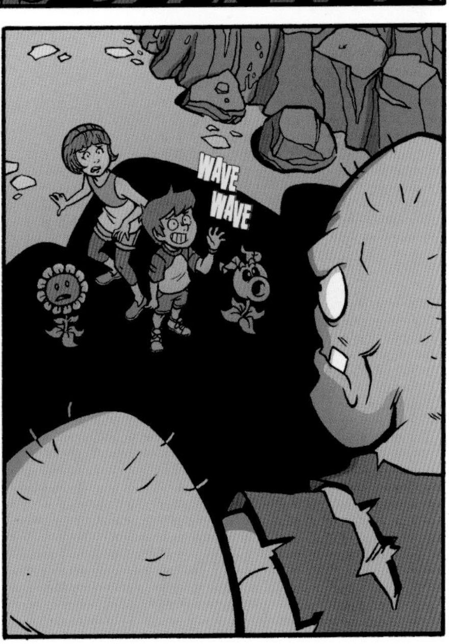
WAVE
WAVE

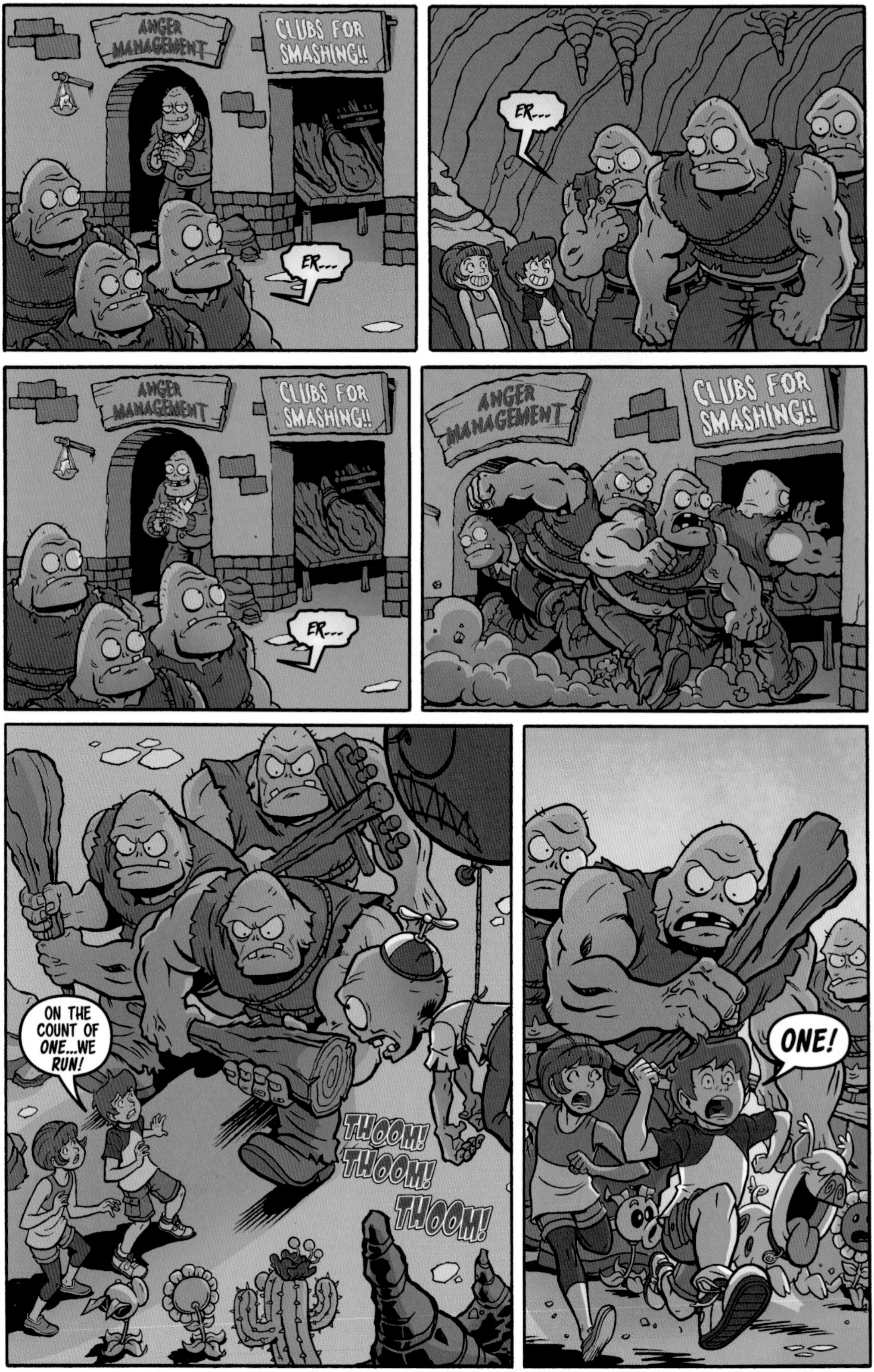
ANGER MANAGEMENT
CLUBS FOR SMASHING!!
ER...
ER...
ANGER MANAGEMENT
CLUBS FOR SMASHING!!
ER...
ANGER MANAGEMENT
CLUBS FOR SMASHING!!
ON THE COUNT OF ONE...WE RUN!
THOOM! THOOM!
THOOM!
ONE!

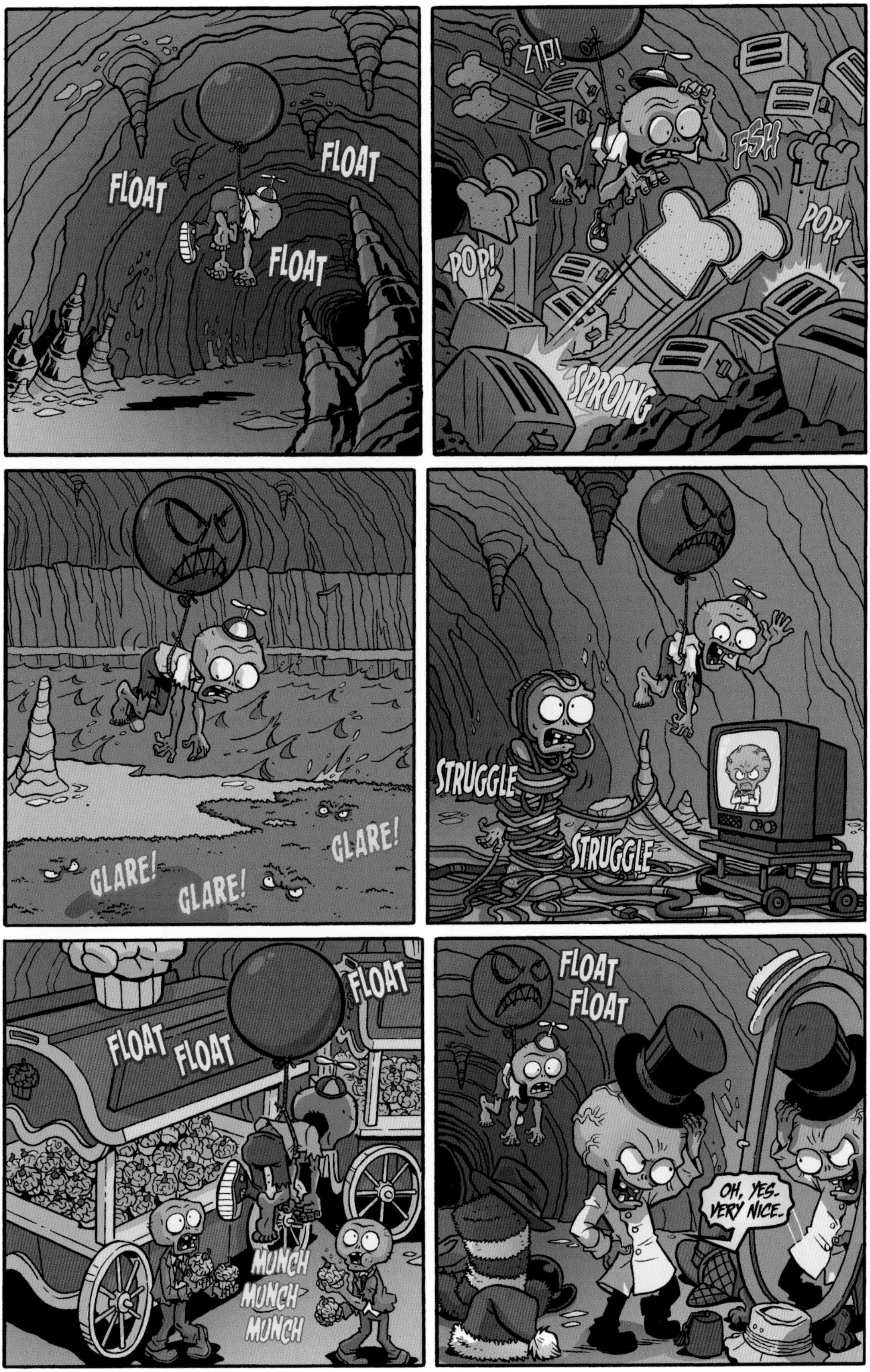
FLOAT
FLOAT
FLOAT
ZIP!
FSH
POP!
POP!
SPROING
GLARE!
GLARE!
GLARE!
STRUGGLE
STRUGGLE
FLOAT
FLOAT
FLOAT
MUNCH
MUNCH
MUNCH
FLOAT
FLOAT
OH, YES. VERY NICE.

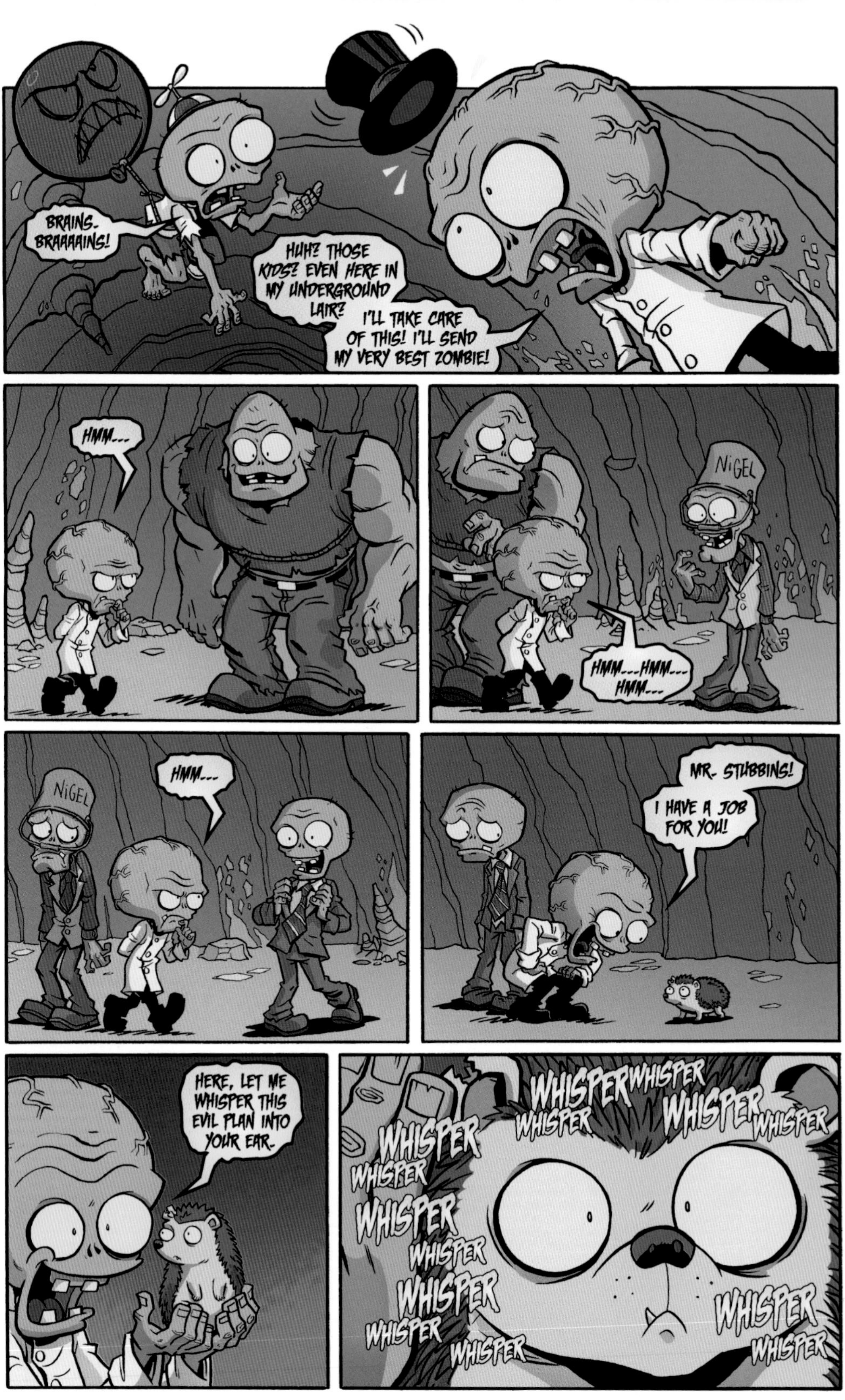
BRAINS. BRAAAAINS!
HUH? THOSE KIDS? EVEN HERE IN MY UNDERGROUND LAIR?
I'LL TAKE CARE OF THIS! I'LL SEND MY VERY BEST ZOMBIE!
HMM...
NIGEL
HMM...HMM... HMM...
NIGEL
HMM...
MR. STUBBINS!
I HAVE A JOB FOR YOU!
HERE, LET ME WHISPER THIS EVIL PLAN INTO YOUR EAR.
WHISPER WHISPER WHISPER WHISPER WHISPER WHISPER WHISPER WHISPER WHISPER WHISPER WHISPER WHISPER WHISPER WHISPER

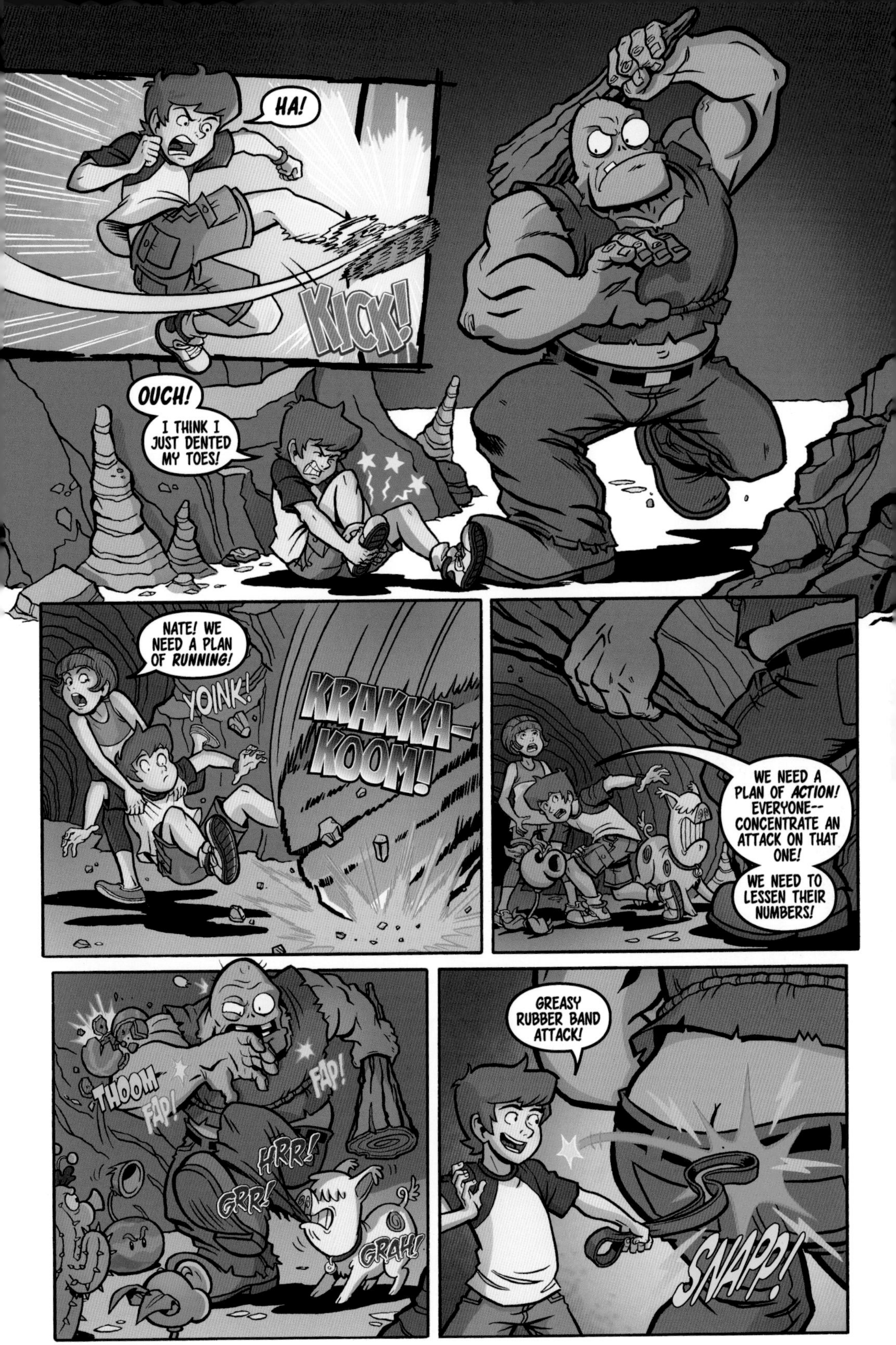
HA!
KICK!
OUCH!
I THINK I JUST DENTED MY TOES!
NATE! WE NEED A PLAN OF RUNNING!
YOINK!
KRAKKA-KOOM!
WE NEED A PLAN OF ACTION! EVERYONE-- CONCENTRATE AN ATTACK ON THAT ONE!
WE NEED TO LESSEN THEIR NUMBERS!
THOOM
FAP!
FAP!
HRR!
GRR!
GRAH!
GREASY RUBBER BAND ATTACK!
SNAPP!

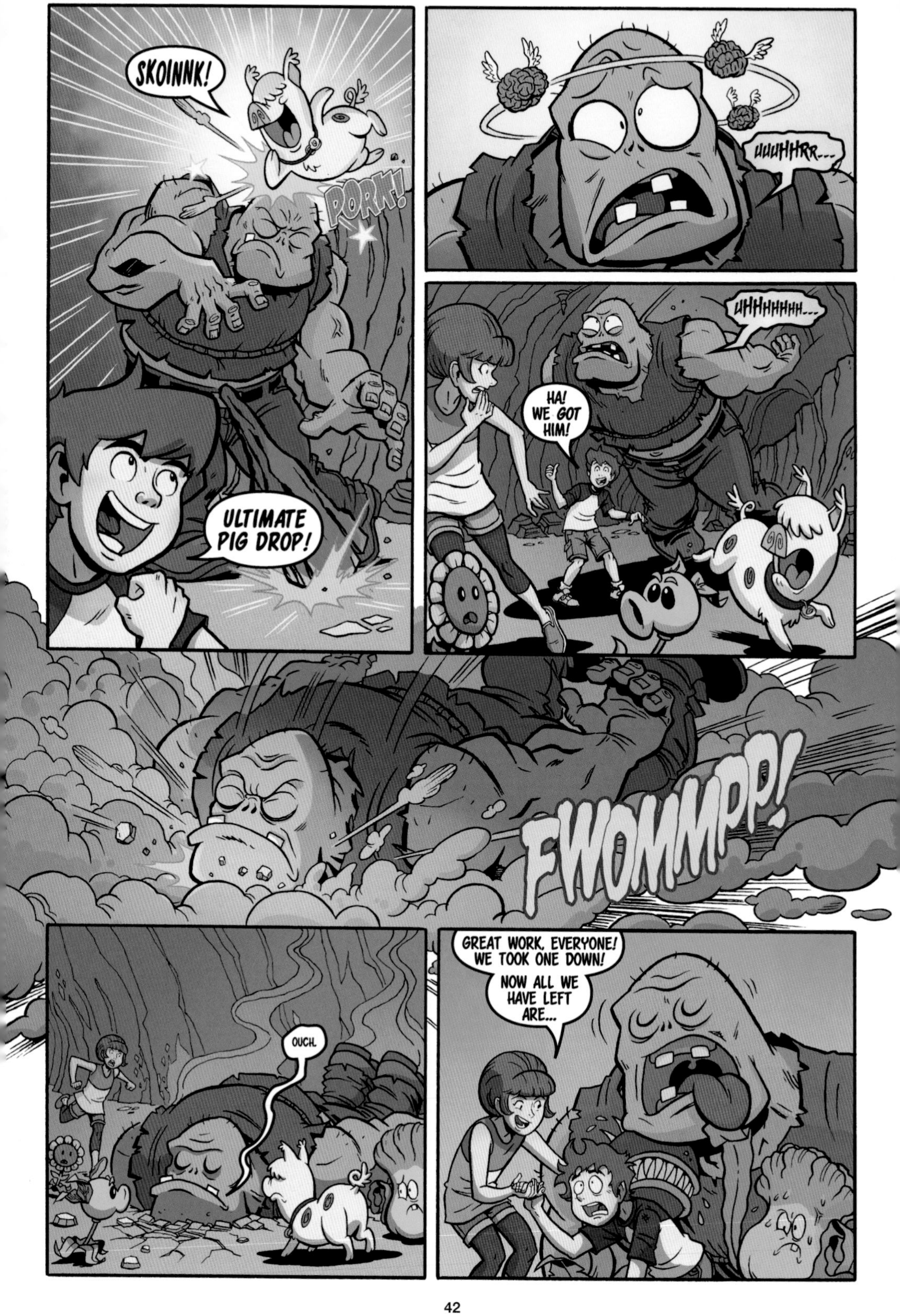

SKOINNK!
PORK!
ULTIMATE PIG DROP!
UUUHHRR...
UHHHHHHH...
HA! WE GOT HIM!
FWOMMPP!
OUCH.
GREAT WORK, EVERYONE! WE TOOK ONE DOWN!
NOW ALL WE HAVE LEFT ARE...

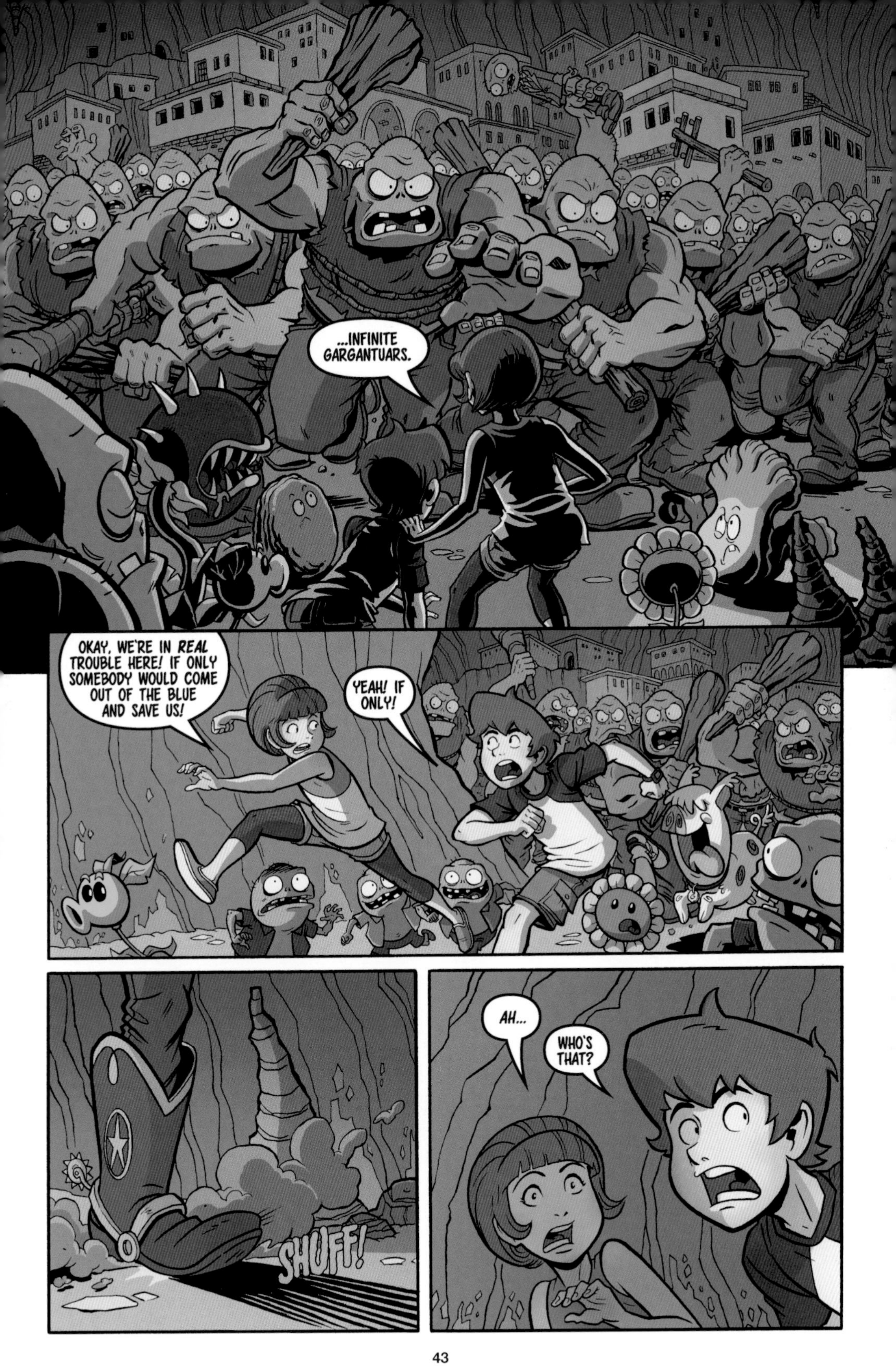
...INFINITE GARGANTUARS.
OKAY, WE'RE IN REAL TROUBLE HERE! IF ONLY SOMEBODY WOULD COME OUT OF THE BLUE AND SAVE US!
YEAH! IF ONLY!
SHUFF!
AH...
WHO'S THAT?

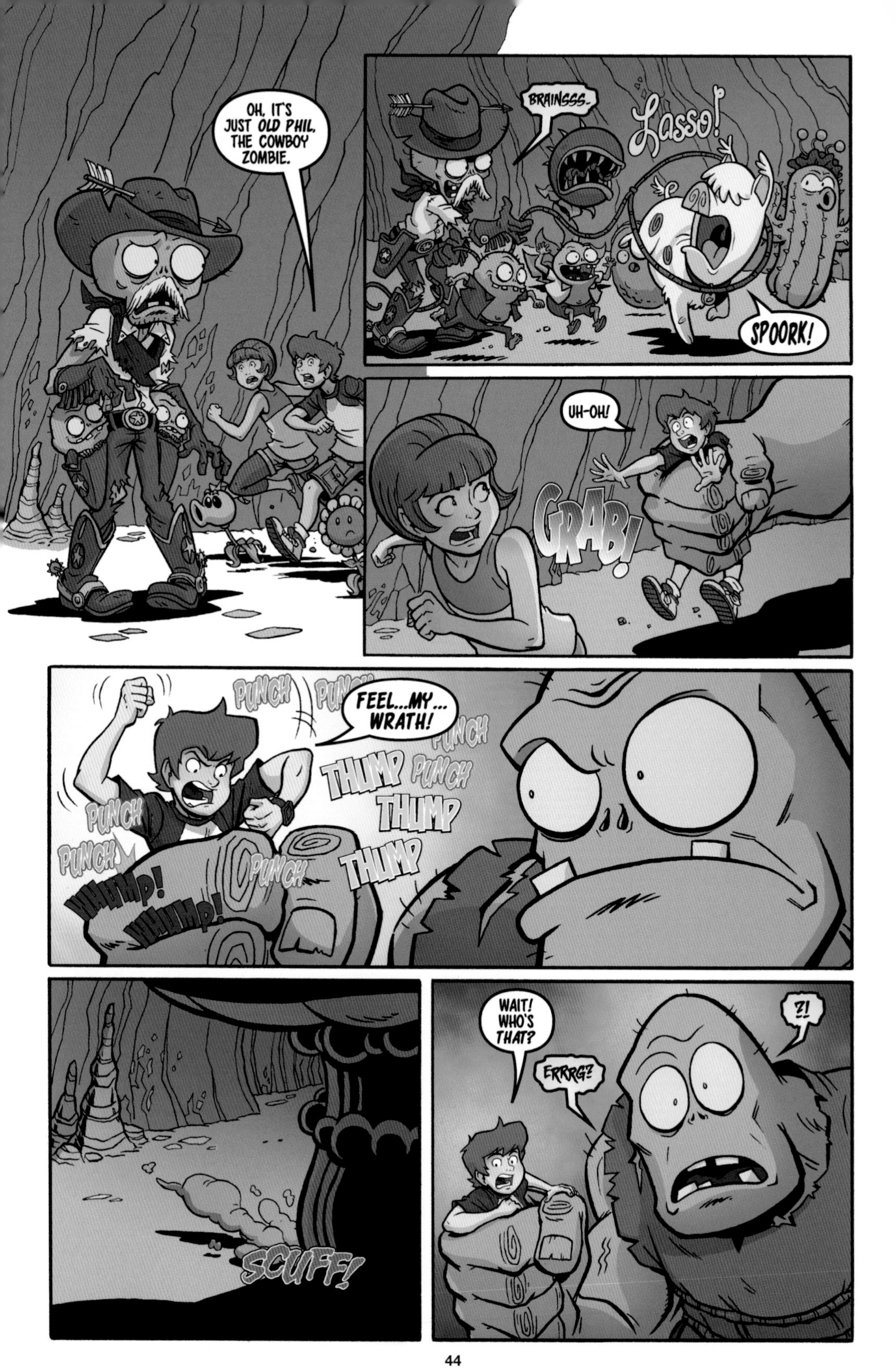
OH, IT'S JUST OLD PHIL, THE COWBOY ZOMBIE.
BRAINSSS...
Lasso!
SPOORK!
UH-OH!
GRAB!
FEEL...MY... WRATH!
PUNCH
PUNCH
PUNCH
THUMP
PUNCH
THUMP
PUNCH
PUNCH
PUNCH
THUMP
WHUMP!
WHUMP!
SCUFF!
WAIT! WHO'S THAT?
ERRRG?
?!

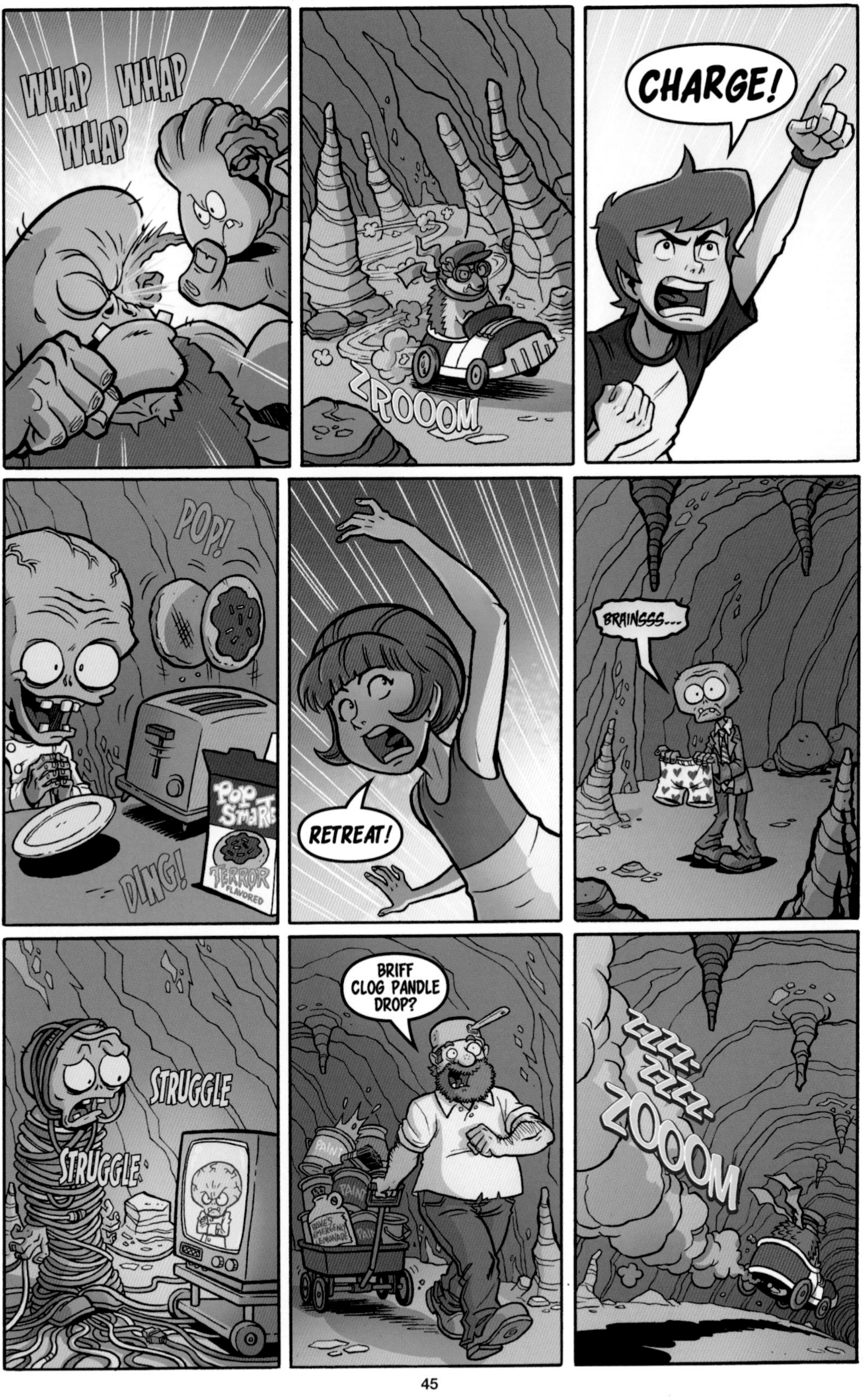
WHAP WHAP
WHAP
ZROOOM
CHARGE!
POP!
DING!
POP SMARTS
TERROR
FLAVORED
RETREAT!
BRAINSSS...
STRUGGLE
STRUGGLE
BRIFF CLOG PANDLE DROP?
PAINT
PAINT
DAVE'S EMERGENCY LEMONADE
ZZZZ-ZZZZ-
ZOOOM

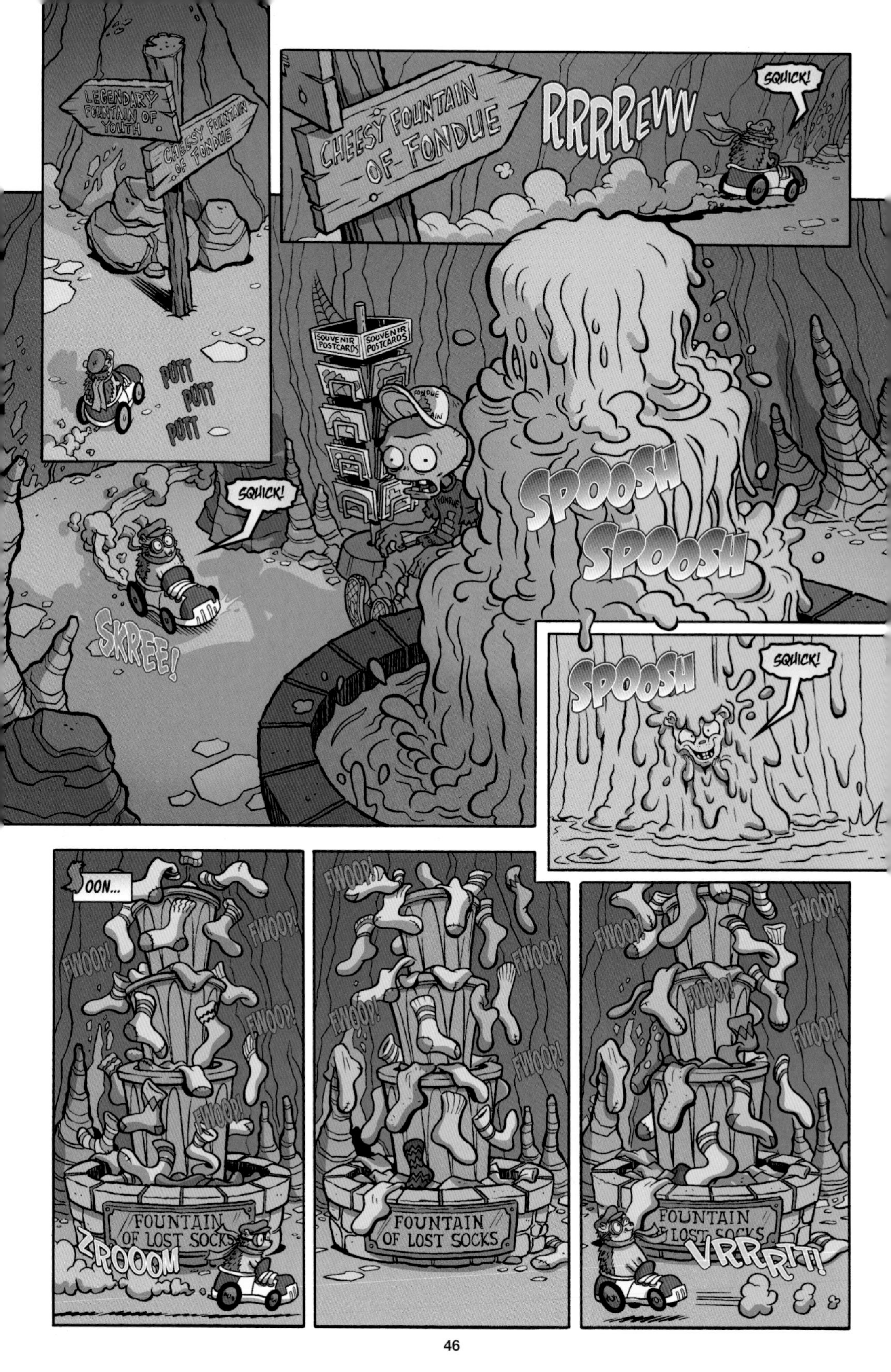
LEGENDARY FOUNTAIN OF YOUTH
CHEESY FOUNTAIN OF FONDUE
PUTT PUTT PUTT
CHEESY FOUNTAIN OF FONDUE
RRRREWW
SQUICK!
SOUVENIR POSTCARDS
SOUVENIR POSTCARDS
SQUICK!
SKREE!
SPOOSH
SPOOSH
SPOOSH
SQUICK!
...OON...
FWOOP!
FWOOP!
FWOOP!
FWOOP!
FOUNTAIN OF LOST SOCKS
ZROOOM
FWOOP!
FWOOP!
FWOOP!
FWOOP!
FOUNTAIN OF LOST SOCKS
FWOOP!
FWOOP!
FWOOP!
FWOOP!
FOUNTAIN OF LOST SOCKS
VRRRTT!

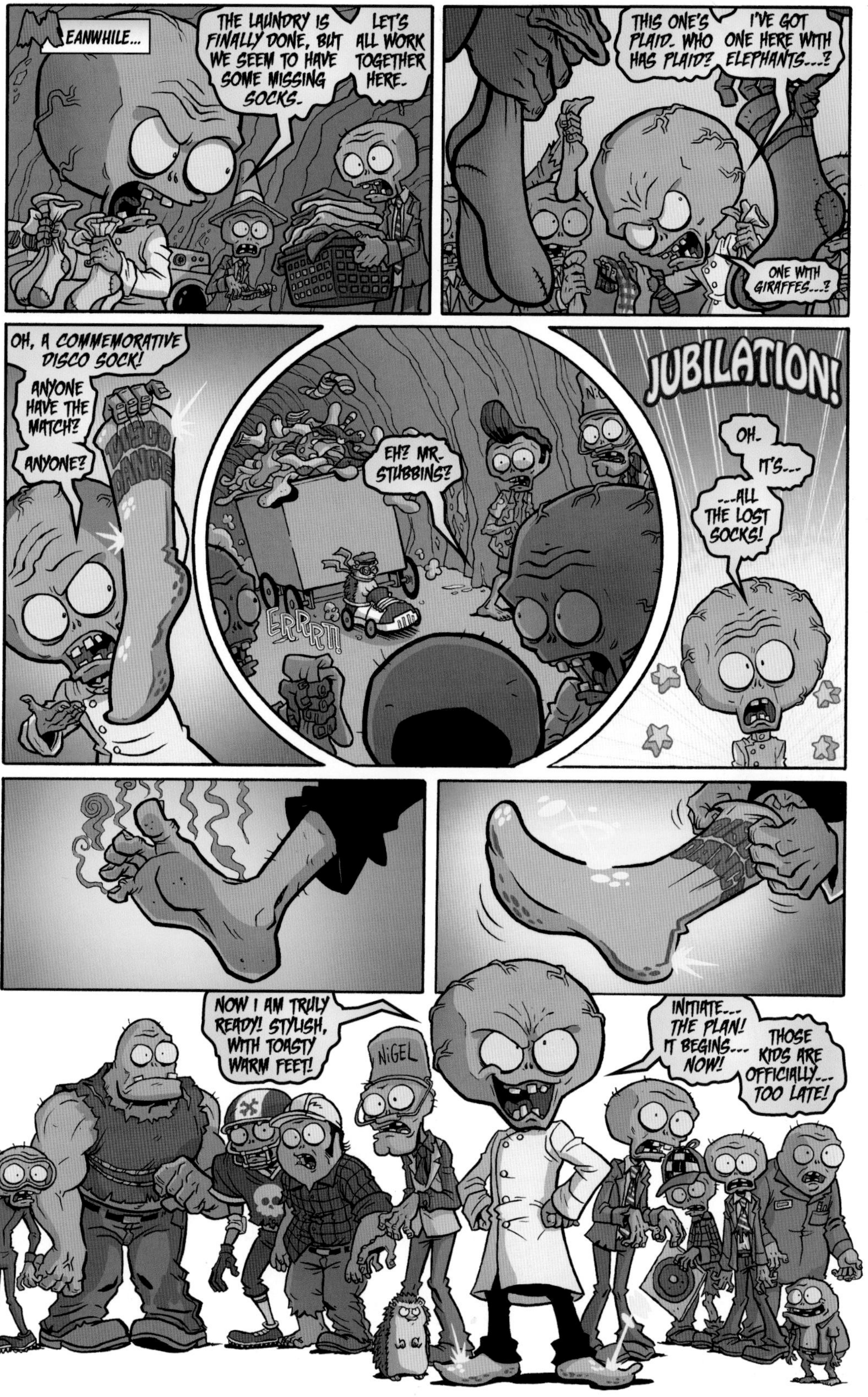
MEANWHILE...
THE LAUNDRY IS FINALLY DONE, BUT WE SEEM TO HAVE SOME MISSING SOCKS.
LET'S ALL WORK TOGETHER HERE.
THIS ONE'S PLAID. WHO HAS PLAID?
I'VE GOT ONE HERE WITH ELEPHANTS...?
ONE WITH GIRAFFES...?
OH, A COMMEMORATIVE DISCO SOCK!
ANYONE HAVE THE MATCH?
ANYONE?
EH? MR. STUBBINS?
ERRRT!
JUBILATION!
OH.
IT'S...
...ALL THE LOST SOCKS!
NOW I AM TRULY READY! STYLISH, WITH TOASTY WARM FEET!
NIGEL
INITIATE... THE PLAN! IT BEGINS... NOW!
THOSE KIDS ARE OFFICIALLY... TOO LATE!

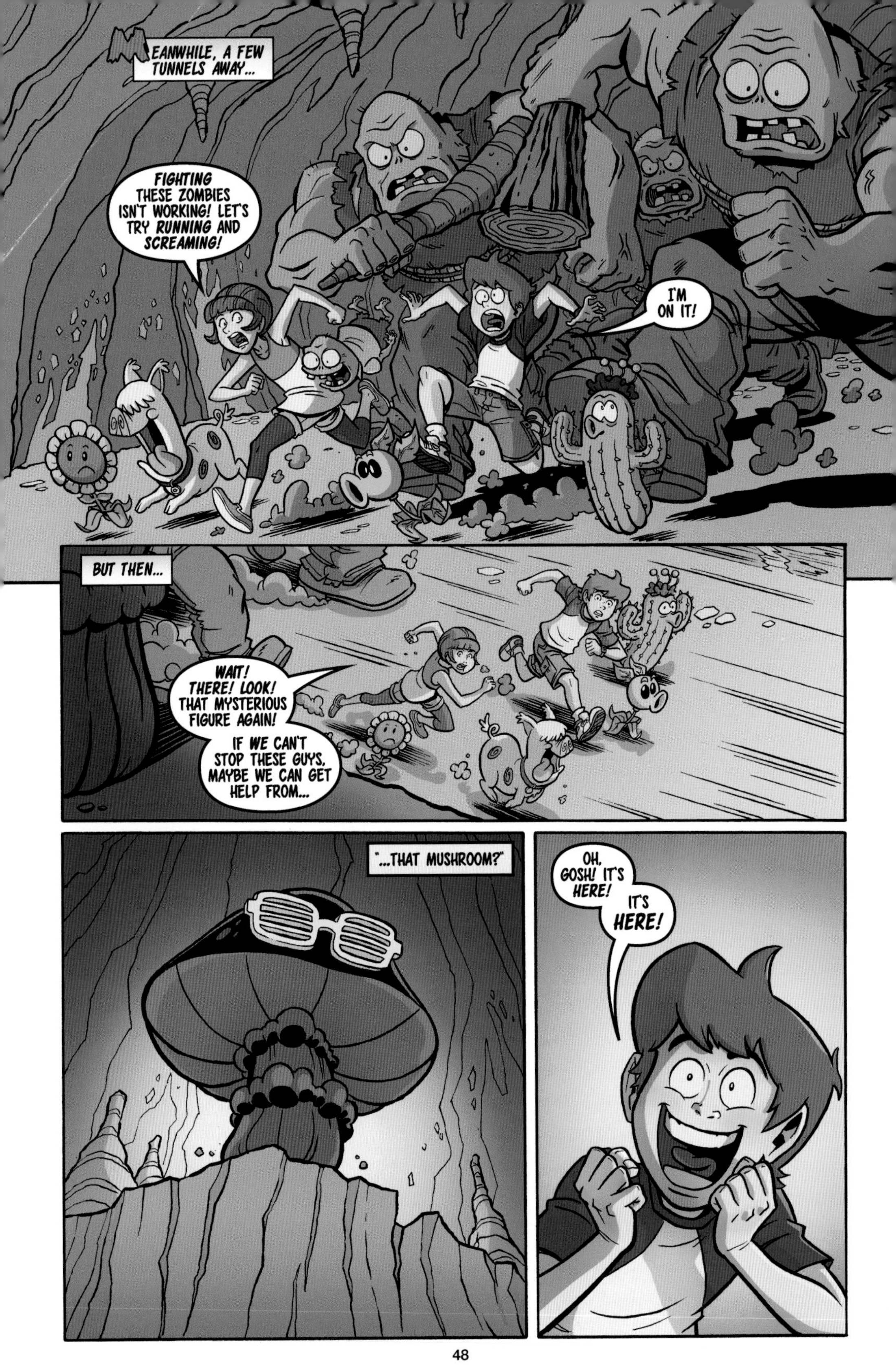
MEANWHILE, A FEW TUNNELS AWAY...
FIGHTING THESE ZOMBIES ISN'T WORKING! LET'S TRY RUNNING AND SCREAMING!
I'M ON IT!
BUT THEN...
WAIT! THERE! LOOK! THAT MYSTERIOUS FIGURE AGAIN!
IF WE CAN'T STOP THESE GUYS, MAYBE WE CAN GET HELP FROM...
"...THAT MUSHROOM?"
OH, GOSH! IT'S HERE!
IT'S HERE!

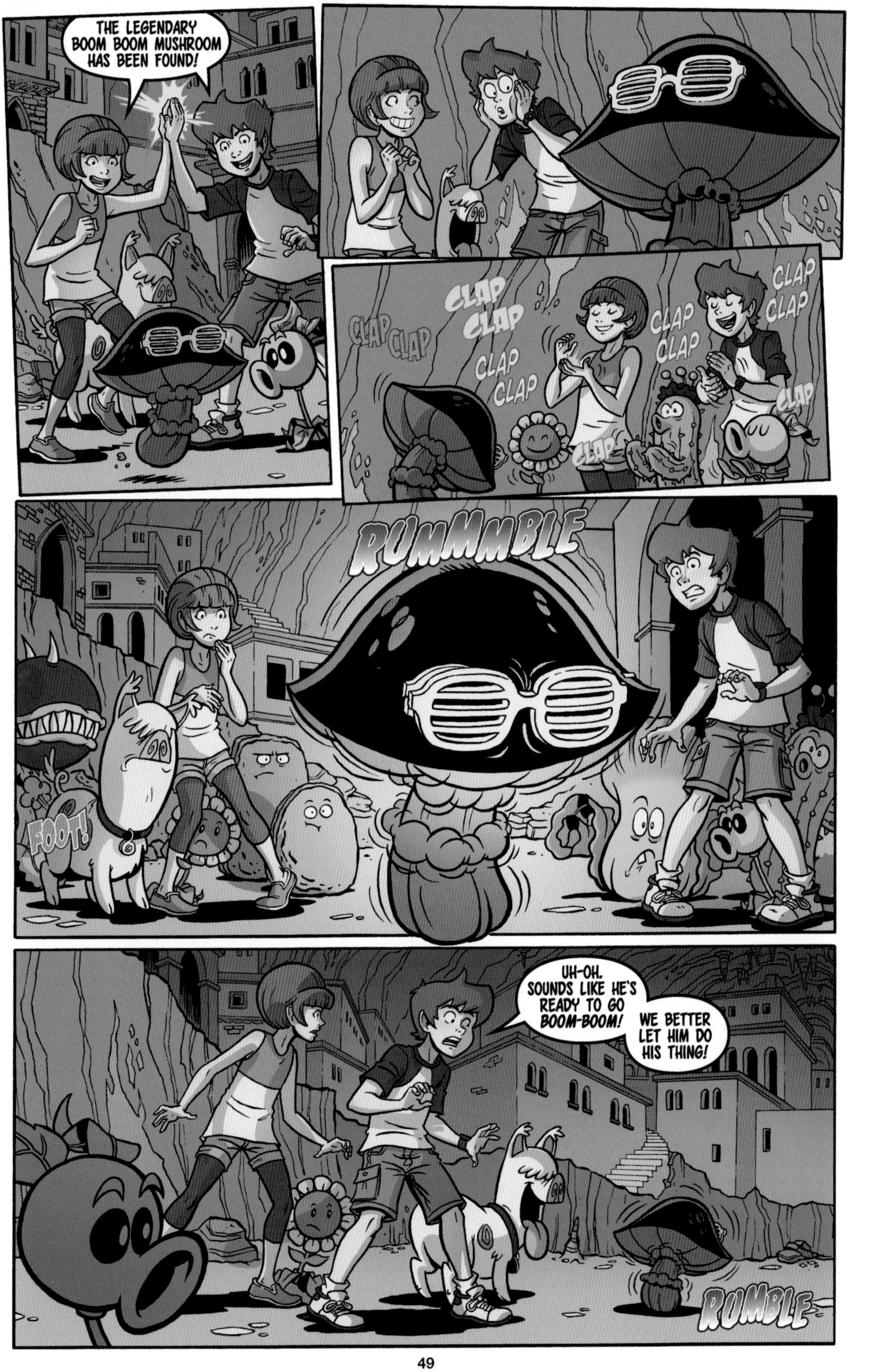
THE LEGENDARY BOOM BOOM MUSHROOM HAS BEEN FOUND!
CLAP CLAP
CLAP CLAP
CLAP CLAP
CLAP CLAP
CLAP CLAP
CLAP
CLAP
RUMMMBLE
FOOT!
UH-OH. SOUNDS LIKE HE'S READY TO GO BOOM-BOOM!
WE BETTER LET HIM DO HIS THING!
RUMBLE

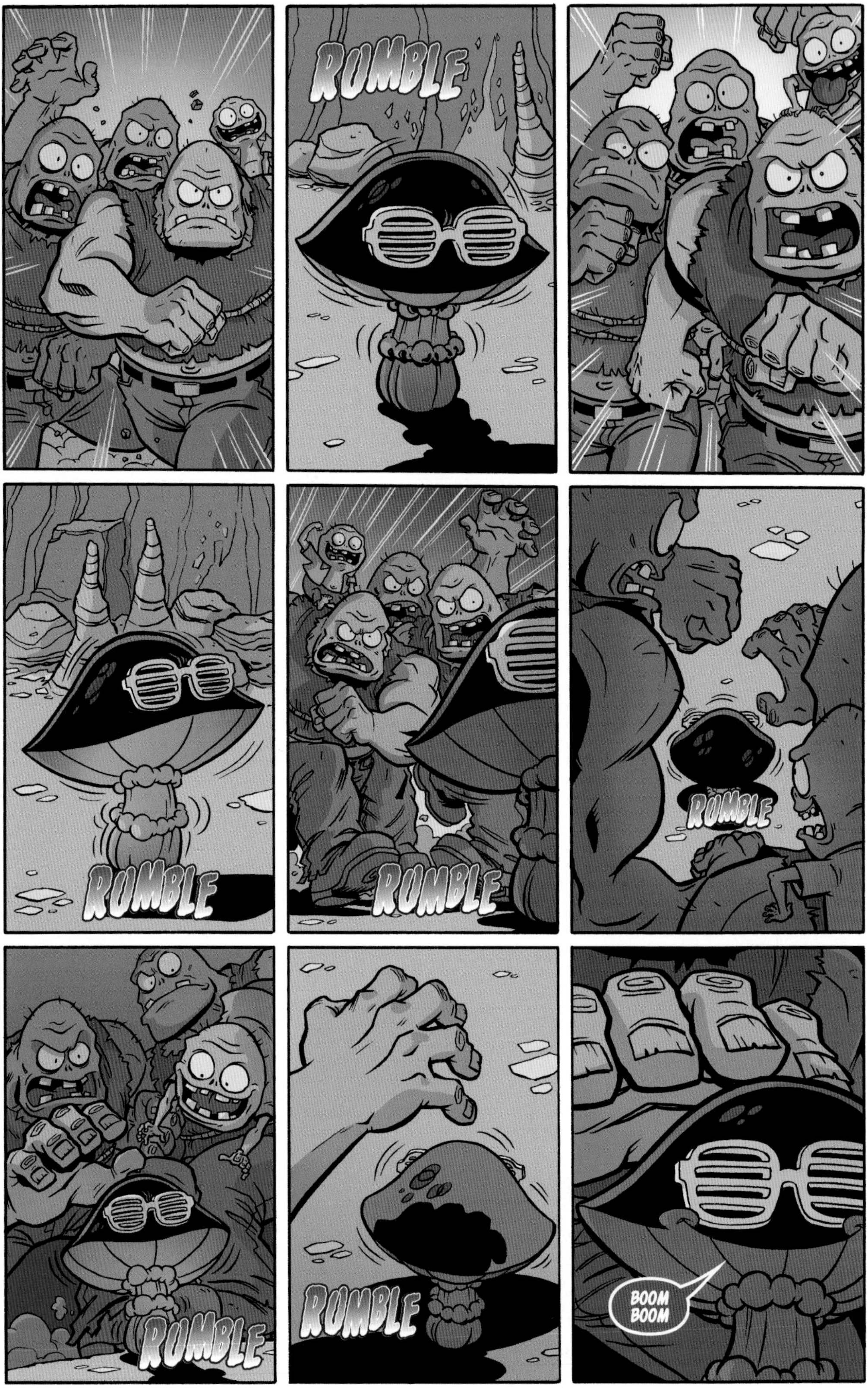
RUMBLE
RUMBLE
RUMBLE
RUMBLE
RUMBLE
RUMBLE
BOOM BOOM

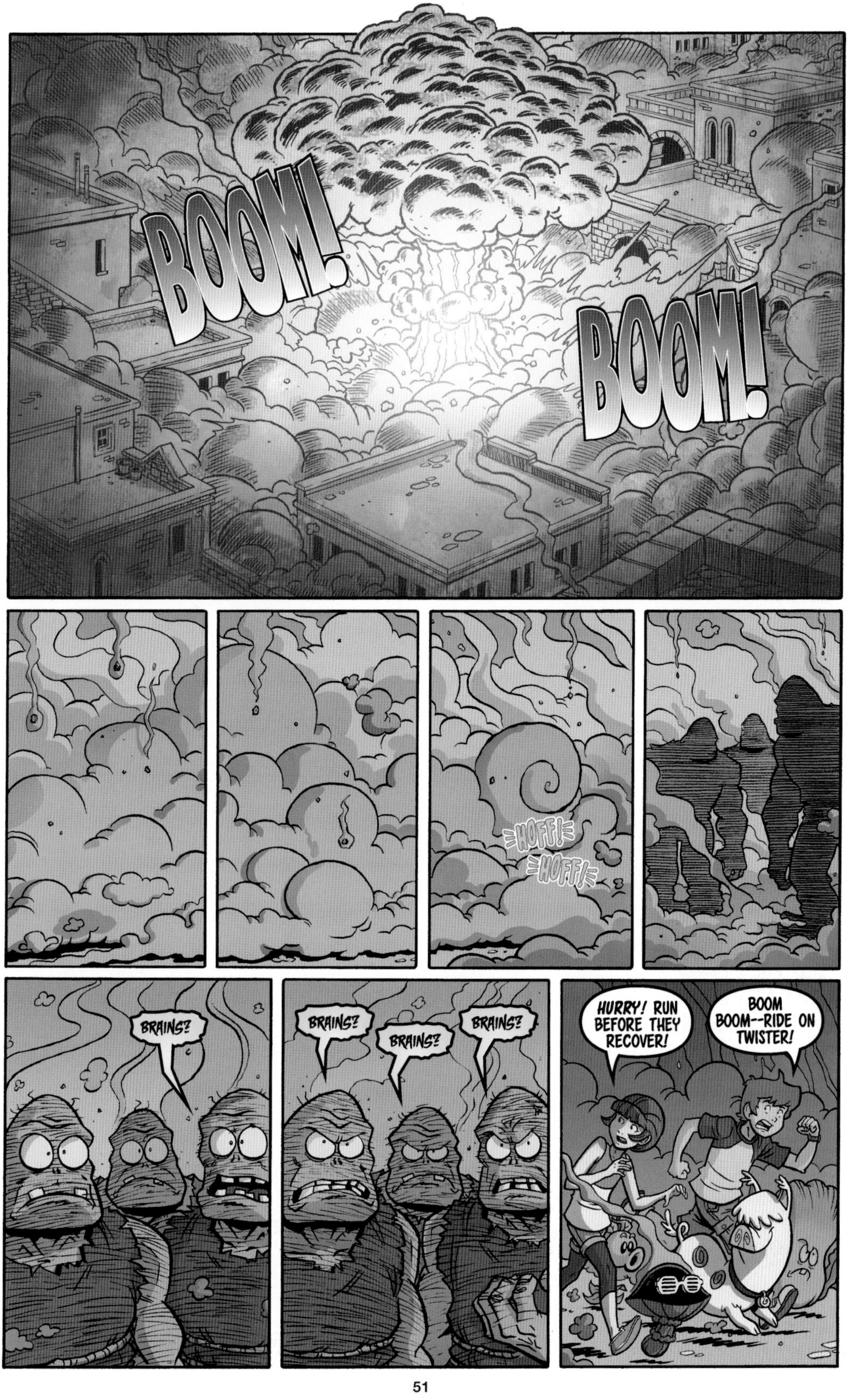
BOOM!
BOOM!
HOFF!
HOFF!
BRAINS?
BRAINS?
BRAINS?
BRAINS?
HURRY! RUN BEFORE THEY RECOVER!
BOOM BOOM--RIDE ON TWISTER!

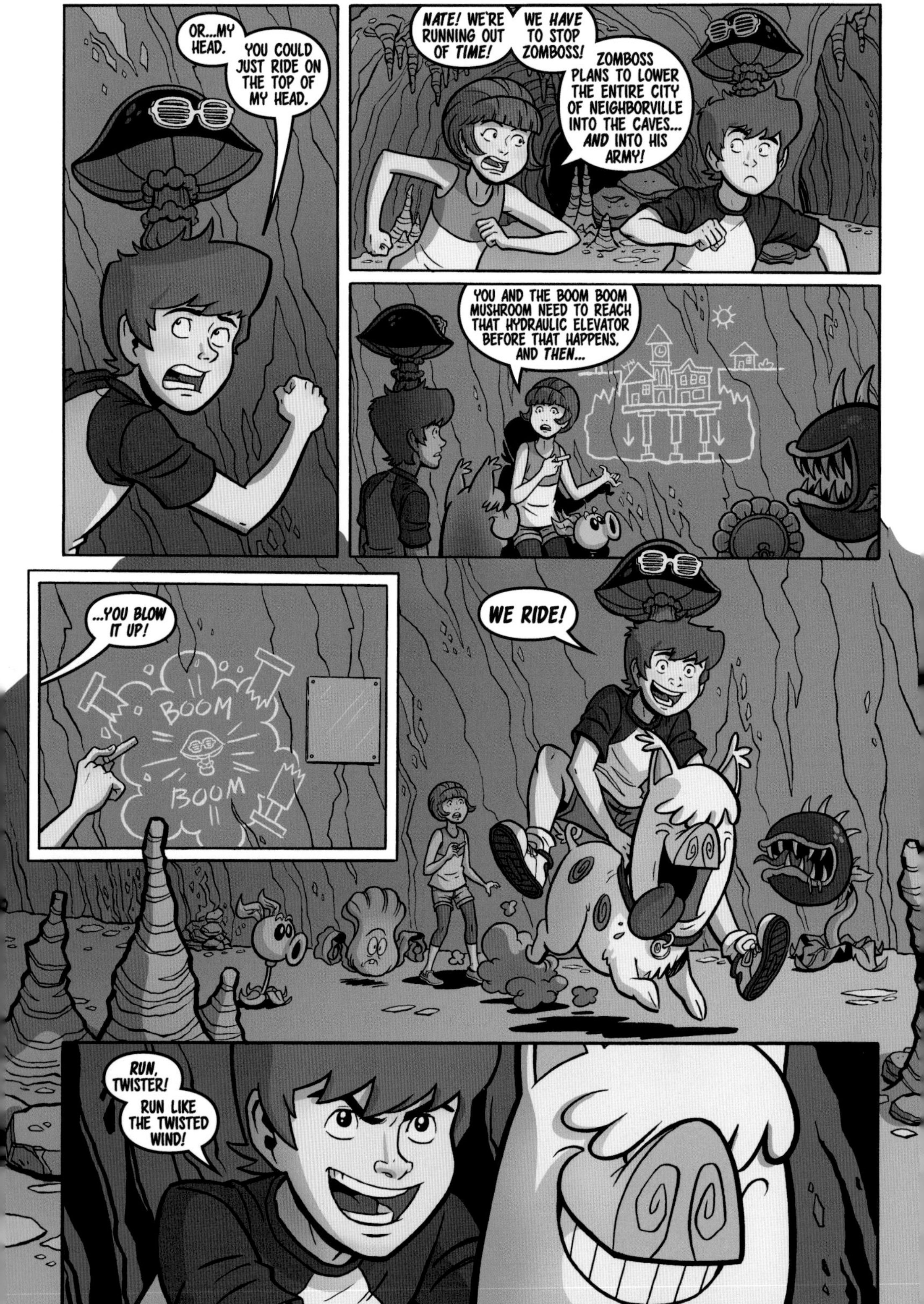
OR...MY HEAD.
YOU COULD JUST RIDE ON THE TOP OF MY HEAD.
NATE! WE'RE RUNNING OUT OF TIME!
WE HAVE TO STOP ZOMBOSS!
ZOMBOSS PLANS TO LOWER THE ENTIRE CITY OF NEIGHBORVILLE INTO THE CAVES... AND INTO HIS ARMY!
YOU AND THE BOOM BOOM MUSHROOM NEED TO REACH THAT HYDRAULIC ELEVATOR BEFORE THAT HAPPENS, AND THEN...
...YOU BLOW IT UP!
BOOM
BOOM
WE RIDE!
RUN, TWISTER!
RUN LIKE THE TWISTED WIND!

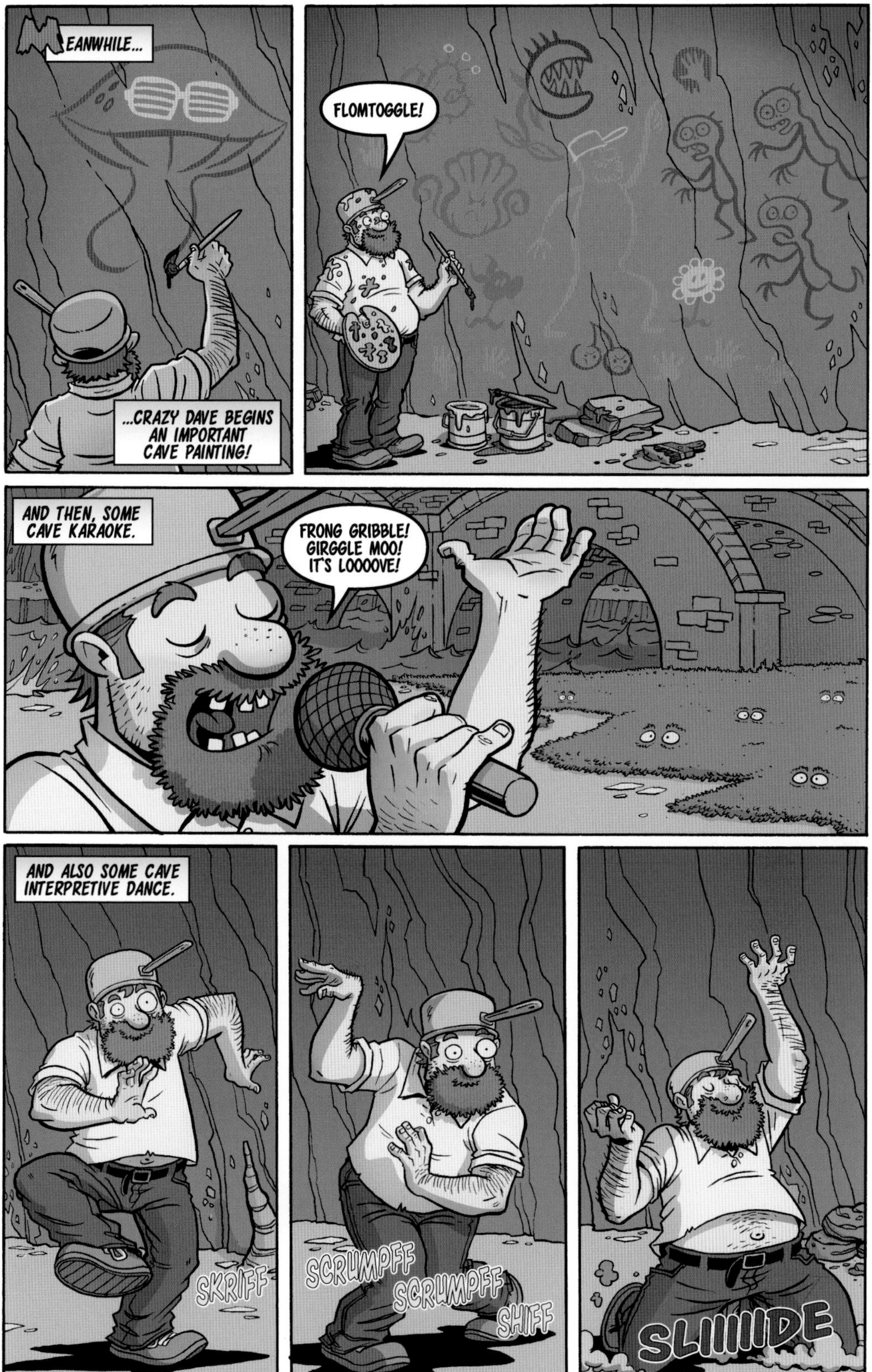
MEANWHILE...
...CRAZY DAVE BEGINS AN IMPORTANT CAVE PAINTING!
FLOMTOGGLE!
AND THEN, SOME CAVE KARAOKE.
FRONG GRIBBLE! GIRGGLE MOO! IT'S LOOOOVE!
AND ALSO SOME CAVE INTERPRETIVE DANCE.
SKRIFF
SCRUMPFF
SCRUMPFF
SHIFF
SLIIIIIDE

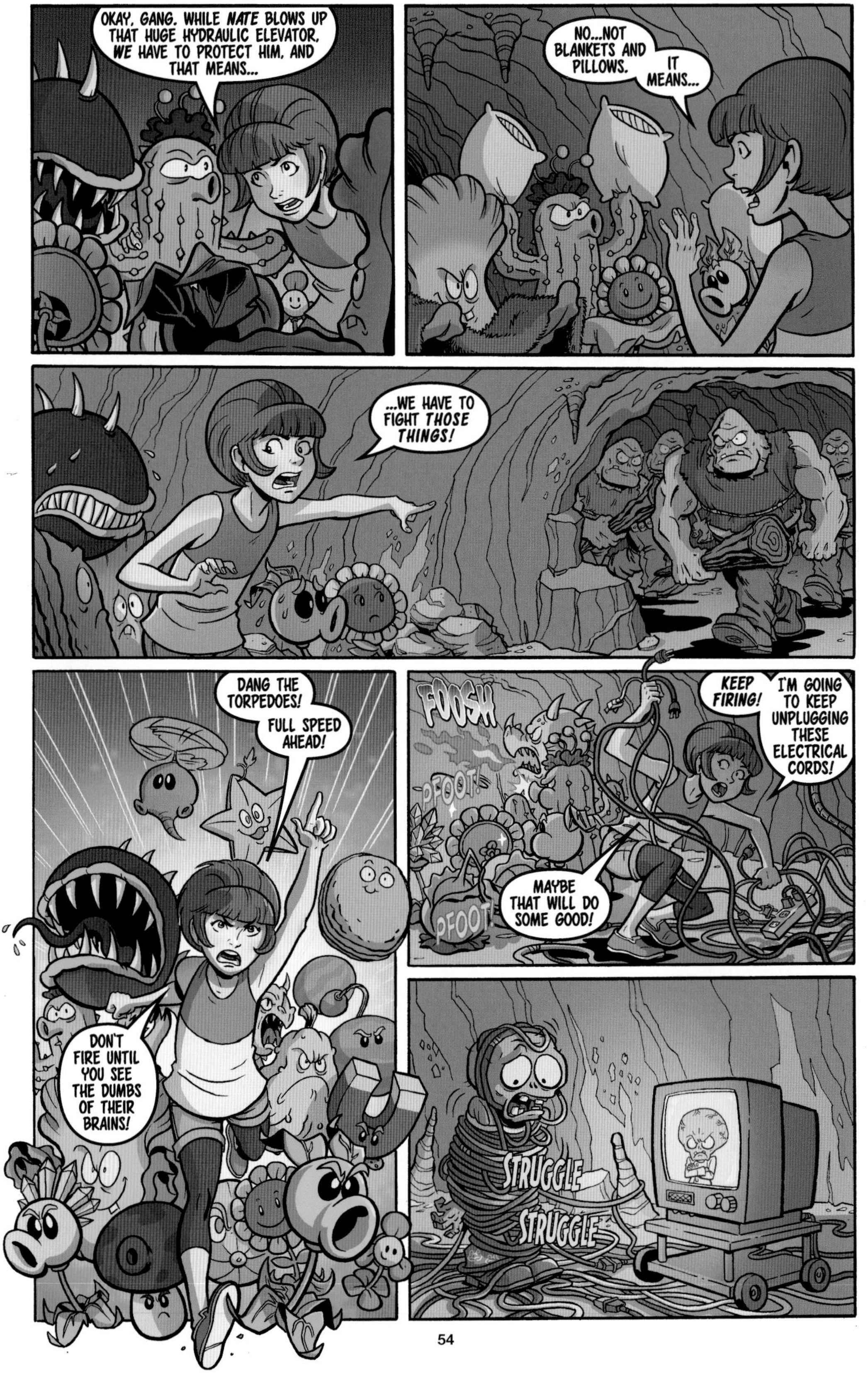
OKAY, GANG. WHILE NATE BLOWS UP THAT HUGE HYDRAULIC ELEVATOR, WE HAVE TO PROTECT HIM, AND THAT MEANS...
NO...NOT BLANKETS AND PILLOWS.
IT MEANS...
...WE HAVE TO FIGHT THOSE THINGS!
DANG THE TORPEDOES!
FULL SPEED AHEAD!
DON'T FIRE UNTIL YOU SEE THE DUMBS OF THEIR BRAINS!
FOOSH
PFOOT!
PFOOT!
KEEP FIRING!
I'M GOING TO KEEP UNPLUGGING THESE ELECTRICAL CORDS!
MAYBE THAT WILL DO SOME GOOD!
STRUGGLE
STRUGGLE

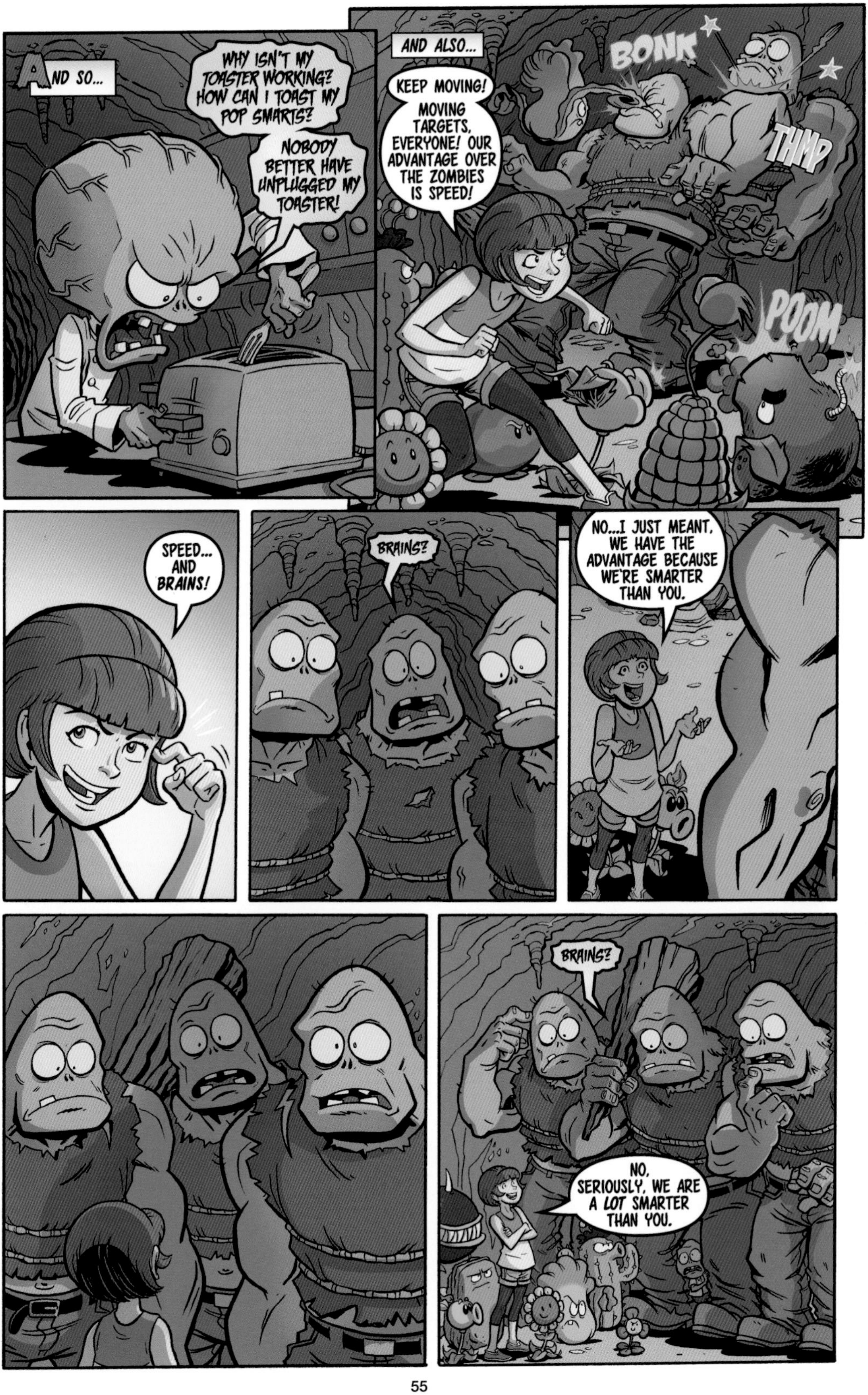
AND SO...
WHY ISN'T MY TOASTER WORKING? HOW CAN I TOAST MY POP SMARTS?
NOBODY BETTER HAVE UNPLUGGED MY TOASTER!
AND ALSO...
KEEP MOVING!
MOVING TARGETS, EVERYONE! OUR ADVANTAGE OVER THE ZOMBIES IS SPEED!
BONK
THMP
POOM
SPEED... AND BRAINS!
BRAINS?
NO...I JUST MEANT, WE HAVE THE ADVANTAGE BECAUSE WE'RE SMARTER THAN YOU.
BRAINS?
NO, SERIOUSLY, WE ARE A LOT SMARTER THAN YOU.

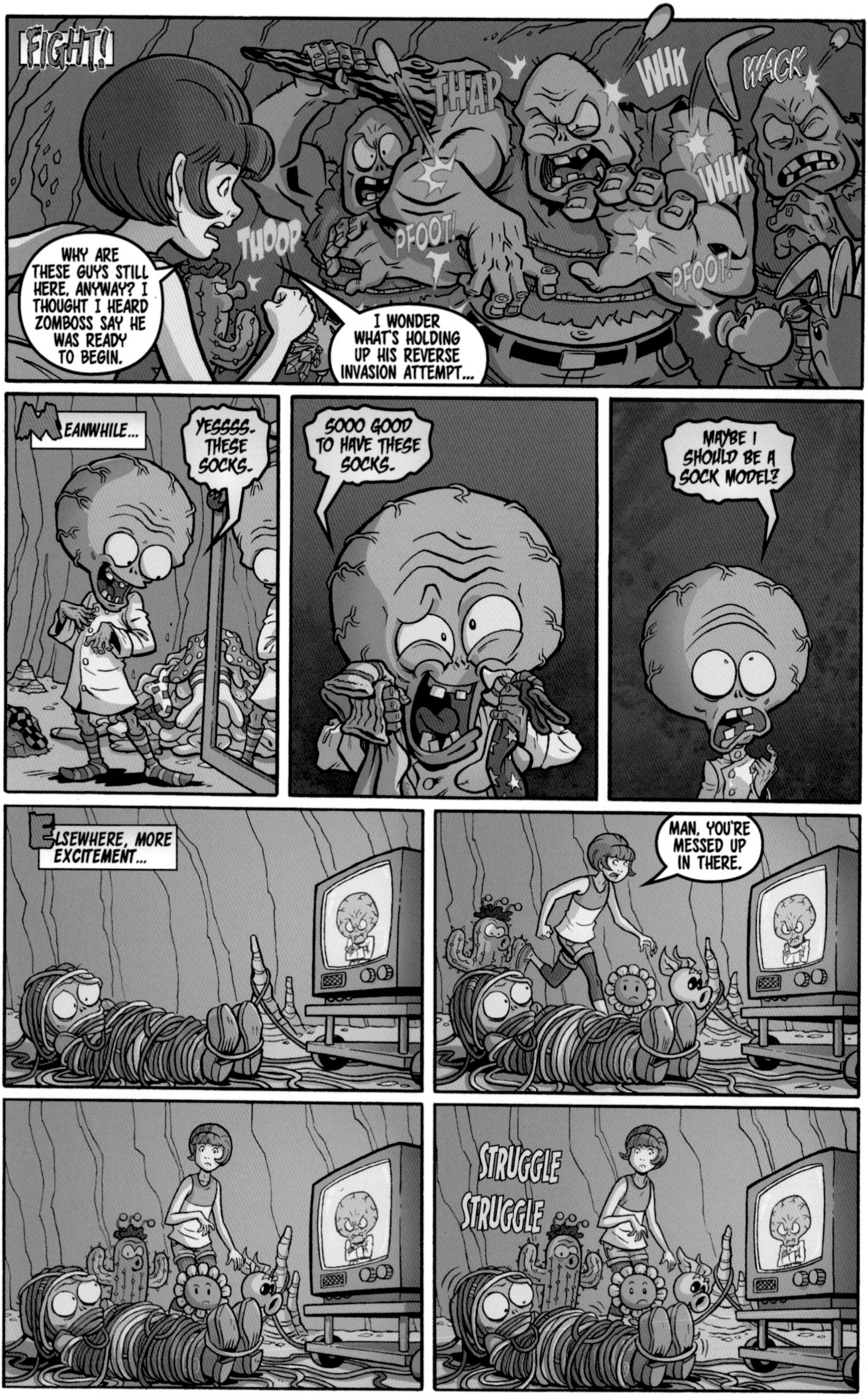
FIGHT!
THAP
WHK
WACK
WHK
THOOP
PFOOT!
PFOOT!
WHY ARE THESE GUYS STILL HERE, ANYWAY? I THOUGHT I HEARD ZOMBOSS SAY HE WAS READY TO BEGIN.
I WONDER WHAT'S HOLDING UP HIS REVERSE INVASION ATTEMPT...
MEANWHILE...
YESSSS. THESE SOCKS.
SOOO GOOD TO HAVE THESE SOCKS.
MAYBE I SHOULD BE A SOCK MODEL?
ELSEWHERE, MORE EXCITEMENT...
MAN, YOU'RE MESSED UP IN THERE.
STRUGGLE
STRUGGLE

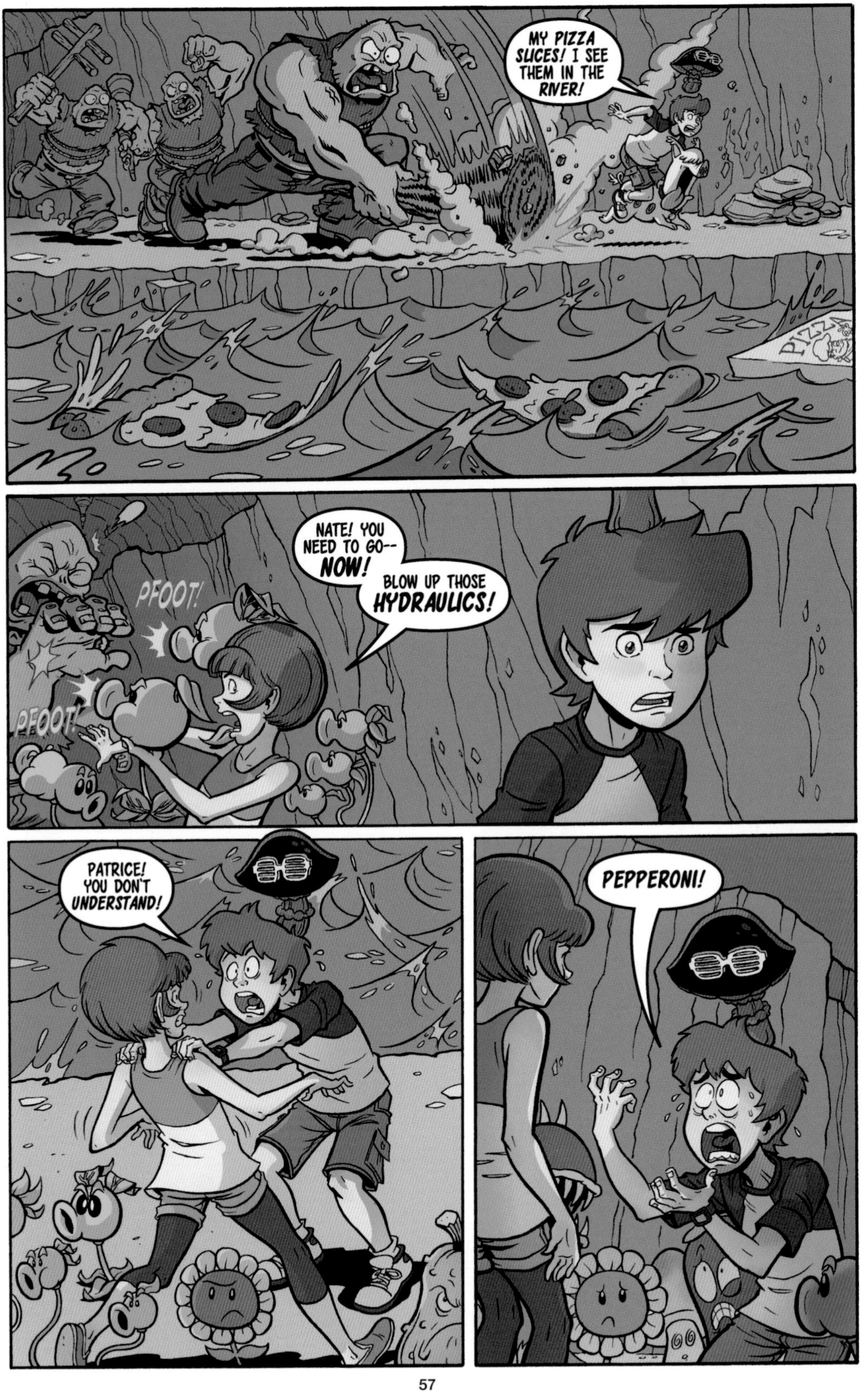
MY PIZZA SLICES! I SEE THEM IN THE RIVER!
PIZZA
PFOOT!
PFOOT!
NATE! YOU NEED TO GO-- NOW!
BLOW UP THOSE HYDRAULICS!
PATRICE! YOU DON'T UNDERSTAND!
PEPPERONI!

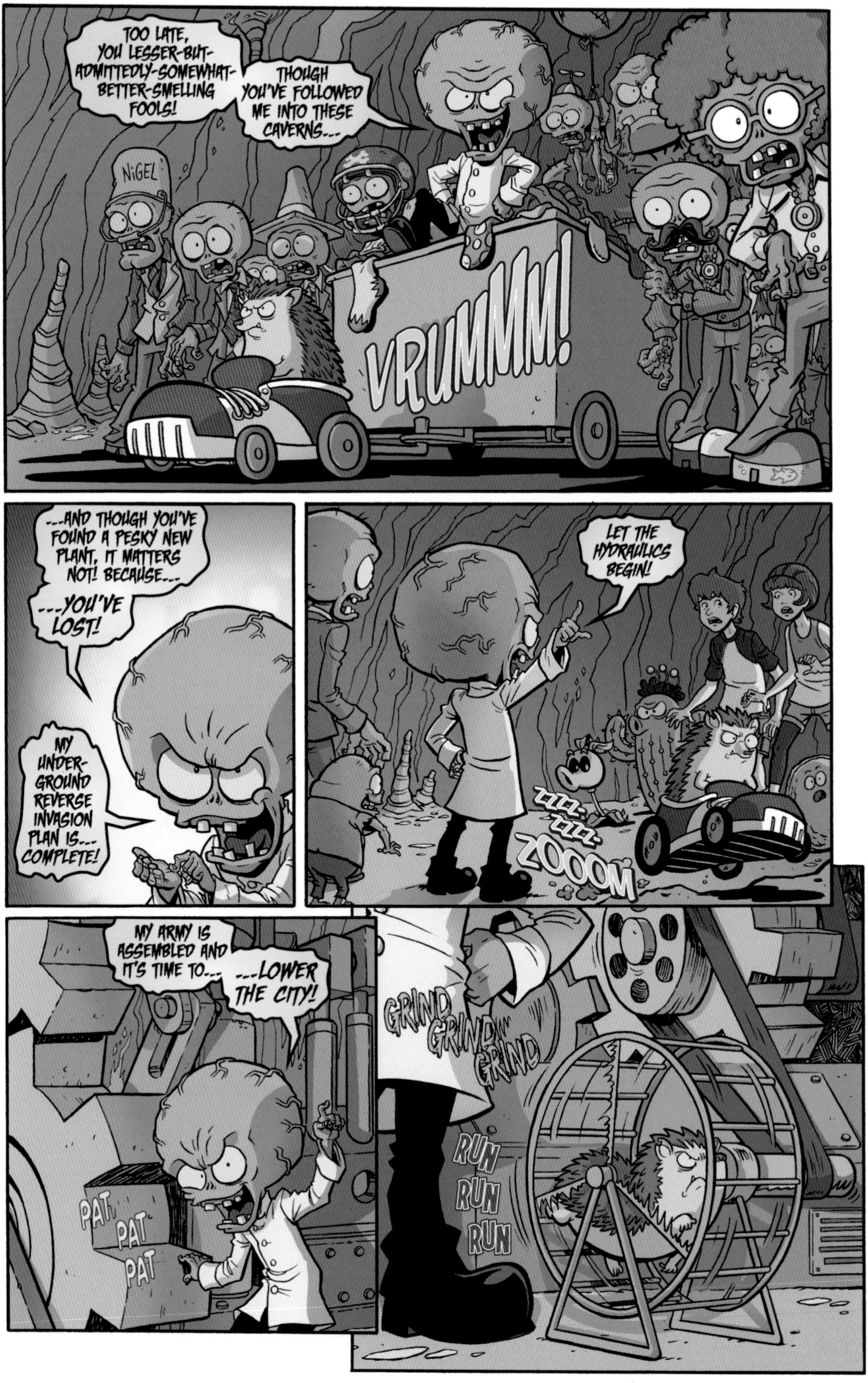
TOO LATE, YOU LESSER-BUT-ADMITTEDLY-SOMEWHAT-BETTER-SMELLING FOOLS!
THOUGH YOU'VE FOLLOWED ME INTO THESE CAVERNS...
NiGEL
VRUMMM!
...AND THOUGH YOU'VE FOUND A PESKY NEW PLANT, IT MATTERS NOT! BECAUSE...
...YOU'VE LOST!
MY UNDER-GROUND REVERSE INVASION PLAN IS... COMPLETE!
LET THE HYDRAULICS BEGIN!
ZZZZ-ZZZZ-ZOOOM
MY ARMY IS ASSEMBLED AND IT'S TIME TO...
...LOWER THE CITY!
GRIND GRIND GRIND
PAT PAT PAT
RUN RUN RUN

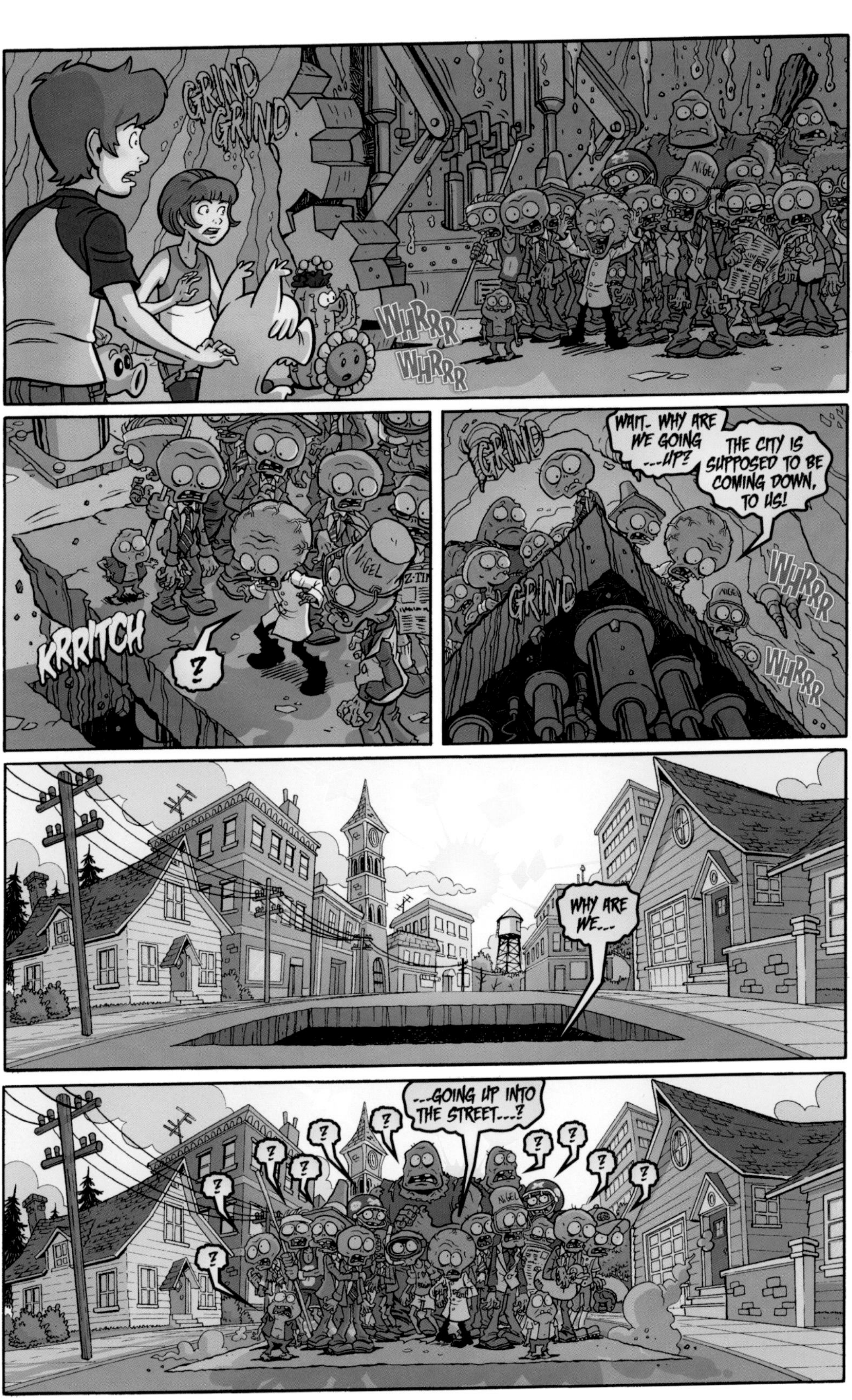

GRIND GRIND
WHRRRR
WHRRRR
KRRITCH
?
GRIND
WAIT- WHY ARE WE GOING ---UP?
THE CITY IS SUPPOSED TO BE COMING DOWN, TO US!
GRIND
WHRRRR
WHRRRR
WHY ARE WE---
---GOING UP INTO THE STREET---?
?
?
?
?
?
?
?
?
?
?
?

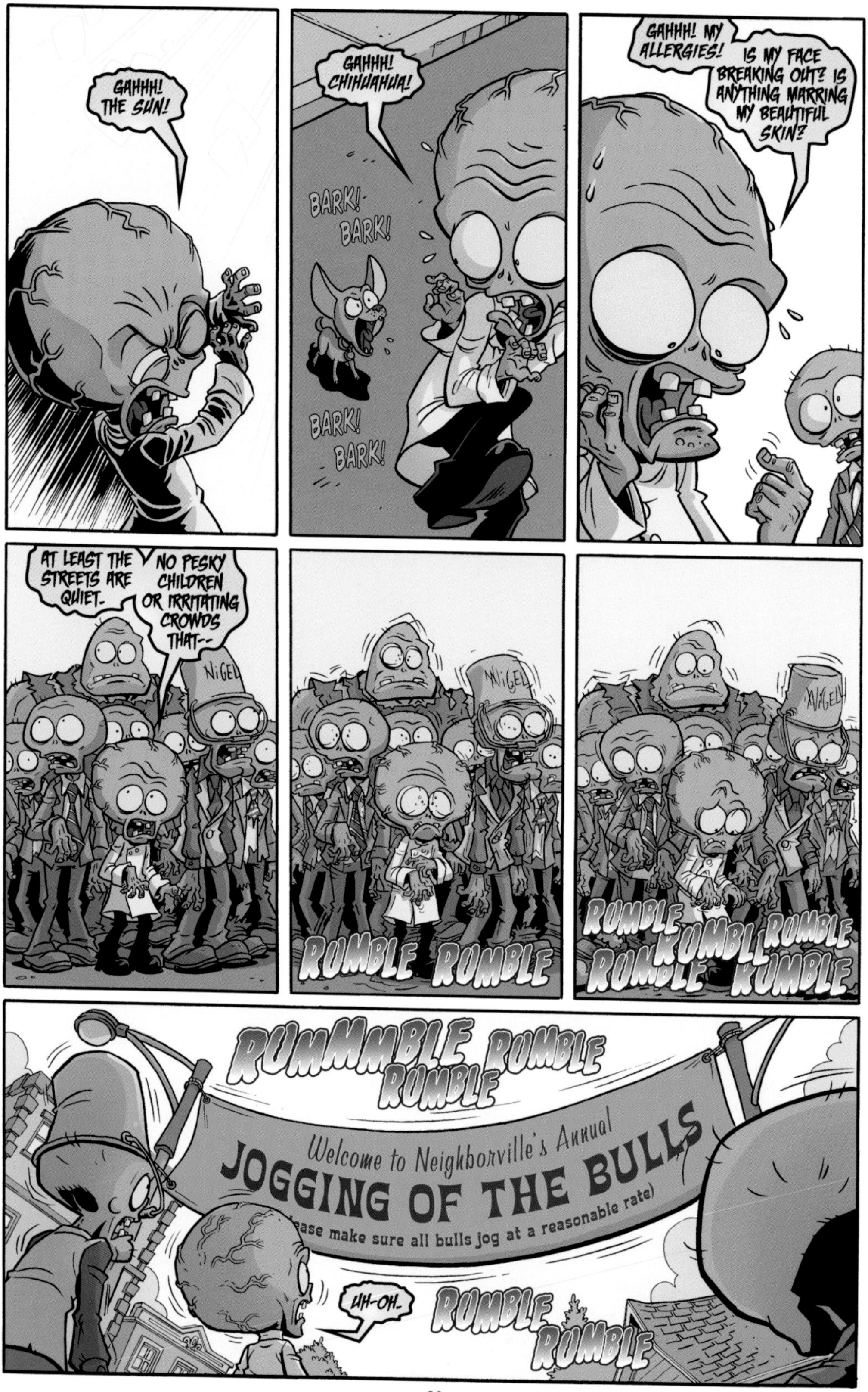
GAHHH! THE SUN!
GAHHH! CHIHUAHUA!
BARK! BARK!
BARK! BARK!
GAHHH! MY ALLERGIES!
IS MY FACE BREAKING OUT? IS ANYTHING MARRING MY BEAUTIFUL SKIN?
AT LEAST THE STREETS ARE QUIET.
NO PESKY CHILDREN OR IRRITATING CROWDS THAT--
NIGEL
RUMBLE RUMBLE
RUMBLE RUMBLE RUMBLE RUMBLE RUMBLE RUMBLE
RUMMMBLE RUMBLE RUMBLE
Welcome to Neighborville's Annual
JOGGING OF THE BULLS
(Please make sure all bulls jog at a reasonable rate)
UH-OH.
RUMBLE RUMBLE

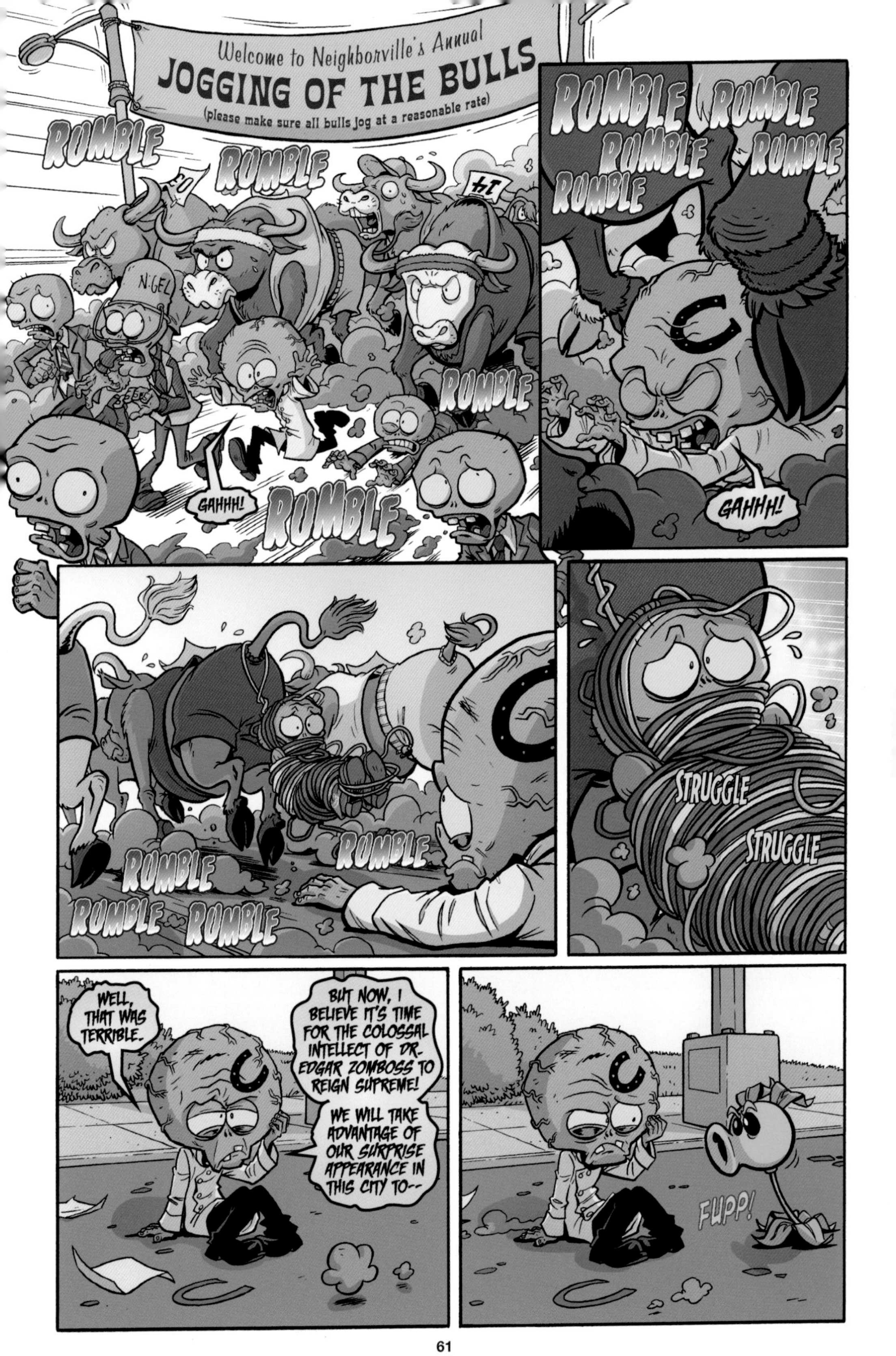

Welcome to Neighborville's Annual
JOGGING OF THE BULLS
(please make sure all bulls jog at a reasonable rate)
RUMBLE
RUMBLE
N-GEL
RUMBLE
GAHHH!
RUMBLE
RUMBLE RUMBLE RUMBLE RUMBLE RUMBLE
GAHHH!
RUMBLE
RUMBLE
RUMBLE RUMBLE
STRUGGLE
STRUGGLE
WELL, THAT WAS TERRIBLE.
BUT NOW, I BELIEVE IT'S TIME FOR THE COLOSSAL INTELLECT OF DR. EDGAR ZOMBOSS TO REIGN SUPREME!
WE WILL TAKE ADVANTAGE OF OUR SURPRISE APPEARANCE IN THIS CITY TO--
FUPP!

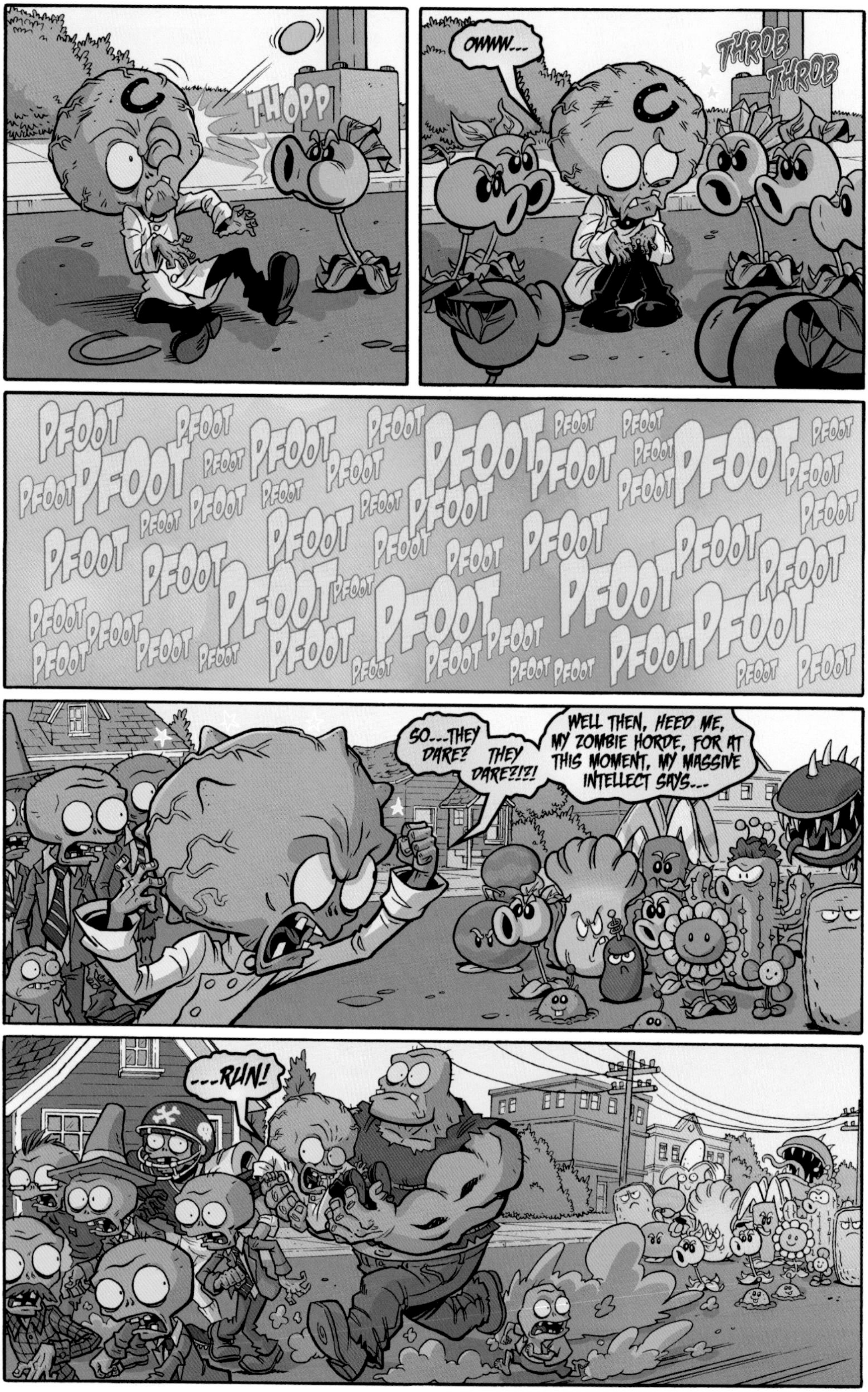
THOPP
OWWW...
THROB THROB
PFOOT PFOOT PFOOT PFOOT PFOOT PFOOT PFOOT PFOOT PFOOT PFOOT
PFOOT PFOOT PFOOT PFOOT PFOOT PFOOT PFOOT PFOOT PFOOT PFOOT
PFOOT PFOOT PFOOT PFOOT PFOOT PFOOT PFOOT PFOOT PFOOT PFOOT
PFOOT PFOOT PFOOT PFOOT PFOOT PFOOT PFOOT PFOOT PFOOT PFOOT
SO...THEY DARE?
THEY DARE?!?!
WELL THEN, HEED ME, MY ZOMBIE HORDE, FOR AT THIS MOMENT, MY MASSIVE INTELLECT SAYS...
...RUN!

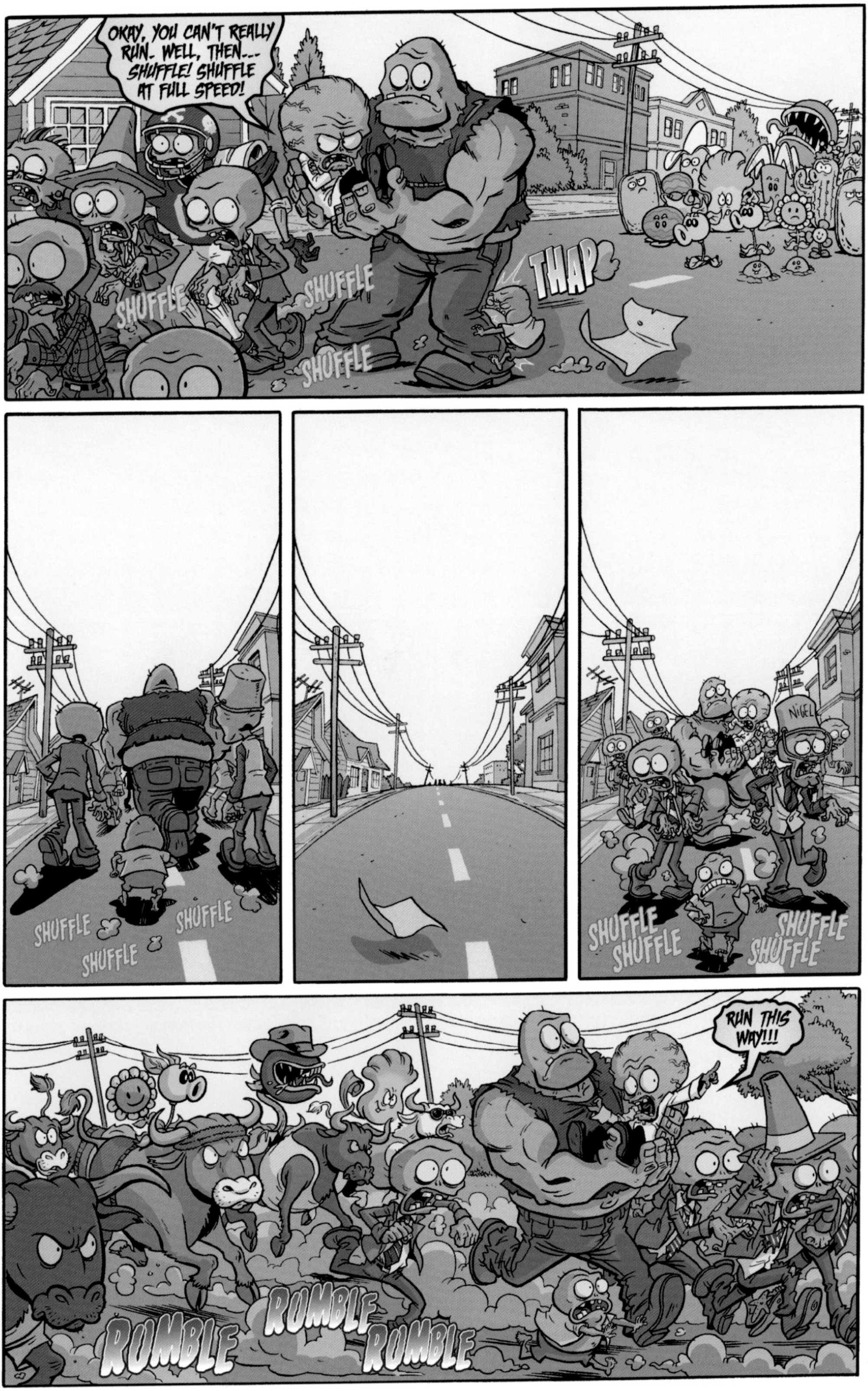
OKAY, YOU CAN'T REALLY RUN. WELL, THEN... SHUFFLE! SHUFFLE AT FULL SPEED!
SHUFFLE
SHUFFLE
SHUFFLE
THAP
SHUFFLE
SHUFFLE
SHUFFLE
NIGEL
SHUFFLE
SHUFFLE
SHUFFLE
SHUFFLE
RUN THIS WAY!!!
RUMBLE
RUMBLE
RUMBLE

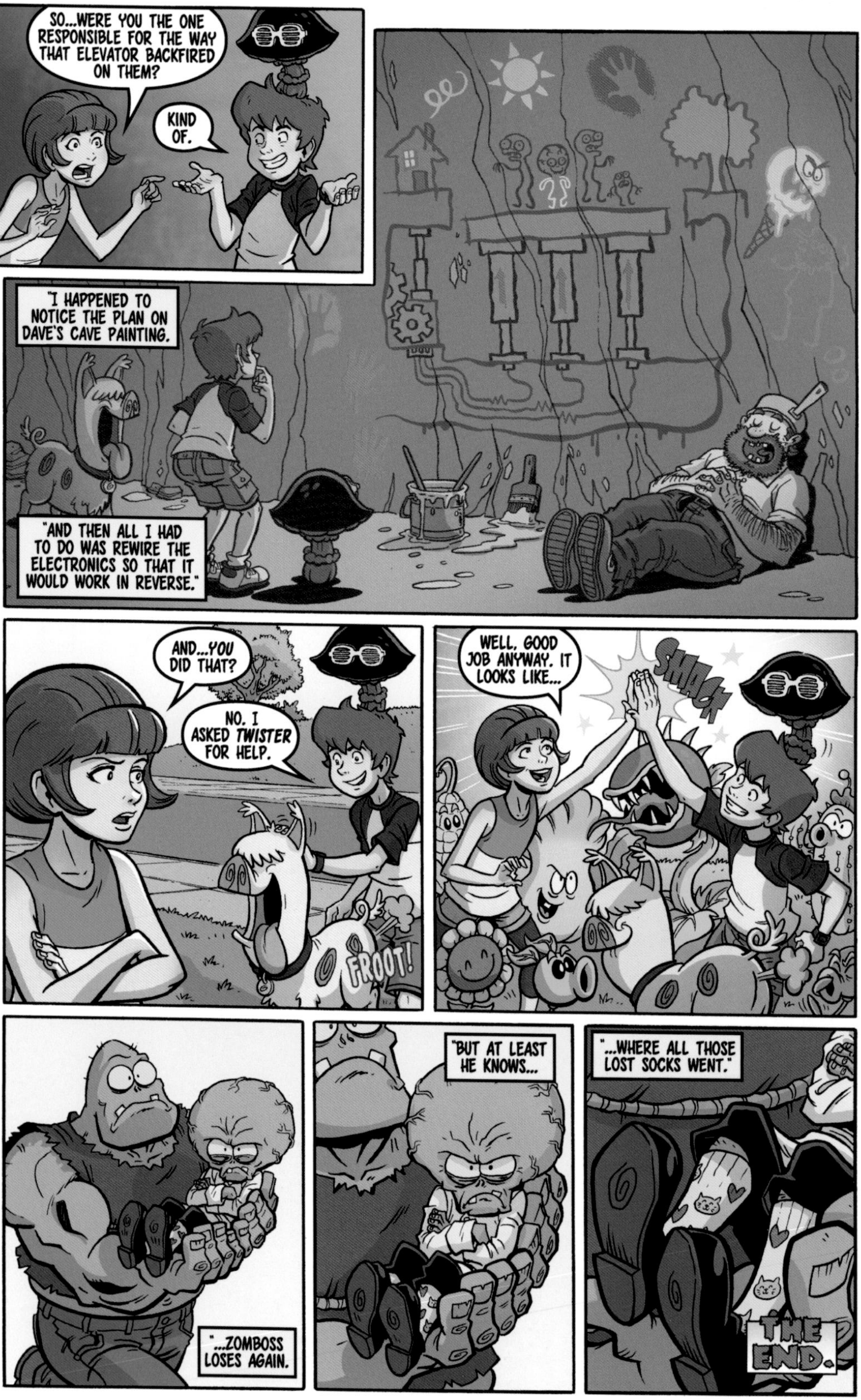
SO...WERE YOU THE ONE RESPONSIBLE FOR THE WAY THAT ELEVATOR BACKFIRED ON THEM?
KIND OF.
"I HAPPENED TO NOTICE THE PLAN ON DAVE'S CAVE PAINTING.
"AND THEN ALL I HAD TO DO WAS REWIRE THE ELECTRONICS SO THAT IT WOULD WORK IN REVERSE."
AND...YOU DID THAT?
NO. I ASKED TWISTER FOR HELP.
FROOT!
WELL, GOOD JOB ANYWAY. IT LOOKS LIKE...
SHMACK
"...ZOMBOSS LOSES AGAIN.
"BUT AT LEAST HE KNOWS...
"...WHERE ALL THOSE LOST SOCKS WENT."
THE END.

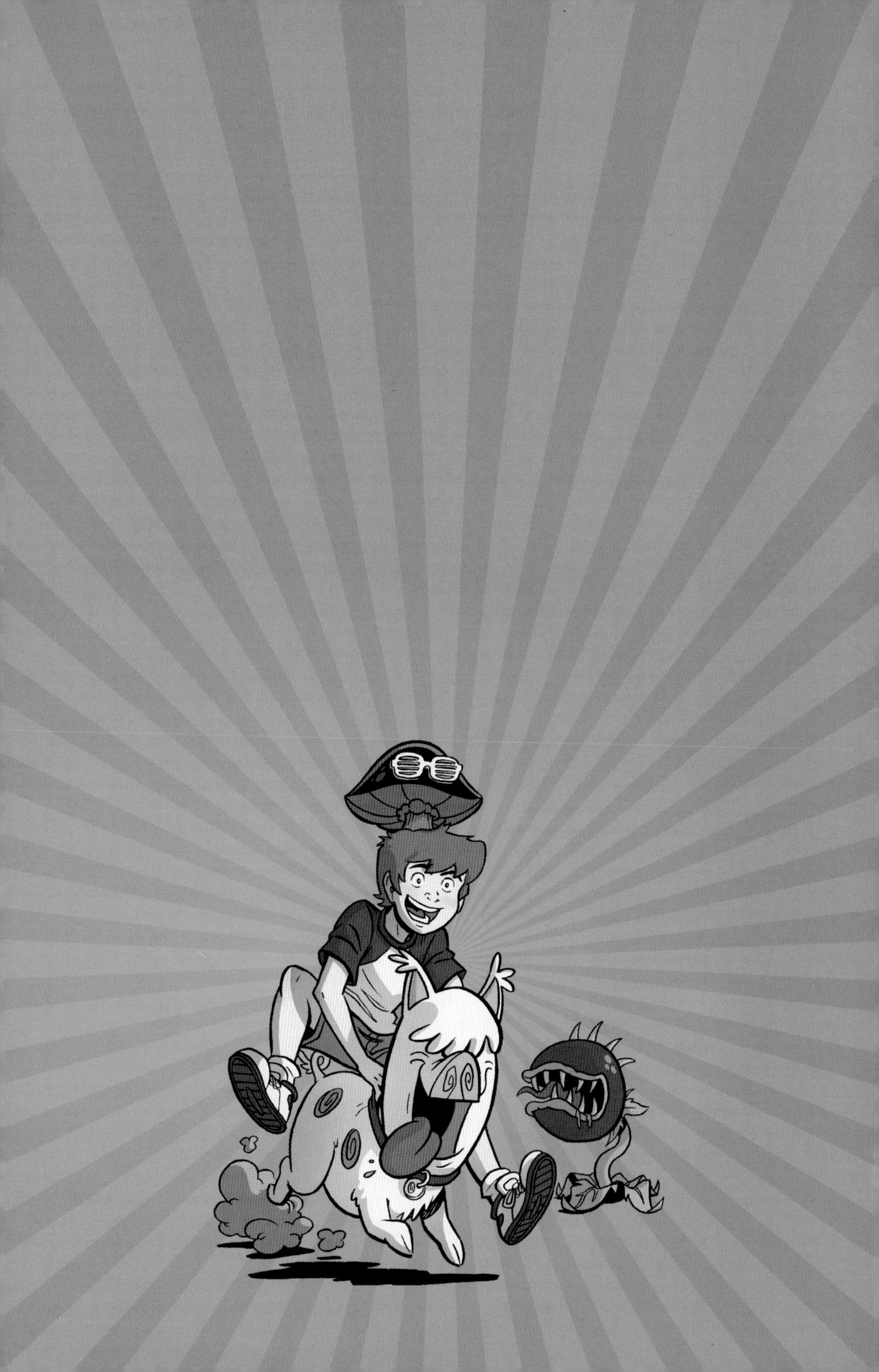

BONUS STORIES

"NOISE FROM THE BOYS"
Written by PAUL TOBIN
Art by CAT FARRIS
Letters by STEVE DUTRO

"THE COUPON"
Written by PAUL TOBIN
Art by MATT J. RAINWATER
Letters by STEVE DUTRO

"THE ADVENTURES OF SHERLOCK BRAINS:
THE ZOMBIE WORLD'S FOREMOST CONSULTING DETECTIVE!"
Written by PAUL TOBIN
Art by RACHEL DOWNING
Letters by STEVE DUTRO

"THE ADVENTURES OF SHERLOCK BRAINS:
THE CASE OF THE PURLOINED POP SMARTS!"
Written by PAUL TOBIN
Art by CHRIS SHERIDAN
Letters by STEVE DUTRO

"TOASTED"
Written by PAUL TOBIN
Art by JEREMY VANHOOZER
Letters by STEVE DUTRO

"THE SCENIC VIEW"
Written by PAUL TOBIN
Art by JEREMY VANHOOZER
Letters by STEVE DUTRO

"ICE SCREAM"
Written by PAUL TOBIN
Art by JEREMY VANHOOZER
Letters by STEVE DUTRO

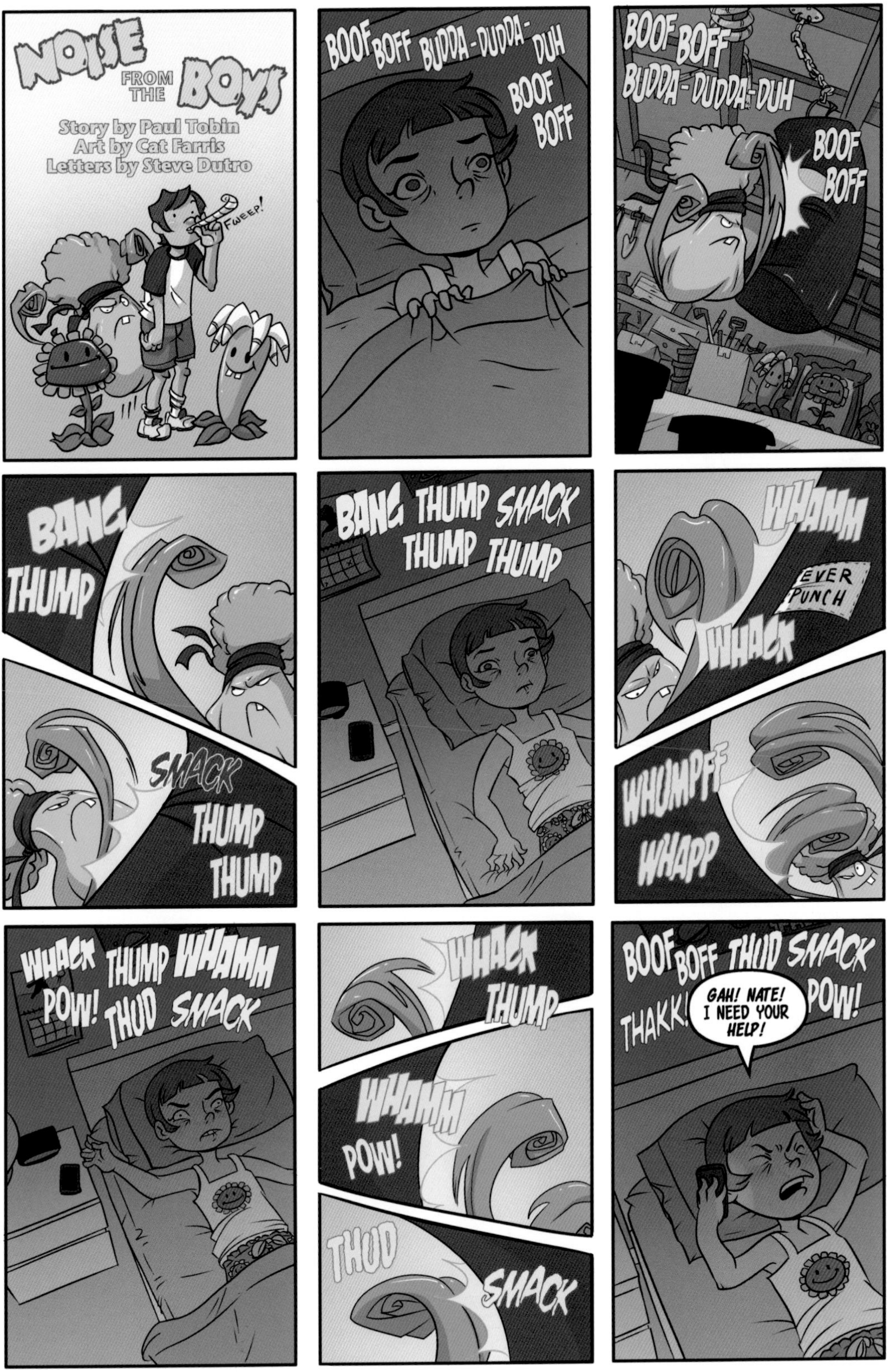
NOISE FROM THE BOYS
Story by Paul Tobin
Art by Cat Farris
Letters by Steve Dutro
FWEEEP!
BOOF BOFF BUDDA-DUDDA-DUH
BOOF BOFF
BOOF BOFF BUDDA-DUDDA-DUH
BOOF BOFF
BANG THUMP
SMACK THUMP THUMP
BANG THUMP SMACK THUMP THUMP
WHAMM
EVER PUNCH
WHACK
WHUMPFF WHAPP
WHACK THUMP WHAMM POW! THUD SMACK
WHACK THUMP
WHAMM POW!
THUD SMACK
BOOF BOFF THUD SMACK THAKK! POW!
GAH! NATE! I NEED YOUR HELP!

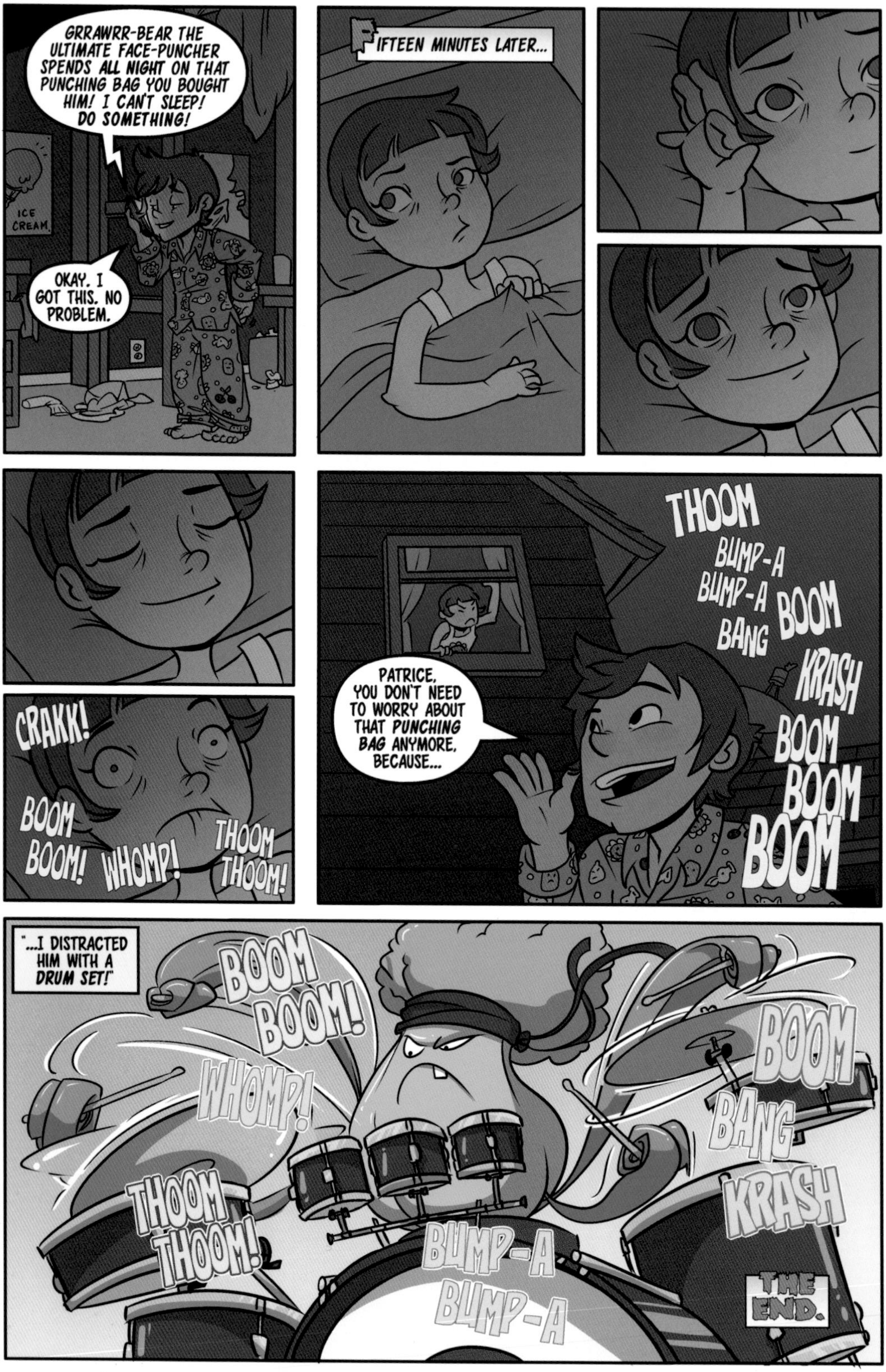
GRRAWRR-BEAR THE ULTIMATE FACE-PUNCHER SPENDS ALL NIGHT ON THAT PUNCHING BAG YOU BOUGHT HIM! I CAN'T SLEEP! DO SOMETHING!
ICE CREAM
OKAY. I GOT THIS. NO PROBLEM.
FIFTEEN MINUTES LATER...
CRAKK!
BOOM BOOM!
WHOMP!
THOOM THOOM!
THOOM
BUMP-A
BUMP-A
BOOM
BANG
KRASH
BOOM
BOOM
BOOM
PATRICE, YOU DON'T NEED TO WORRY ABOUT THAT PUNCHING BAG ANYMORE, BECAUSE...
"...I DISTRACTED HIM WITH A DRUM SET!"
BOOM BOOM!
WHOMP!
THOOM THOOM!
BUMP-A BUMP-A
BOOM
BANG
KRASH
THE END.

The Coupon

Story by Paul Tobin
Art by Matt J. Rainwater
Letters by Steve Dutro

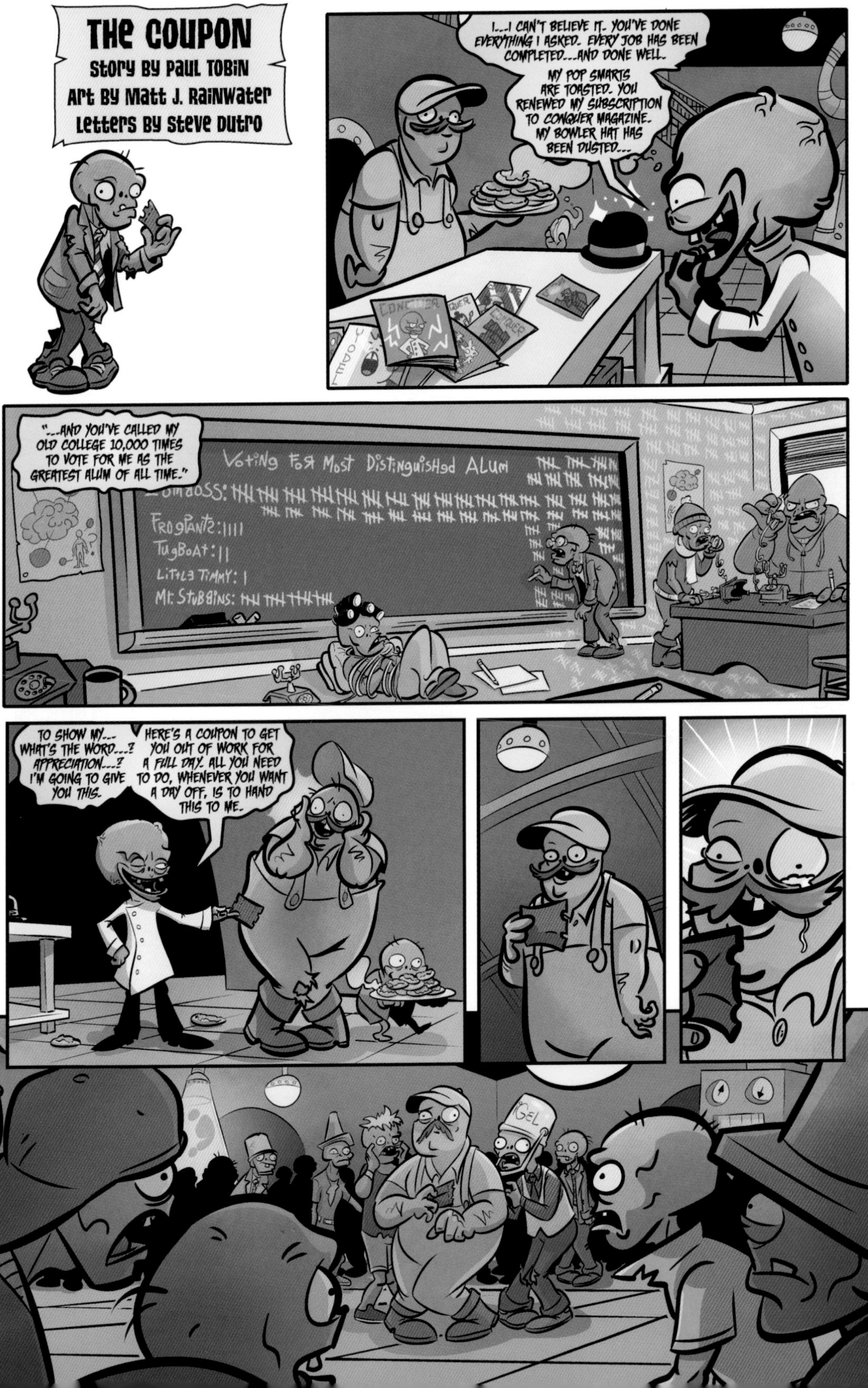
I...I CAN'T BELIEVE IT. YOU'VE DONE EVERYTHING I ASKED. EVERY JOB HAS BEEN COMPLETED...AND DONE WELL.
MY POP SMARTS ARE TOASTED. YOU RENEWED MY SUBSCRIPTION TO CONQUER MAGAZINE. MY BOWLER HAT HAS BEEN DUSTED...
CONQUER
"...AND YOU'VE CALLED MY OLD COLLEGE 10,000 TIMES TO VOTE FOR ME AS THE GREATEST ALUM OF ALL TIME."
Voting For Most Distinguished Alum
FrogPantz: 1111
TugBoAt: 11
Little Timmy: 1
Mr. StuBBins:
TO SHOW MY... WHAT'S THE WORD...? APPRECIATION...? I'M GOING TO GIVE YOU THIS.
HERE'S A COUPON TO GET YOU OUT OF WORK FOR A FULL DAY. ALL YOU NEED TO DO, WHENEVER YOU WANT A DAY OFF, IS TO HAND THIS TO ME.
GEL

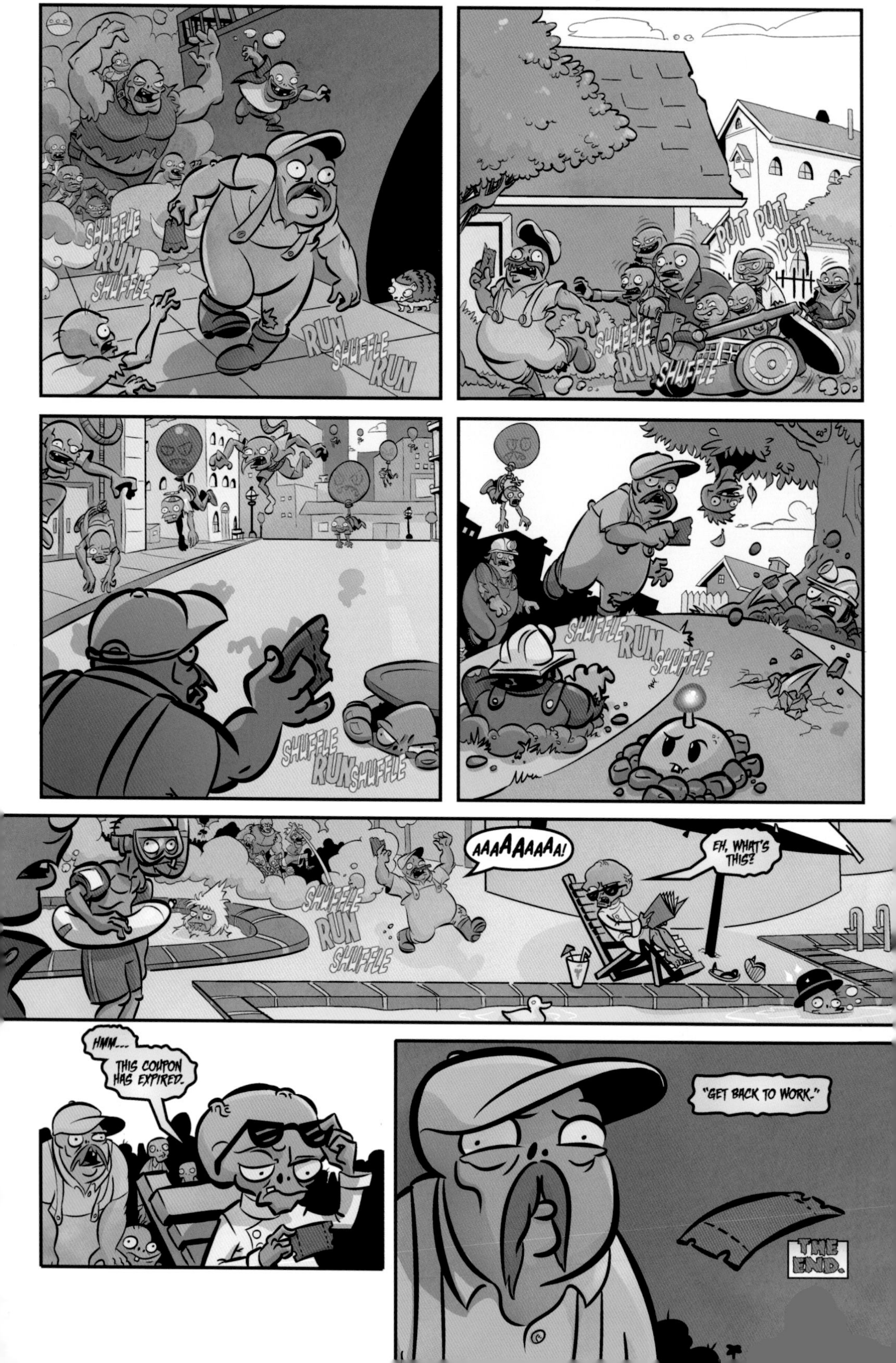
SHUFFLE RUN SHUFFLE
RUN SHUFFLE RUN
PUTT PUTT PUTT
SHUFFLE RUN SHUFFLE
SHUFFLE RUN SHUFFLE
SHUFFLE RUN SHUFFLE
SHUFFLE RUN SHUFFLE
AAAAAAAAA!
EH, WHAT'S THIS?
HMM...
THIS COUPON HAS EXPIRED.
"GET BACK TO WORK."
THE END.

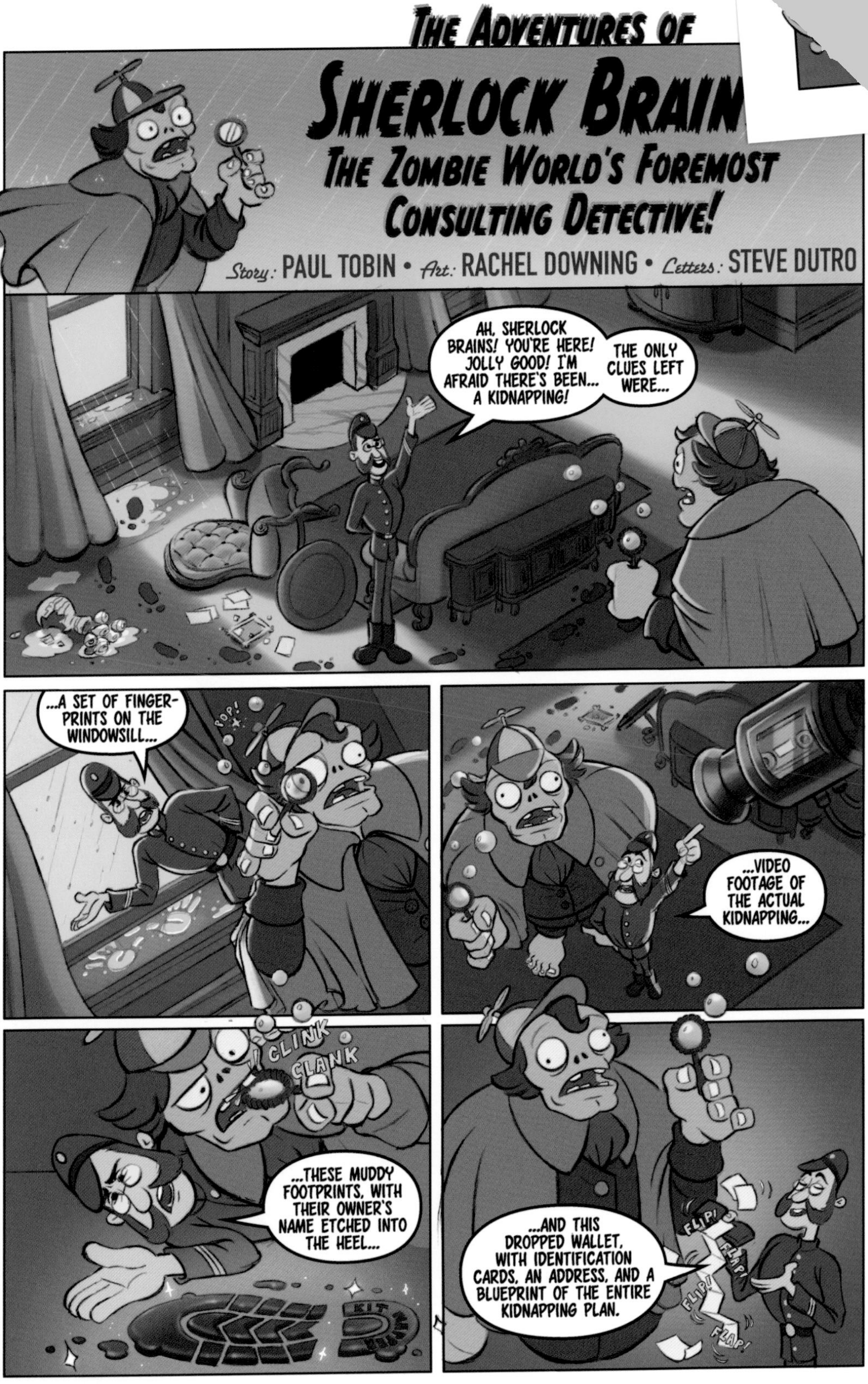
THE ADVENTURES OF
SHERLOCK BRAIN
THE ZOMBIE WORLD'S FOREMOST CONSULTING DETECTIVE!
Story: PAUL TOBIN • Art: RACHEL DOWNING • Letters: STEVE DUTRO
AH, SHERLOCK BRAINS! YOU'RE HERE! JOLLY GOOD! I'M AFRAID THERE'S BEEN... A KIDNAPPING!
THE ONLY CLUES LEFT WERE...
...A SET OF FINGER-PRINTS ON THE WINDOWSILL...
POP!
...VIDEO FOOTAGE OF THE ACTUAL KIDNAPPING...
CLINK
CLANK
...THESE MUDDY FOOTPRINTS, WITH THEIR OWNER'S NAME ETCHED INTO THE HEEL...
KIT
...AND THIS DROPPED WALLET, WITH IDENTIFICATION CARDS, AN ADDRESS, AND A BLUEPRINT OF THE ENTIRE KIDNAPPING PLAN.
FLIP!
FLAP!
FLIP!
FLAP!

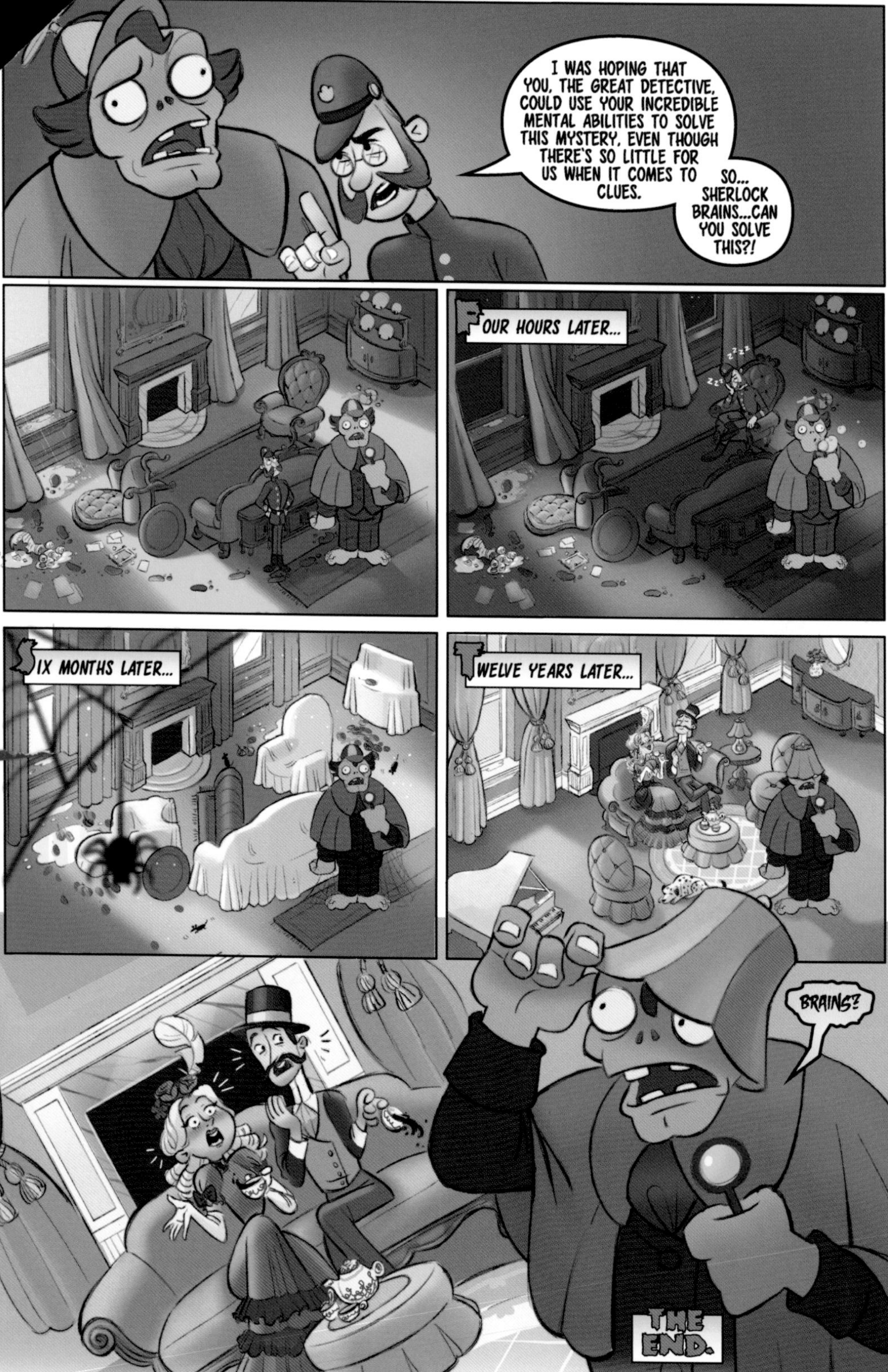
I WAS HOPING THAT YOU, THE GREAT DETECTIVE, COULD USE YOUR INCREDIBLE MENTAL ABILITIES TO SOLVE THIS MYSTERY, EVEN THOUGH THERE'S SO LITTLE FOR US WHEN IT COMES TO CLUES.
SO... SHERLOCK BRAINS...CAN YOU SOLVE THIS?!
FOUR HOURS LATER...
SIX MONTHS LATER...
TWELVE YEARS LATER...
BRAINS?
THE END.

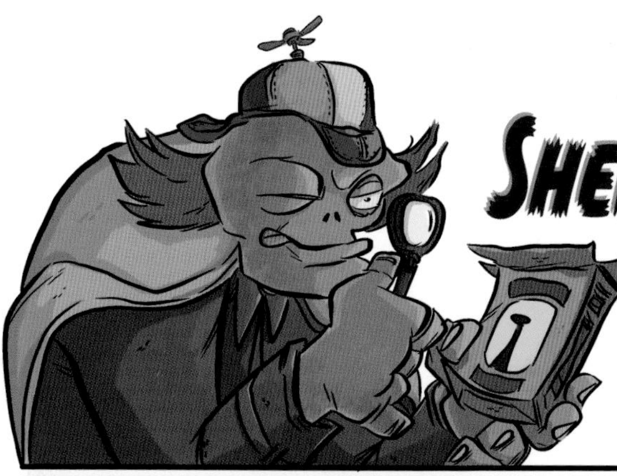

The Adventures of Sherlock Brains:

The Case of the Purloined Pop Smarts!

Story: PAUL TOBIN
Art: CHRIS SHERIDAN
Letters: STEVE DUTRO

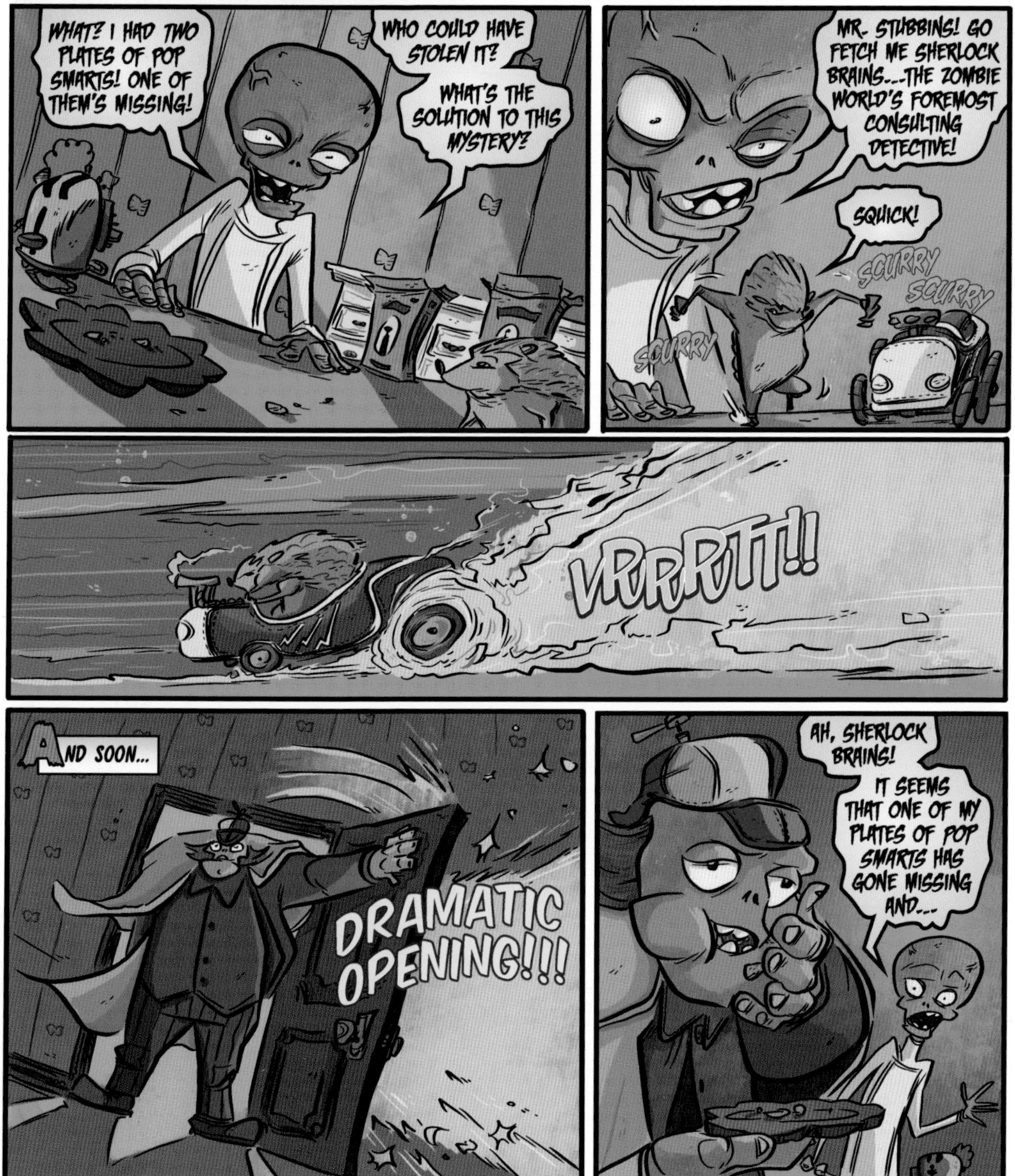
WHAT? I HAD TWO PLATES OF POP SMARTS! ONE OF THEM'S MISSING!
WHO COULD HAVE STOLEN IT?
WHAT'S THE SOLUTION TO THIS MYSTERY?
MR. STUBBINS! GO FETCH ME SHERLOCK BRAINS...THE ZOMBIE WORLD'S FOREMOST CONSULTING DETECTIVE!
SQUICK!
SCURRY
SCURRY
SCURRY
VRRRRTT!!
AND SOON...
DRAMATIC OPENING!!!
AH, SHERLOCK BRAINS!
IT SEEMS THAT ONE OF MY PLATES OF POP SMARTS HAS GONE MISSING AND...

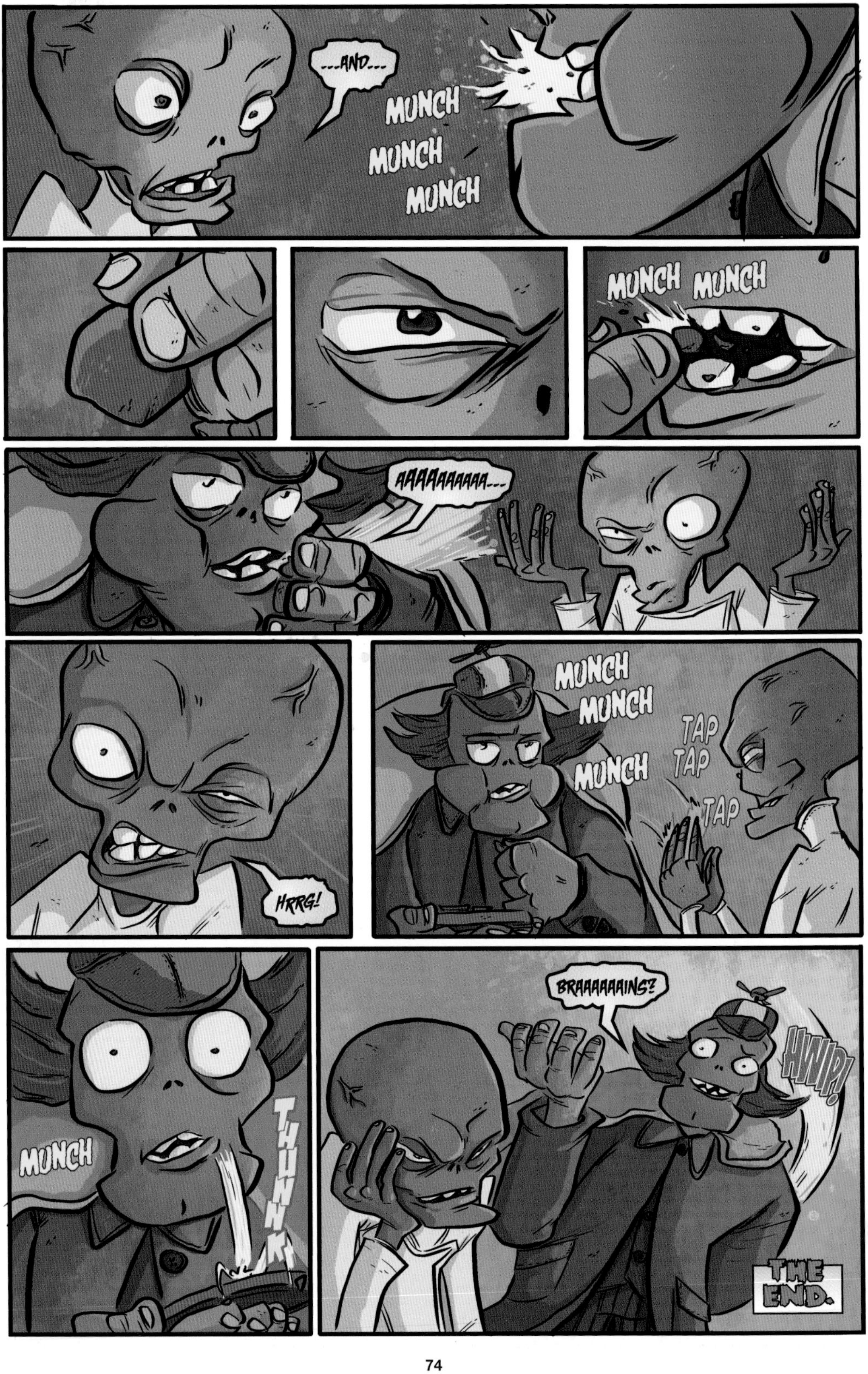
...AND...
MUNCH
MUNCH
MUNCH
MUNCH MUNCH
AAAAAAAAAA...
HRRG!
MUNCH
MUNCH
MUNCH
TAP
TAP
TAP
MUNCH
THUNK!
BRAAAAAAINS?
HWIP!
THE END.

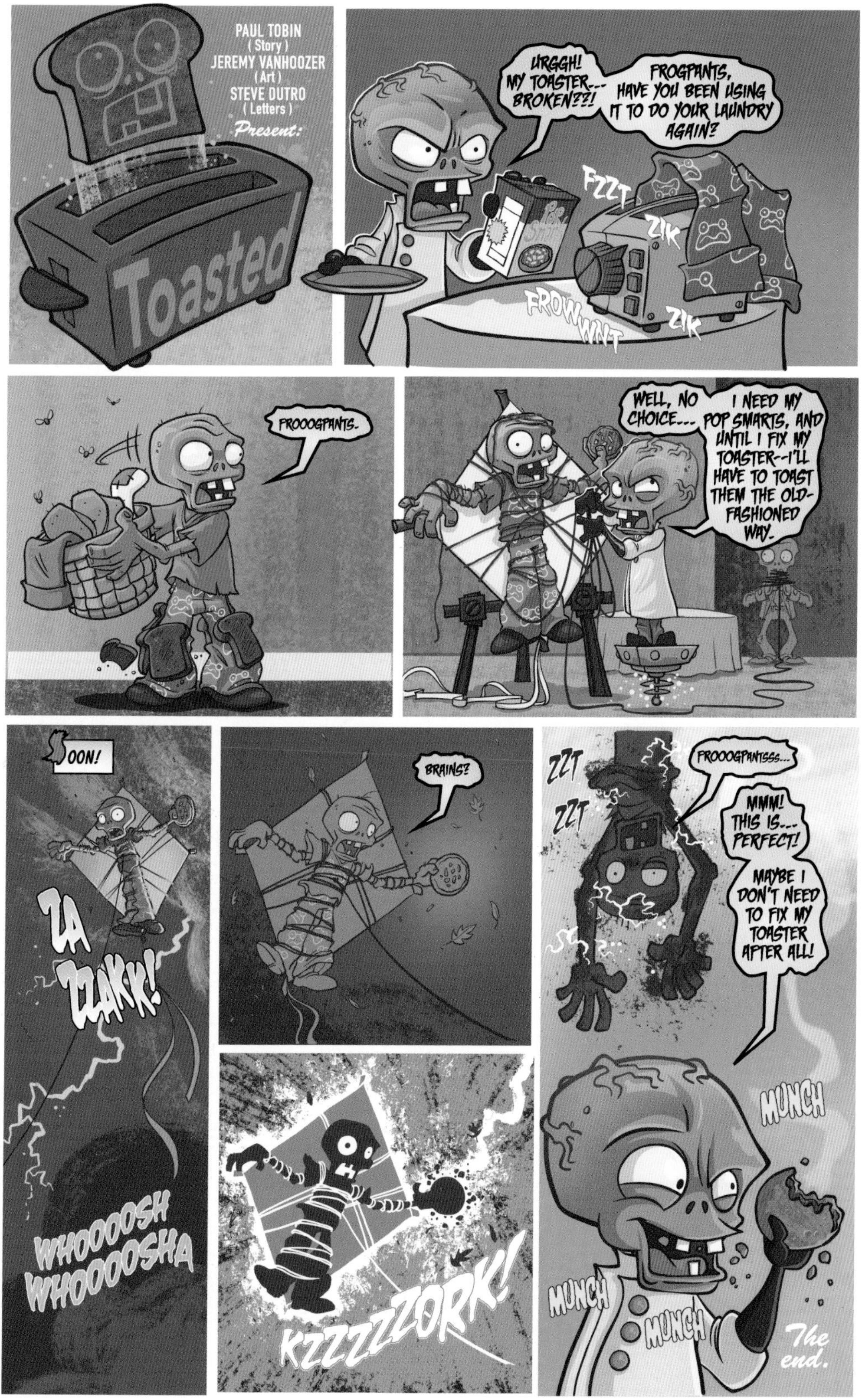
PAUL TOBIN
(Story)
JEREMY VANHOOZER
(Art)
STEVE DUTRO
(Letters)
Present:
Toasted
URGGH! MY TOASTER... BROKEN???!
FROGPANTS, HAVE YOU BEEN USING IT TO DO YOUR LAUNDRY AGAIN?
FZZT
ZIK
FROWWNT
ZIK
FROOOGPANTS.
WELL, NO CHOICE...
I NEED MY POP SMARTS, AND UNTIL I FIX MY TOASTER--I'LL HAVE TO TOAST THEM THE OLD-FASHIONED WAY.
SOON!
ZA
ZZAKK!
WHOOOOSH
WHOOOOSHA
BRAINS?
KZZZZZZORK!
ZZT
ZZT
FROOOGPANTSSS...
MMM! THIS IS... PERFECT!
MAYBE I DON'T NEED TO FIX MY TOASTER AFTER ALL!
MUNCH
MUNCH
MUNCH
The end.

THE SCENIC VIEW

STORY: PAUL TOBIN ART: JEREMY VANHOOZER LETTERS: STEVE DUTRO

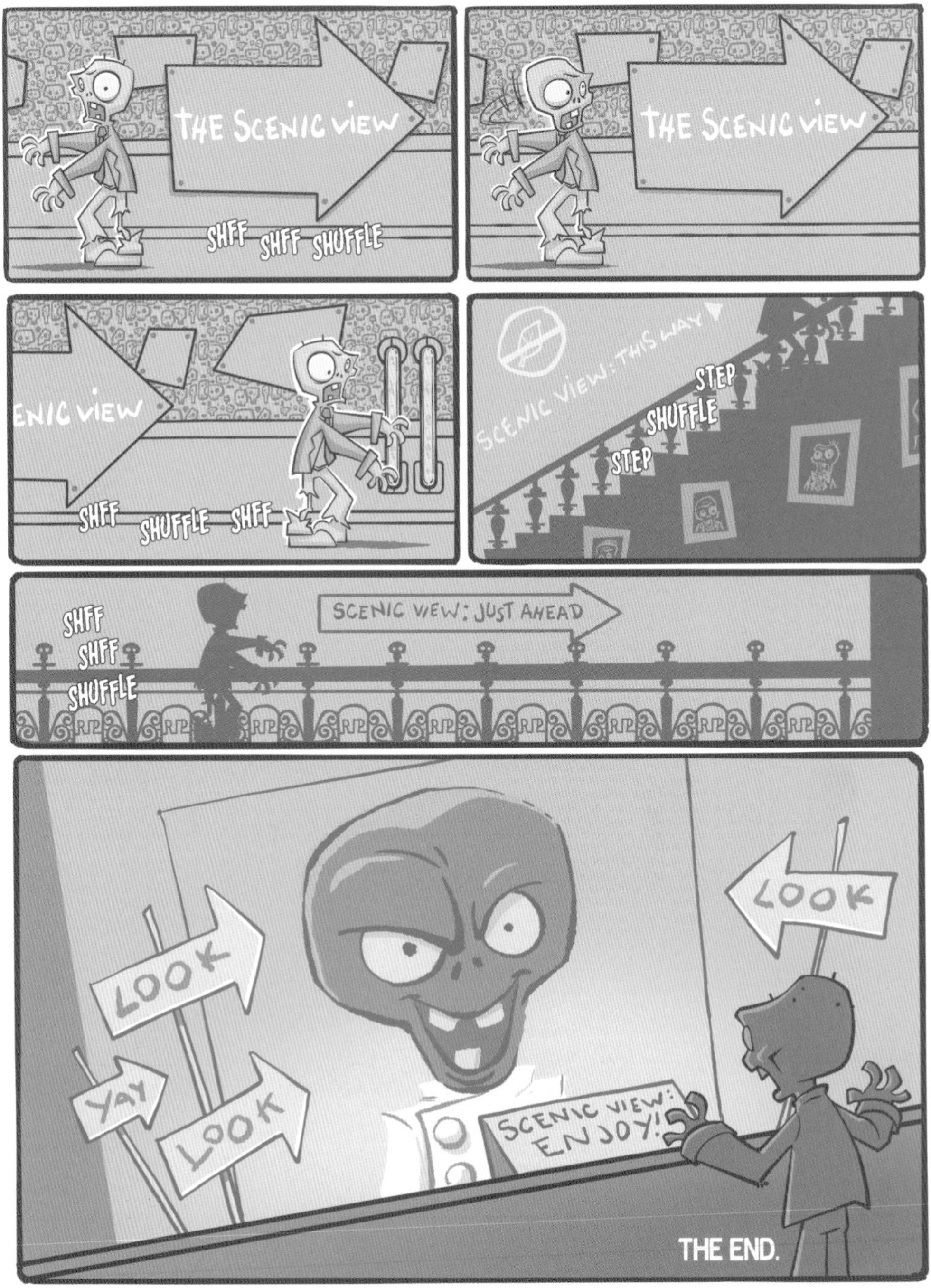
THE SCENIC VIEW
SHFF SHFF SHUFFLE
THE SCENIC VIEW
ENIC VIEW
SHFF SHUFFLE SHFF
SCENIC VIEW: THIS WAY
STEP
SHUFFLE
STEP
SHFF
SHFF
SHUFFLE
SCENIC VIEW: JUST AHEAD
RIP
LOOK
YAY
LOOK
SCENIC VIEW: ENJOY!
LOOK
THE END.

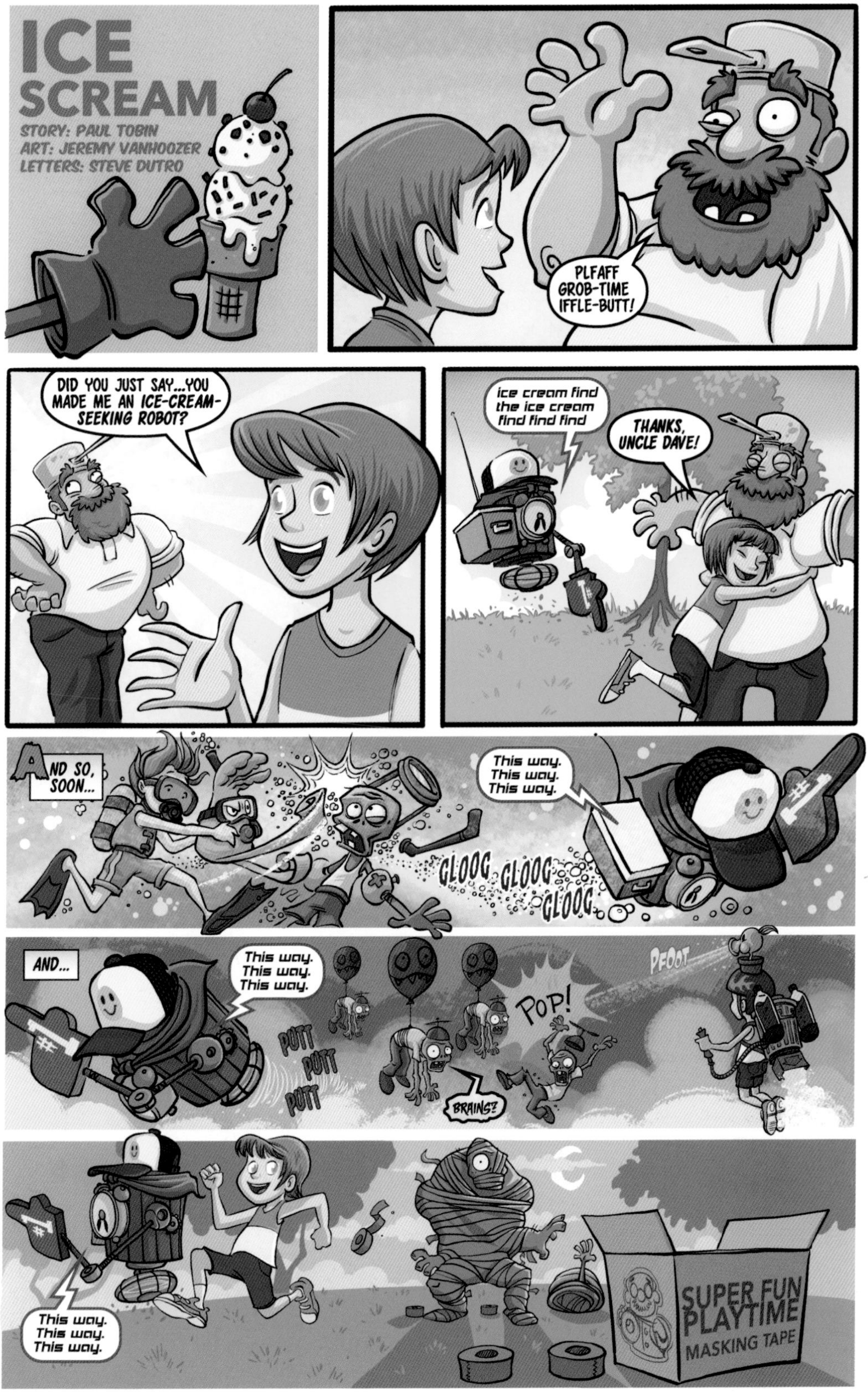
ICE SCREAM
STORY: PAUL TOBIN
ART: JEREMY VANHOOZER
LETTERS: STEVE DUTRO
PLFAFF GROB-TIME IFFLE-BUTT!
DID YOU JUST SAY...YOU MADE ME AN ICE-CREAM-SEEKING ROBOT?
ice cream find the ice cream find find find
THANKS, UNCLE DAVE!
AND SO, SOON...
This way. This way. This way.
GLOOG GLOOG GLOOG
AND...
This way. This way. This way.
PFOOT
POP!
PUTT PUTT PUTT
BRAINS?
This way. This way. This way.
SUPER FUN PLAYTIME MASKING TAPE

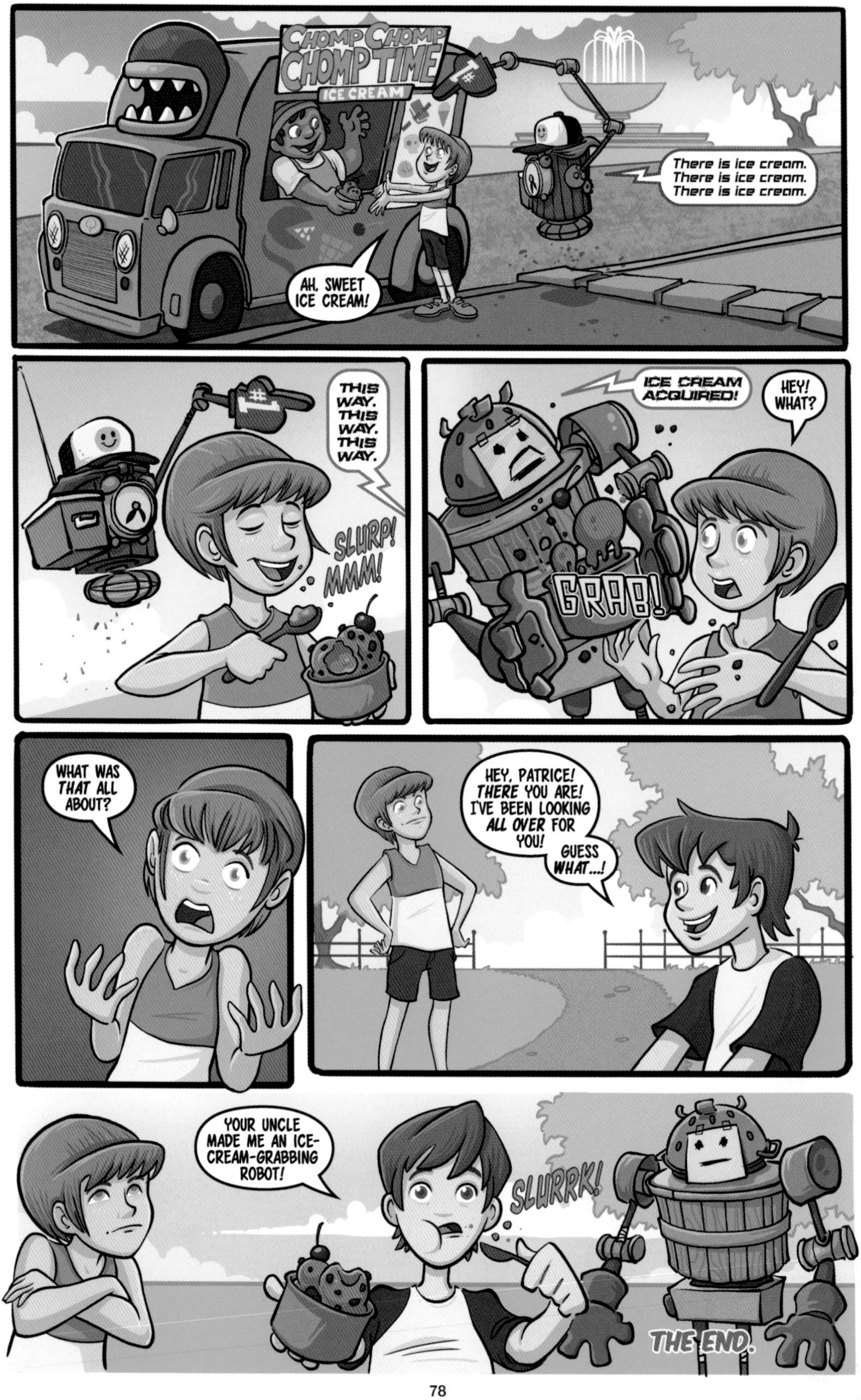
CHOMP CHOMP CHOMP TIME
ICE CREAM
There is ice cream.
There is ice cream.
There is ice cream.
AH, SWEET ICE CREAM!
THIS WAY. THIS WAY. THIS WAY.
SLURP! MMM!
ICE CREAM ACQUIRED!
HEY! WHAT?
GRAB!
WHAT WAS THAT ALL ABOUT?
HEY, PATRICE! THERE YOU ARE! I'VE BEEN LOOKING ALL OVER FOR YOU!
GUESS WHAT...!
YOUR UNCLE MADE ME AN ICE-CREAM-GRABBING ROBOT!
SLURRK!
THE END.

PLANTS VS. ZOMBIES #10
cover inks by JACOB CHABOT

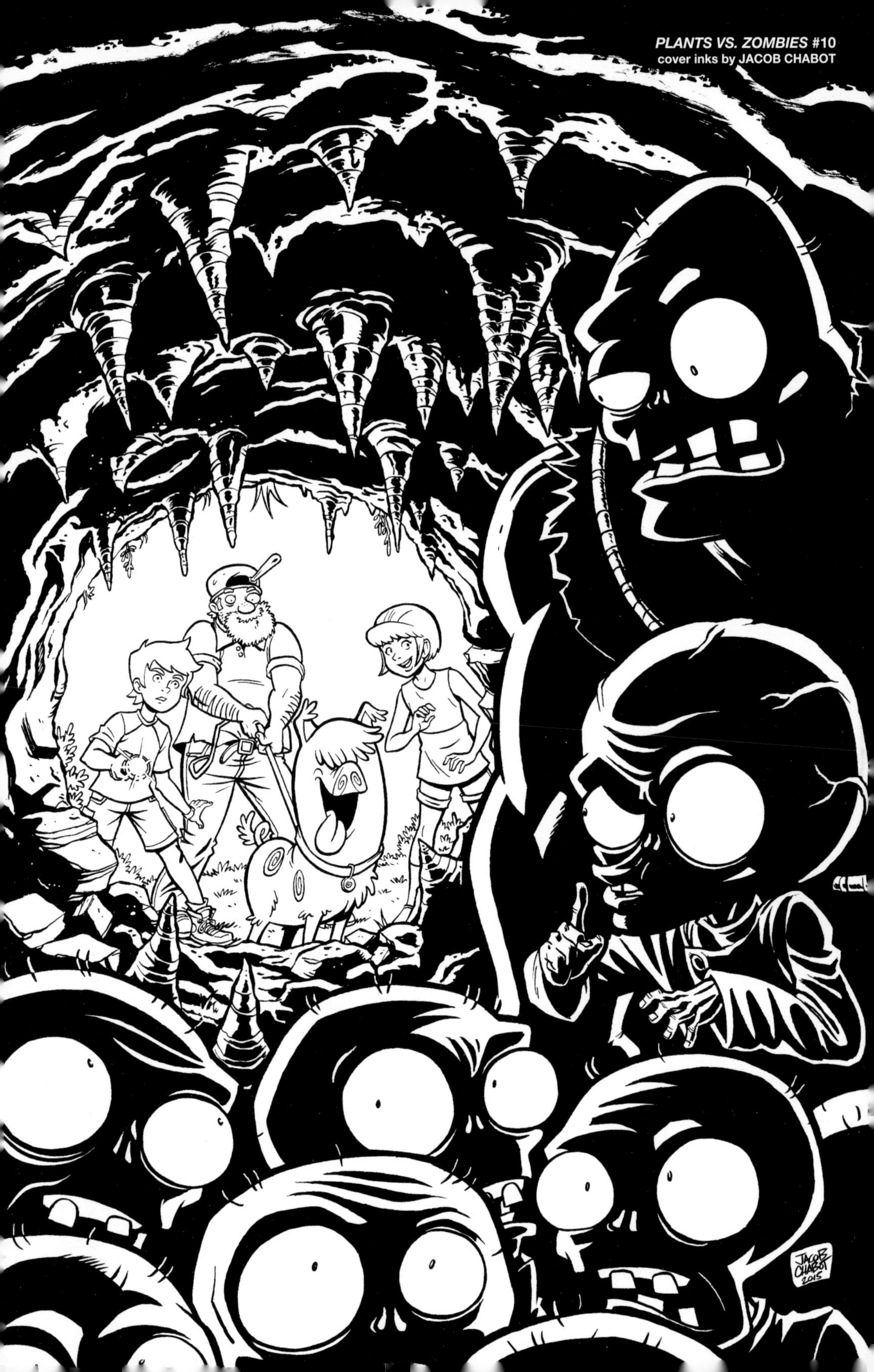
JACOB CHABOT 2015

***PLANTS VS. ZOMBIES* #11**
cover inks by JACOB CHABOT

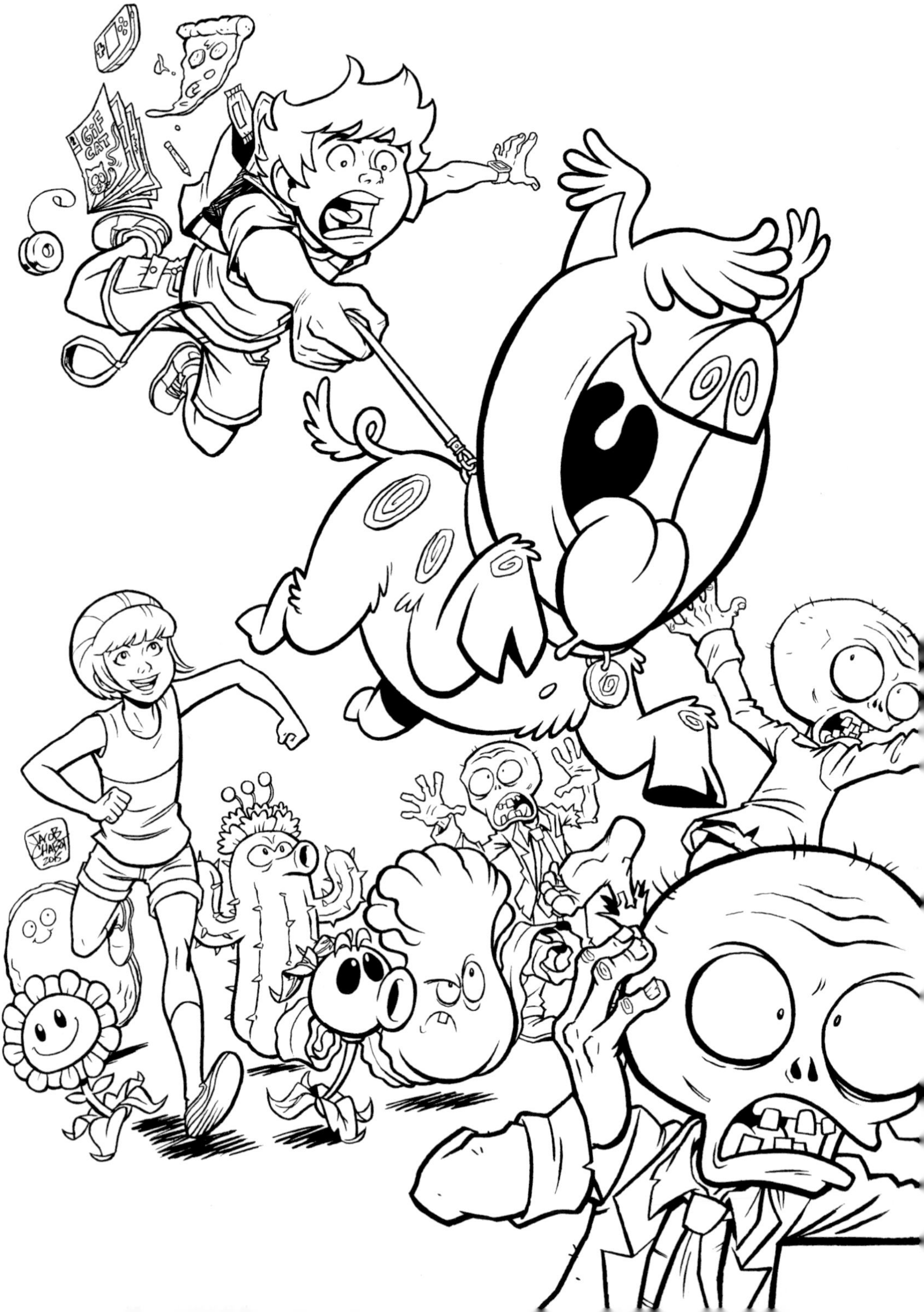
GIF CAT

***PLANTS VS. ZOMBIES* #11**
cover by JACOB CHABOT

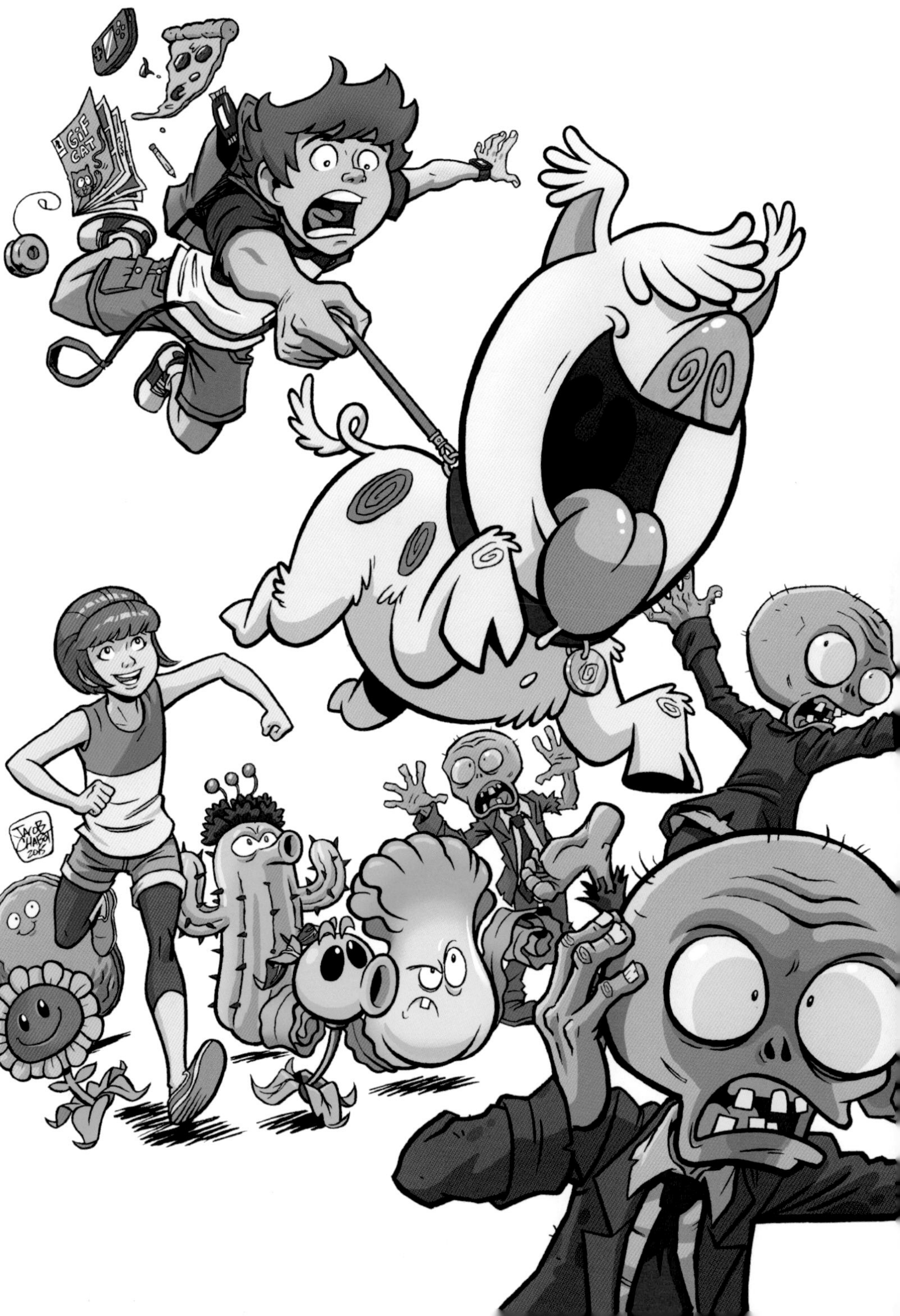
GIF CAT
JACOB CHABOT

PLANTS VS. ZOMBIES #12
cover inks by JACOB CHABOT

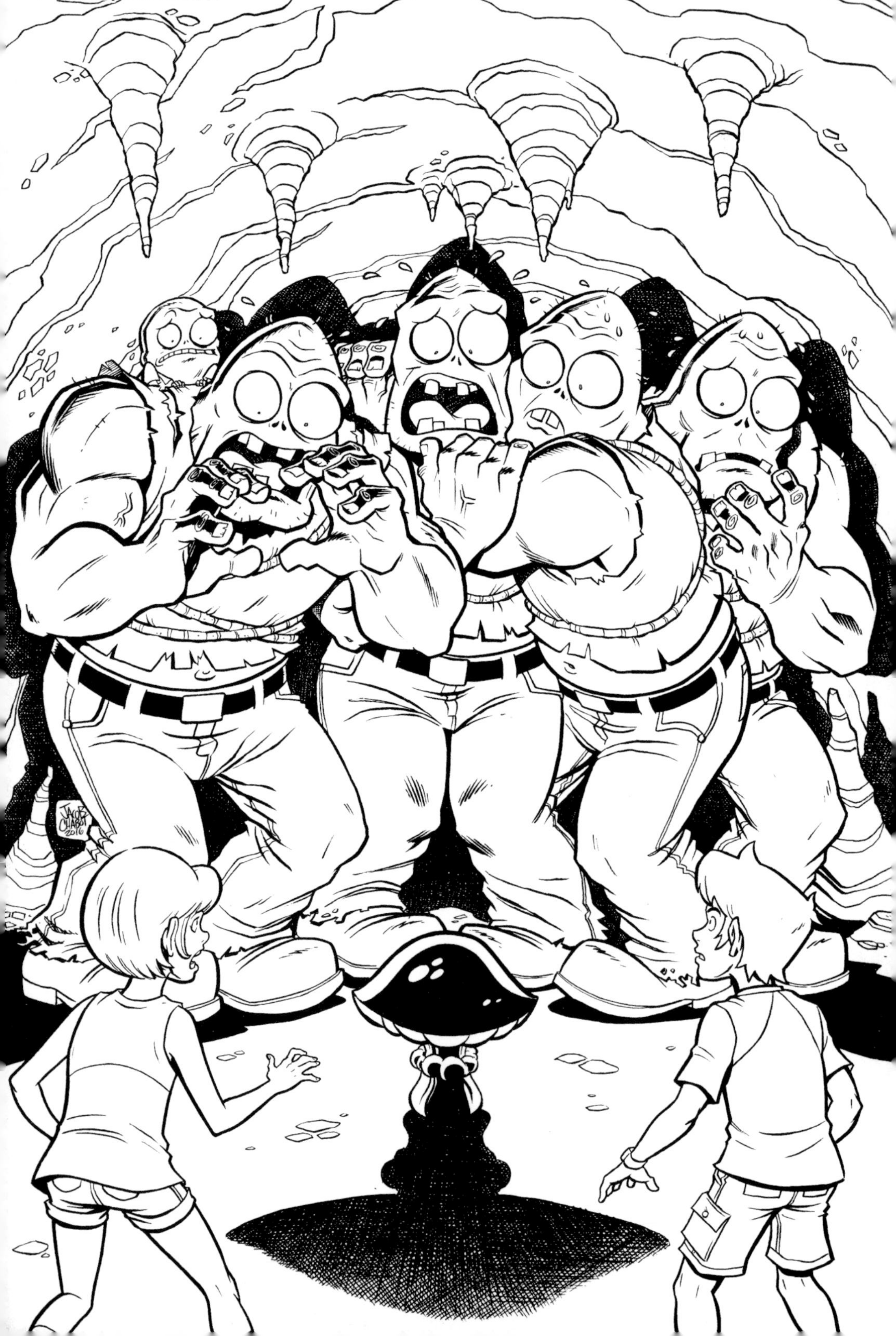

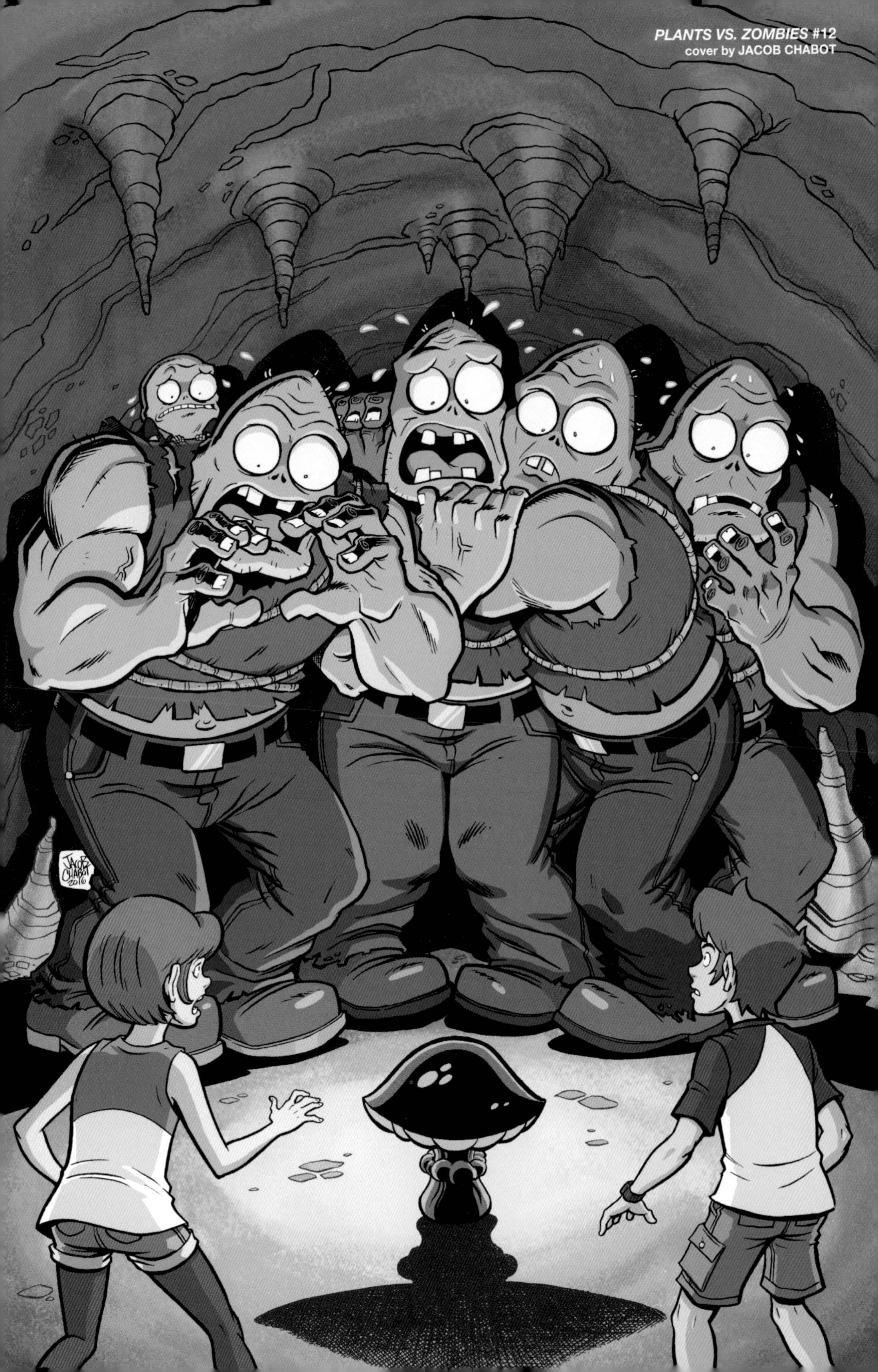
JACOB CHABOT 2016

PLANTS VS. ZOMBIES #12
cover by JACOB CHABOT

CREATOR BIOS

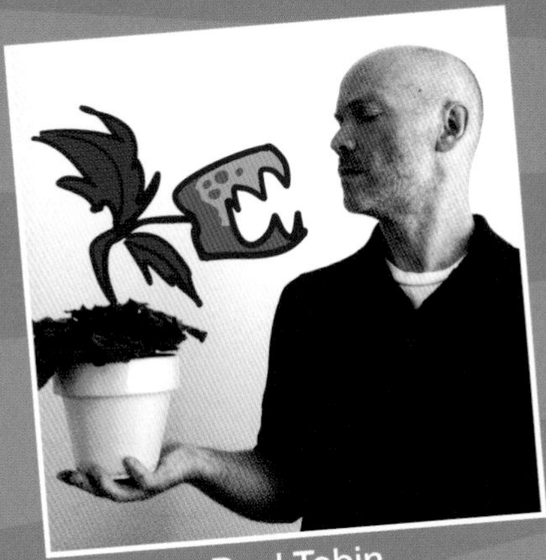

Paul Tobin

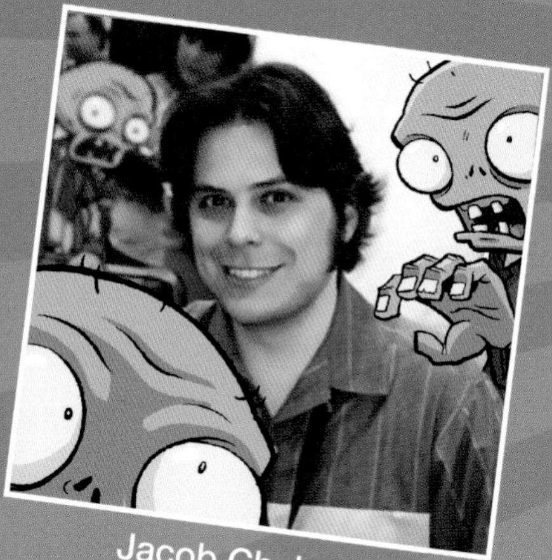

Jacob Chabot

PAUL TOBIN is a critically acclaimed freckled person who has a detailed plan for any actual zombie invasion, based on creating a vast perfume and cologne empire—both of which would be vitally important in a zombie-infested world. Paul was once informed he "walks funny, like, seriously," but has recovered from this childhood trauma to write hundreds of comics for Marvel, DC, Dark Horse, and many others, including such creator-owned titles as *Colder* and *Bandette*, as well as *Prepare to Die!*—his debut novel. His *Genius Factor* series of novels about a fifth-grade genius and his war against the Red Death Tea Society began in March 2016 from Bloomsbury Publishing. Despite his many writing accomplishments, Paul's greatest claim to fame is his ability to win water levels in *Plants vs. Zombies* without using any water plants.

JACOB CHABOT is a New York City–based cartoonist and illustrator. His credits include work for *SpongeBob Comics*, *Simpsons Comics*, Marvel Comics, *Hello Kitty*, and his own Eisner-nominated book *The Mighty Skullboy Army* (published by Dark Horse Comics). He also has almost all the achievements in *Plants vs. Zombies Garden Warfare*, and if he could stop drawing for a minute, maybe he could finish them all!

Matt J. Rainwater

Steve Dutro

Residing in the cool, damp forests of Portland, Oregon, **MATT J. RAINWATER** is a freelance illustrator whose work has been featured in advertising, web design, and independent video games. On top of this, he also self-publishes several comic books, including *Trailer Park Warlock*, *Garage Raja*, and *The Feeling Is Multiplied*—all of which can be found at MattJRainwater.com. His favorite zombie-bashing strategy utilizes a line of Bonk Choys with a Wall-nut front guard and Threepeater covering fire.

STEVE DUTRO is an Eisner Award–nominated comic book letterer from northern California who can also drive a tractor. He graduated from the Kubert School and has been in the comics industry for decades, working for Dark Horse (*The Fifth Beatle*, *I Am a Hero*, *The Evil Dead*, *Eden*), Viz, Marvel, and DC. Steve's last encounter with zombies was playing zombie paintball in a walnut orchard on Halloween. He tried to play the *Plants vs. Zombies* video game once, but experienced a full-on panic attack and resolved to stick with calmer games . . . like *Gears of War*.

ALSO AVAILABLE FROM DARK HORSE!

THE HIT VIDEO GAME CONTINUES ITS COMIC BOOK INVASION!

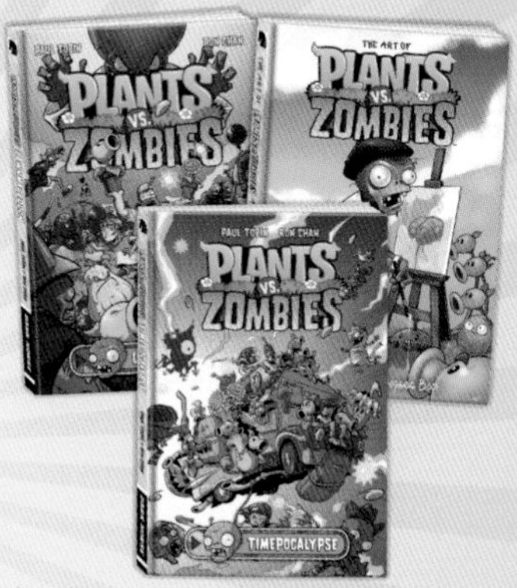
PLANTS vs. ZOMBIES
THE ART OF
PLANTS vs. ZOMBIES
PLANTS vs. ZOMBIES
TIMEPOCALYPSE

PLANTS VS. ZOMBIES: LAWNMAGEDDON
Crazy Dave—the babbling-yet-brilliant inventor and top-notch neighborhood defender—helps his niece Patrice and young adventurer Nate Timely fend off a zombie invasion that threatens to overrun the peaceful town of Neighborville in *Plants vs. Zombies: Lawnmageddon*! Their only hope is a brave army of chomping, squashing, and pea-shooting plants! A wacky adventure for zombie zappers young and old!
ISBN 978-1-61655-192-6 | $9.99

THE ART OF PLANTS VS. ZOMBIES
Part zombie memoir, part celebration of zombie triumphs, and part anti-plant screed, *The Art of Plants vs. Zombies* is a treasure trove of never-before-seen concept art, character sketches, and surprises from PopCap's popular *Plants vs. Zombies* games!
ISBN 978-1-61655-331-9 | $9.99

PLANTS VS. ZOMBIES: TIMEPOCALYPSE
Crazy Dave helps Patrice and Nate Timely fend off Zomboss's latest attack in *Plants vs. Zombies: Timepocalypse*! This new standalone tale will tickle your funny bones and thrill your brains through any timeline!
ISBN 978-1-61655-621-1 | $9.99

PLANTS VS. ZOMBIES: BULLY FOR YOU
Patrice and Nate have followed Crazy Dave throughout time—but are they ready to investigate a strange college campus to keep the streets safe from zombies?
ISBN 978-1-61655-889-5 | $9.99

PLANTS VS. ZOMBIES: GARDEN WARFARE
Based on the hit video game, this comic tells the story leading up to the events in *Plants vs. Zombies: Garden Warfare 2*!
ISBN 978-1-61655-946-5 | $9.99

PLANTS VS. ZOMBIES: GROWN SWEET HOME
Armed with newfound knowledge of humanity, Dr. Zomboss launches a strike at the heart of Neighborville . . . and also sparks a series of all-star plant-versus-zombie brawls!
ISBN 978-1-61655-971-7 | $9.99

PLANTS VS. ZOMBIES: PETAL TO THE METAL
Crazy Dave takes on the incredibly tough *Don't Blink* video game—and he also challenges Dr. Zomboss to a race to determine the future of Neighborville!
ISBN 978-1-61655-999-1 | $9.99

PLANTS VS. ZOMBIES: BOOM BOOM MUSHROOM
The gang discover "Zomboss's Secret Plan for Raising a Zombie Army Underground and Then Swallowing the Entire City of Neighborville Whole!" A rare mushroom must be found in order to save the humans aboveground!
ISBN 978-1-50670-037-3 | $9.99

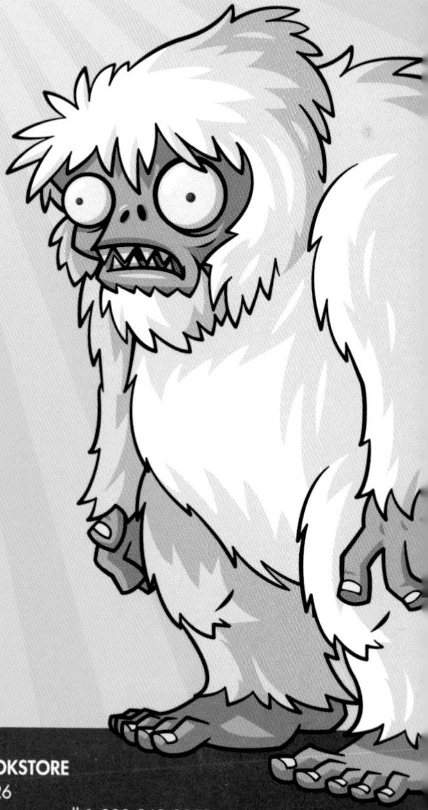

AVAILABLE AT YOUR LOCAL COMICS SHOP OR BOOKSTORE
To find a comics shop in your area, call 1-888-266-4226
For more information or to order direct visit **DarkHorse.com** or call 1-800-862-0052

MORE DARK HORSE ALL-AGES TITLES

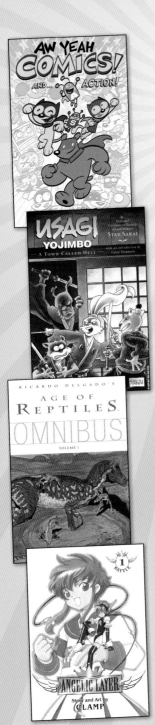

AW YEAH
COMICS!
AND...
ACTION!

AW YEAH COMICS! AND . . . ACTION!

Cornelius and Alowicious are just your average comic book store employees, but when trouble strikes, they are . . . Action Cat and Adventure Bug! Join their epic all-ages adventures as they face off—with the help of Adorable Cat and Shelly Bug—against their archnemesis, Evil Cat, and his fiendish friends!

ISBN 978-1-61655-558-0 | $12.99

USAGI
YOJIMBO
A Town Called Hell
Stan Sakai
SAKAI

USAGI YOJIMBO

In his latest adventure, the rabbit *ronin* Usagi finds himself caught between competing gang lords fighting for control of a town called Hell, confronting a *nukekubi*—a flying cannibal head—and crossing paths with the demon Jei!

Volume 25: Fox Hunt
ISBN 978-1-59582-726-5 | $16.99

***Volume 26: Traitors of the Earth* | $16.99**
ISBN 978-1-59582-910-8

***Volume 27: A Town Called Hell* | $16.99**
ISBN 978-1-59582-970-2

RICARDO DELGADO'S
AGE OF
REPTILES
OMNIBUS
VOLUME 1

AGE OF REPTILES OMNIBUS

When Ricardo Delgado first set his sights on creating comics, he crafted an epic tale about the most unlikely cast of characters: dinosaurs. Since that first Eisner-winning foray into the world of sequential art he has returned to his critically acclaimed *Age of Reptiles* again and again, each time crafting a captivating saga about his saurian subjects.

ISBN 978-1-59582-683-1 | $24.99

1
BATTLE
ANGELIC LAYER
Story and Art by
CLAMP

ANGELIC LAYER BOOK 1

Junior-high student Misaki Suzuhara just arrived in Tokyo to live with her TV-star aunt and attend the prestigious Eriol Academy. But what excites Misaki most is Angelic Layer—an arena game where you control a miniature robot fighter with your mind! Can Misaki's enthusiasm and skill take her to the top of the arena?

ISBN 978-1-61655-021-9 | $19.99

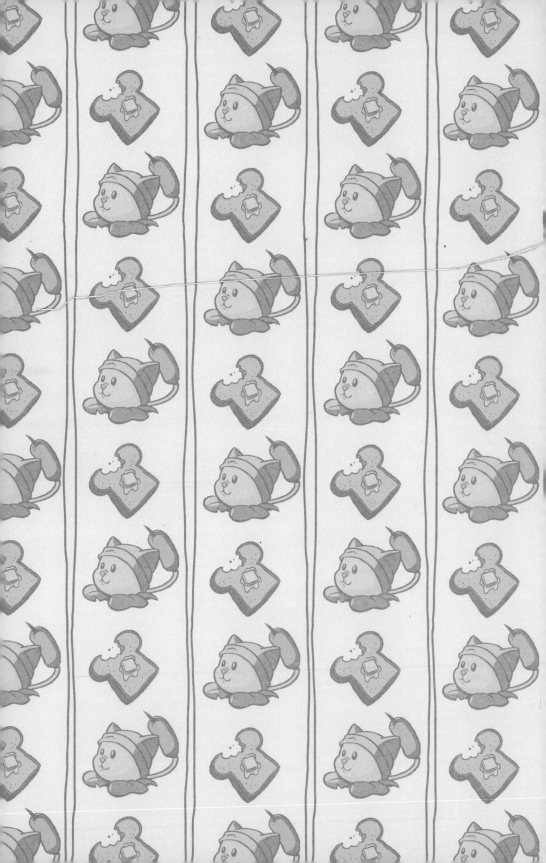